Seasons of Love and War

War

Book One

by

Brenda Ashworth Barry

Published by
Melange Books, LLC
White Bear Lake, MN 55110
www.melange-books.com

Seasons of Love and War, Book One ~
Copyright © 2014 by Brenda Ashworth Barry

ISBN: 978-1-61235-843-7 Print

Dedication

To my dear friend Cindy Watson who has been my biggest fan. Thank you for being there from the very beginning and loving my story along with being an Auntie to Kaylob and Beth Ann.

To my wonderful husband who served in the US Air Force for twenty one years and helped me with so much military information.

To Mom and Dad you are the best and have cheered me on.

To the memory and inspiration of K.S. who loved me forever and a day.

To Mona and Denise who inspired me to write about childhood best friends.

To all my BETA Readers, thank you and I love all of you.

To my coach, Lori Deboer, who pushed me hard and kept faith in me.

To Joyce Sterling Scarbrough, my friend and editor who has helped me immensely.

To all my family and friends—thank you for the love and support—you know who you are.

To my brother, Chuck, who is not here, but always wanted me to write a book. I miss you.

And to the branches of the United States Military Services, and every military person past and present, including my brother Joe, who fought in the Vietnam War.

Thank you for your service to this country.

And last but not least, to Melange and the staff who have been amazing to work with.

Chapter One

A hush fell over the sweltering jungles as Kaylob Shawn O'Brien and Walt Shaffer anchored their bodies to the putrid ground alive with fire ants and spiders. Although the humid air grew thick with giant mosquitoes, Kaylob focused on worse threats like snakes, tarantulas, and the Viet Cong.

The moon cast a mellow glow over the landscape in contrast to the chaos below. The stench of sulfur brought Kaylob back to the moment. He looked over at Walt, his inseparable buddy since boot camp. He liked the guy. He was the brother Kaylob had never had.

"Stick close, kid," Kaylob whispered. "Don't wanna get my ass shot trying to rescue you."

"No way, man." Shaffer placed his hand on Kaylob's shoulder. "Gotta get you home to the redhead."

Kaylob nodded and swatted away a bug. "Groovy, and we gotta get you home to your mama too. When's she sending some more of those chocolate chip cookies?"

"Kiss my... ass."

They shared a quiet laugh but stopped abruptly as an eerie silence blanketed the air. Kaylob raised his finger to his lips and stared at Shaffer. In the next instant the silence was shattered. Something exploded close to them. Dirt particles stung Kaylob's face. They needed to move.

"Shaffer, follow me."

Kaylob moved through the bush, flinching as more grenades blasted around them. The deafening sounds sent mud and rock flying into the air. He glanced back. No Shaffer. Son of a bitch. Where was he?

Silhouettes of enemy soldiers appeared against the moon. They closed in as the smell of smoke, earth, and death enveloped him. Shit. He'd lost sight of Shaffer. A figure emerged out of the darkness, not more than a foot away.

"Shaffer, is that you?"

No one answered. Then, a shot rang out and something warm hit his arm. A dark splotch of blood spread over his uniform. Kaylob watched Walt pause

1

and saw his eyes widen. As if in slow motion, Walt crumpled and hit the ground.

Damn it, no… Oh God, no…

Kaylob dropped his M16 in the mud, pulled his buddy into his arms and saw his eyes roll back. Shaffer took a last rattling gasp. Tears slid down Kaylob's face as he rocked his best friend.

Shaffer body was there, but he was gone. It was over.

"Walt, I'm so sorry." Kaylob sobbed. "I swear I'm gonna kill those bastards who did this to you." He kissed his friend's head. "I love you, buddy. Your death won't be in vain, I promise."

Kaylob felt like his heart was shattered, but he knew he had to pull it together. You had to stay focused in war or it could mean your life or the lives of others. No way would he let those bastards kill any more of his buddies. He'd hated it when he'd been drafted, but now he felt dedicated to help his brothers-in-arms.

The fighting continued all around him, but Kaylob barely heard anything as he laid Shaffer in the thick underbrush of the jungle, vowing to return. The Army didn't leave its dead behind, and he sure as shit wasn't going to leave his best friend.

More bombs blasted fire, shrapnel, and dirt. Fury roared through him. He picked up his M16, his face dripping with sweat and tears as he fired his weapon into the night. Damn them, and damn this war.

All he wanted in that moment was to settle the score, and he would find a way or die trying. As much as he loved Beth Ann, he couldn't let his friend die in vain. He'd seen too much goddamn death.

Once again he fired his gun into the night. "Walt, this is for you."

Chapter Two

Two weeks later, Beth Ann Rose rushed into her apartment, drenched through to her skin. Water dripped on the wood floor as she shook off her umbrella. The flooded mess outside made her later than normal. With Kaylob gone, she usually didn't care what time she got home. She hated the empty apartment without him, but she had to come home because it was a mess and needed some deep cleaning.

The leotards stuck to her skin, so she dashed into the bathroom to remove them. Crap, the hamper was almost full, but she managed to shove them down while she turned on the water to let it get warm. The shower called her name after such a long day.

When she got out, she brushed her teeth and fixed her hair. The face staring back at her from the mirror showed brown eyes filled with sadness. She missed Kaylob so much her heart was crying. Every day she worried about him. Every time the phone rang or someone knocked at her door, she was afraid it would be bad news. Lately she'd been having nightmares about him that made her wake up drenched in sweaty fear.

She reached over and turned on the radio to try and chill out. A song from the Jackson Five came drifting out, and she sang along with tears stinging her eyes. Faith, yes she had that. When she got to the part that said 'I'll be there...' she had to turn it off before she lost it.

The war sucked, and she hated that he was over there fighting. He had to go even though he'd been in culinary school because he'd just started and wasn't protected from the draft. All they'd wanted to do was get married and start their dreams. She wanted to do Broadway, which was why they were in Riverside, but the draft and the war had postponed most of their plans.

After she finished with her hair, she went to the bedroom and sank down on the bed. Her heart and soul felt hollow without Kaylob. She had loved him even before she knew what love was. His blond hair and blue eyes with that dimple in his chin made him stand out from all the other guys, and his unique, deep masculine voice turned a lot of girls' heads. Yes, he was gorgeous, but that wasn't all that made her swoon. It was who he was on the inside that she loved the most.

"Dear God," she said, turning her eyes heavenward, "I just want him home."

Chapter Three

Kaylob stepped off the plane, happy to get away from the overly friendly stewardess who had flirted with him the entire flight, even after he told her he had a fiancée. Man, he was glad to be back home and couldn't wait to find a phone and tell Beth Ann he was home early. He wasn't looking forward to telling her why he'd gotten to come home early, but he'd deal with that later. Right now he just wanted to see her again.

When he reached the landing, two protesters who looked no older than nineteen ran toward him holding picket signs. Before he even had a chance to register what they were doing, they both spit at him.

"War Dog. Baby Killer." one of them shouted. "You should die, bastard pig."

The woman was tall and angry, her face twisted with disgust. Kaylob wanted to pay her back, but he would never do that to a girl. The guy with her looked like a punk kid. His hair was dirty, and his eyes appeared dilated as if he was stoned. Kaylob pushed him out of the way and wanted to kick his ass, but he decided instead to escape.

Wiping the spittle off his face with his handkerchief, he walked away and pushed through the other war protesters, reminding himself that he couldn't act like he was still in 'Nam. Behind him, the ragtag cadre rushed toward other uniformed soldiers getting off the plane. Why didn't those hippies understand?

Jesus, the soldiers were trying to protect the U.S. and were getting spit at. What in the hell was this world coming to? Hippies, drugs, free sex. He might be old-fashioned, but at least he understood respect.

He picked up his duffel bag from the carousel and found a payphone so he could call Beth Ann, but the number was busy. He tried again and again and thought about getting the operator to interrupt the call, but decided it would be fun to show up at the apartment and surprise her. He stepped outside to get a cab to Riverside and got stung by the rain and wind blowing ferociously at him.

An older gentleman of at least fifty in a business suit was waiting beside him and examined Kaylob's uniform. "Comin' back from the war, Corporal?"

5

"Yes, sir," Kaylob answered.

"Let me tell you, you're doing a fine job. Those pinko commie punk kids need a damn haircut and to get a job. Either that or get their fricken asses kicked. I'd do it myself if it weren't for my back. Goddamn chinks."

Kaylob felt bad for the man, but he still winced at the slur. "Korea, sir?"

The older man placed his hand on his back. "Yeah, 8th Army. Fricken chink sliced a couple of nerves in my back with a bayonet. The pricks captured me and held me for two years. I was glad to get out alive."

He paused and looked down the street. "Hey, listen, gotta go. Cab's here. This damn wind and rain are bad. Fight the good fight, okay, Corporal?" He waved at Kaylob and started toward the cab.

"Yes, sir," Kaylob called after him.

He noticed the man walked with a limp as he got into the taxi. Damn, he couldn't imagine being captured and held prisoner for two years. He could go through a lot, but he didn't think he could survive being away from Beth Ann that long. After the man's taxi drove away, another one pulled up, splashing water onto Kaylob's boots. He didn't give a damn about that. The only one thing he cared about was getting home to Beth Ann.

He glanced at his wristwatch and knew she was only about an hour away.

* * * *

Beth Ann rolled her eyes. "I already told you I can't go to the movies with you tonight, Frankie." She sighed. "I have to clean this place. It's a mess."

"So you're making me go all alone." He sounded pitiful.

"Frankie Russo, don't you dare try to lay a guilt trip on me. Call Carol, she'll go with you."

"Hell no she won't. She's at one of her NOW meetings, probably burning some more bras or something important like that."

Beth Ann cracked up. "They don't just burn bras."

"How would you know? You've never been there."

"Carol tells me things."

The pause told her he was coming up with a smart-aleck comment.

"Maybe I should go volunteer to be the bra collector." He laughed.

"Frankie, you need to settle down and stop being such a playboy."

"I am settled down. I'm on the couch right now, deciding who'll be the lucky girl I invite over to keep me company. Hell, maybe I can help her burn her bra." He chuckled again.

Beth Ann shook her head. Women loved Frankie's dark curly hair and green eyes, and being Italian didn't hurt either. Of course, women were smitten with Kaylob too. Floozies came on to him all the time just like they did

6

Frankie. The difference was that Kaylob ignored them while Frankie took names and numbers.

"Hello? Beth Ann, did I lose you?"

"No, I was just thinking about Kaylob." Her voice broke from just saying his name.

"Want me to come over?" Frankie said. "Are you okay, honey?"

"I'm fine"." She, tried to sound like it. "Cleaning will take my mind off him, at least for a few seconds."

"You know," Frankie said, all the teasing gone from his voice, "someday when I'm old—like thirty something—and I fall in love, I want it to be like you and Kaylob. You two have loved each other forever, and it's always been the real deal. I remember watching you both when we were kids. The guy was head over heels in love even then, just like you were with him. Everyone knew it."

"Yeah, I guess it showed. Frankie, do you think I'm sexy?"

"Christ, where did that come from? Why are you asking me that?"

"Because of what you just said. It took Kaylob until I was eighteen to be my steady boyfriend because he always said he was too old for me and he wasn't that much older. We've never ... well you know. Honest, Frankie, do you think I'm sexy?"

"You're my best friend, and I refuse to answer that." He inhaled deeply. "Besides, you know Kaylob's a square. He thinks you should be married first."

"Frankie, why did you leave Harvard and move to Riverside?" She had always wondered about that, but he never wanted to talk about it. Case closed was all he'd ever said.

"Hey, what's with all the questions tonight? You giving up your dream of Broadway and thinking of being a lawyer?" He laughed. "How's all that training and your dancing coming along? I know your singing is perfect. Jesus, Beth Ann, you've always had such talent. I always kinda felt like you gave up a lot of your childhood for this dream of yours."

"I know I missed out on a lot, but it's always been my dream and still is. I'm so sore right now though. Carol works me hard and the school does too."

"Good, let's talk about that instead of all those dumb questions." He laughed again.

"Fine, if my best friend won't even tell me I'm sexy, then I must not be."

"That's absurd. You know you're a fox. Look, I have to get off the phone and get more settled for tonight."

"All right, I have to go clean anyway," she said, laughing. "Bye, Frankie."

"Bye, you little redheaded brat," he said. "Call if you need me."

"Okay, I will."

She put the phone back on the cradle and looked around. The bedroom was the worst mess, so she'd start in there. After getting her dust spray and rag, she

7

began with the tables on either side of the bed. She loved the way her apartment was set up. From the bedroom you could see all the way into the living room and kitchen, but the pocket doors gave her some privacy if someone came over or spent the night.

She sprayed her rag and picked up the treasure box Kaylob had made for her, and tears filled her eyes as she remembered the day he'd given it to her. It was June of 1969, the day she'd graduated from high school. Her parents had surprised her with a new car and taken her out to dinner. When they got home, Kaylob had been waiting and asked if he could steal her away for a while.

She'd been waiting years for him to officially ask her to be his girl and to stop worrying about being too old for her. She hoped that was why he wanted to talk to her alone.

He took her to his house, and they'd spent at least thirty minutes kissing before he handed her a beautifully wrapped gift. The handmade treasure box had taken her breath away—until she lifted the top and saw that he had filled it with Polaroid snapshots of their times together, but no going-steady ring. Heartbroken, she'd ran out the door and left the gift behind.

When she finally spoke to him after two days of crying her eyes out, all she told him was to go away and leave her alone.

That entire summer, they hadn't spoken so much as one word. She'd seen him from a distance but that was all. At one point, she had almost gone on a date with Blake Tanner. When he'd shown up to take her out, all she'd done was cry on his shoulder and tell him she wasn't over Kaylob yet. Besides, she was leaving soon for Riverside. He had been so nice and understanding, even when she'd told him her heart was occupied and out of service.

When August came and she was packing up her belongings to move, she heard a knock at the front door and was astonished to see Kaylob standing there, holding the beautiful treasure chest he'd made for her. When he asked her to be his girl and said he wanted to go to Riverside with her so they could live together, she could hardly believe it, especially coming from someone as old-fashioned as Kaylob. When he told her he loved her, that was all it took.

Now, standing in her messy apartment, she held the treasure box close. "Oh, Kaylob, I miss you so much."

She placed it back on the table and swiped away a few tears. After she finished dusting, she decided to tackle her closet. She pulled out all her shoes, including her bunny slippers. Once again, she was flooded with memories of Kaylob. He loved those pink bunny slippers on her. Was that his idea of sexy? He'd given them to her on their first Christmas together in their apartment.

That Christmas day, they had decided to do something special for each other, something that would last for years. They'd each written a love letter to the other and had buried them unread in a sealed glass bottle.

Beth Ann had found the perfect spot to bury them—underneath the old oak tree at their favorite park downtown. They had marked the spot by pacing five steps back from their initials carved in the tree, amongst all the others engraved there too. Beth Ann told Kaylob that bearing all that love must have kept it alive for so long. They made a promise to come back there on their twenty-fifth wedding anniversary to open and read their love letters to each other.

Clutching the silly bunny slippers to her heart, she said another prayer that both the tree and Kaylob would still be alive to keep their date.

* * * *

Beth Ann began cleaning again when a rattling at the front door startled her. Who the heck was trying to get into her apartment? There were robbers all over the place, and she'd heard about some break-ins in the neighborhood. She grabbed the first shoe her hand touched and stepped into the living room. She'd clobber the holy hell out of them. After all, shoes could be a deadly weapon.

Before she reached the door, it began to open slowly. With her heart racing, she drew back her hand in a stance like a Kung fu master.

"Kaylob?" She couldn't believe her eyes as she stood with her arm still drawn back ready to throw.

He laughed and pointed at the bunny slipper. "Don't let it bite me, it might have rabies."

She dropped her weapon and launched herself into his arms, causing them both to fall into the wall.

"Kaylob—oh my God, you're home. Oh, honey, I can't believe you're here." Tears streamed down her face, and she felt like her heart would explode with happiness.

"For someone so tiny, you almost knocked me on my butt. C'mere, my little tiger." He growled and wrapped his arms around her.

"I love you, I love you, I love you. I've missed you so much." The words were hard to get out because her lips were pressed against his. "I've been so worried. Thank God you're home."

He picked her up and spun her around. "Baby, you look beautiful. I've missed you more than you'll ever know."

Little sobs came from her throat as he held her. "My honey—oh God, Kaylob. Am I in a dream? I was just thinking about you."

"No, baby, it's not a dream. I'm here holding you."

He carried her to the couch and sat down with her on his lap, holding her while he waited for her tears to dry. His lips felt so good, and his arms were exactly what she needed. His love was what she needed most.

This wonderful man with such beautiful ... worried eyes? Why did he look upset? She felt a little tingle in her stomach. Something was wrong—she could feel it.

"I love you, baby girl," he said. "God, I've missed you."

Their lips touched and his tongue found its way home, making her forget everything but the taste of his mouth.

When they could finally bear to separate their lips, she leaned back and looked into his eyes. "Kaylob, have I told you how proud I am of you?" Her eyes filled with tears again.

"No, baby, but it's nice to hear. Have I told you how special you are? How the thought of you brought sunshine into my life during my darkest moments?"

That must be what was bothering him. "Did you have a lot of dark moments, honey? Was it really bad for you over there? Do you want to talk about it?"

He shook his head. "Not tonight, sweetheart. Tonight is just about me and you."

"Then just hold me, Kaylob. I want to feel your arms around me all night."

"You got it, baby."

That rainy September night, they held onto each other tightly, neither of them wanting to let go. He was like the air she breathed. She loved him so much it made her wonder how safe it was to love so deeply. What would she be without her Kaylob?

Chapter Four

The next morning rushed into their apartment uninvited as street traffic outside mixed with the clanging garbage trucks and pouring rain to create a maddening symphony. Beth Ann woke and considered the idea of complaining about the noise. Then she realized that being awake gave her more time to check out her fiancé sleeping soundly through the clamor outside.

She glanced at the clock and saw it was way past eleven. Much later than they usually slept, but no surprise after cuddling and making out off and on all night. At one point, she'd thought they might finally go all the way, but he'd stopped as usual. Kaylob was the poster child for restraint.

He was home early after six months, one week, and three days of combat duty. Thank goodness he would be out of the service soon. At least he didn't have to go back to war. Now they could concentrate on their wedding and possibly move up their plans.

Beth Ann gazed at his sleeping form and felt her heart swell. She loved him so much, it was as if her love for him had become a part of her. From the moment she'd seen him look at her with those blue eyes of his, she had been a goner. By the age of twelve, every time he'd looked at her she had thought she had the flu. It hadn't taken long for her to discover that what Kaylob did to her was not a bug. Not of the viral kind anyway.

One thing for certain. She would never let him travel out of the country without her again. If he got stationed in Africa, she would go with him. Her passport was ready, and she was willing.

She moved ever so slowly to his side and caught a whiff of his masculine aroma, a fresh hint of leather with a bit of spice from his cologne. God, he caused her head to spin with desire. She couldn't wait until they were married and together completely. She moved her hand to his stomach and rubbed it lightly. His muscles were amazing, and she loved the feel of them. In a split second, he caught her hand and raised it to his lips to kiss her palm.

"Beth Ann, you can't do that to me, you dangerous woman. What am I going to do with you?" He sat up to kiss her lips and then got up off the bed.

After he made a quick run to the bathroom, he went into the living room and waved for her to follow. With a pout she knew would do her no good, she crawled out of bed and walked over to where he sat to plop down on his lap. He let out a grunt and shifted her weight, unable to hide his arousal through his pajamas.

"You're a little redheaded minx, you know that?"

His face lit up with a warm, radiant smile, giving her a chance to admire his deep blue eyes. His sun-streaked blond hair still looked good despite being cut to military regulations.

"Beth Ann, do you know how much I love you?" He spoke in a bottomless baritone as he ran his fingers a touch away from her breast.

She shivered and her heart fluttered. "Kaylob, stop teasing me."

He kissed her nose. "What's the matter?"

"You know, Mr. Not-So-Innocent. Yes, I know you love me."

Leaning into his shoulder, she gazed up at him, impressed at how much he towered over her even while sitting. His hands, arms, and muscular frame made him look like a lumberjack.

"I was thinking," she said, letting her hand run through his buzz cut, "that we could push up the wedding date." She gave him a cajoling look.

His next kiss was incomplete. He appeared distressed. She sat up and held his gaze, hoping for an explanation. She sensed a shift in the way he held her. His arms were warm and his kisses sweet, but something wasn't right. The tension in his body made her feel the same.

He coughed and stared at the floor. "Becoming your husband is something I look forward to with all my heart. There's something you need to know, sweetheart."

She moved her head from his chest and released a deep sigh. He was nervous—that was pretty darn clear. The rain outside along with the grind from a garbage truck were the only sounds in the room. A thunderclap made her jump, and his arms tightened around her. They felt protective as always, but she recognized his look of trepidation. Oh God, what was wrong?

"Kaylob, what's the matter? You can tell me."

He lifted her chin and kissed her again. "You know how I was able to come home early and surprise you?"

"Yes, and I'm very happy you did. I love surprises, and having you home early is the best one ever."

"I only got to come home early because ..." He paused to sigh deeply. "Because I agreed to return, baby. I'm doing a second tour."

She leaned back to look at him, shock flooding her senses. This couldn't be true.

"What do you mean by a second tour? I told you I'd go anyplace they stationed you. I have my passport and—"

"I'm going back to Vietnam."

All she could do was stare at him. Surely she hadn't heard him right. He was going back to the war? Why would he do that? They couldn't make him. The military couldn't force him to fight in that war again. Just the thought nauseated her.

The rainstorm outside swelled in waves, matching her mood. After all the years of waiting, she couldn't bear this now. They were engaged and supposed to be getting married soon. All those promises he'd made to her before he left. No way in hell was he going to Vietnam again.

Okay, she had to breathe. She swallowed and took a deep breath. "What do you mean you're going back?"

"I have to go back to Vietnam, Beth Ann. The guys need me over there."

She got up off his lap and started pacing around the room, her mind reeling from his words. "How can they make you do that? We need a lawyer. I'm calling Frankie." She headed for the phone. "He'll know what to do. Why are they sending you back when they let those dropouts and politicians' kids get out of the draft? This isn't right." She picked up the phone and started to dial.

Kaylob walked over, wrapped his arms around her, and took the telephone gently out of her hand. "No, sweetheart. Don't call Frankie."

"Why not? He's studying to be a lawyer. He'll know what to do."

With the look of a parent ready to tell a child their favorite pet had to be put down, Kaylob hung up the phone and held her tighter.

She recognized that expression—guilt. He had made the choice to leave again. Anger quickly took the place of the fear and outrage she'd been feeling moments ago. How could he agree with them? Did he really think that leaving her to fight this war was okay?

She pushed him away. "You agreed to this, didn't you? Why didn't you tell them no?"

"Sweetheart, I'm going back because I left guys over there that need me. I can't leave them behind. They're my brothers."

Nothing he said made sense. All she could hear him saying was that he was going back. "No, you can't just decide this without me. We'll talk about this together and decide what's best. We're engaged."

He shook his head. "It's too late. I already signed."

Her face felt like angry coals. She couldn't believe he hadn't even talked it over with her.

"What about leaving me here? Aren't I as important as your brothers over there?"

He put his hands gently on her shoulders, his blue eyes full of tenderness as he looked into hers. "Of course you are, but you're not in any danger, Beth Ann. You're safe here with all our friends. My guys in 'Nam need me."

Rage rapidly replaced her seething anger.

"Yes, I am in danger. I'm in danger every day without you."

His eyebrows lifted. "What kind of danger?"

"I'm in danger of losing my stinking mind. It doesn't matter how many people I have, I want you."

She turned and ran into the bathroom, locking the door behind her.

* * * *

Kaylob started after her to try to make her understand, but he decided to give her some time to absorb the news. He knew he should have told her as soon as he got back and felt guilty for that. He didn't want to make things worse. He'd go fix breakfast. Maybe that would calm her down.

He went into the kitchen and started the percolator, adding a little cinnamon to the coffee the way she liked it. He pulled out some eggs and some potatoes that looked a little old. Not great, but it would have to do. He wondered if she'd really cooked anything while he was gone.

After he set the table and placed glasses of orange juice beside the plates, Beth Ann came out of the bathroom. For a minute he felt relief. Then he saw her face. She walked over to the table and stared down at the place setting. He opened his mouth to say something.

"How dare you not talk this over with me? I'm your fiancée. Did you even think about my feelings?"

"Of course I did, and you know your feelings matter. You mean everything to me, Beth Ann." He took a step toward her, but she held up her hand to keep him from coming closer.

"Right. Didn't you see how bad it hurt me when you left the first time? I've been stressed and worried every day. I guess that doesn't matter so long as you're with your brothers in Vietnam." Tears streamed down her face.

His heart was being squeezed by a giant fist. He just wanted to put his arms around her and make her feel better. "Baby, I'm sorry. Come here and let me hold you."

"Don't touch me."

He took a step closer "But, baby, please—"

"I told you to stay away." She glared at him.

"But baby ..." The sound of thunder echoed through their apartment.

14

Without as much as a word she threw the orange juice at the wall and it splattered all over him. "I don't want to hear any more of your excuses. Why don't you just go now if you're going to leave me anyway."

Her words hurt him as though he'd been cut by shards from the broken orange juice glass. He stared at her a moment as the juice dripped from his face, then he turned slowly and walked to the bathroom, feeling like a complete ass for tilting her world this way. He'd thought he could make her understand, but maybe that was hoping for too much. How could anyone who hadn't been there to see all the horrors of war understand it?

He got in the shower, remembering the look that had been on Walt's face when he died. He leaned his head against the shower wall and watched the water and juice mixed with his tears as they washed down the drain.

When he got out of the shower he slipped on his robe and went back to the living room. The apartment was quiet. The evidence was as he glanced around and knew Beth Ann had gone. He called her mom to see if she had called, but Jean said she hadn't heard from her. After he made a few more calls with no luck he started to feel the first inklings of panic.

The truth was he had known she would be upset, but not this upset. Now she was out there alone in a storm, and anything could happen to her in a city with as much crime as there was in Riverside. He had to find her no matter how bad the storm and no matter how long it took. He threw on some clothes when a crack of thunder coaxed him to move even faster.

When he stepped outside, he noticed the streets the absence of the usual flood of cars because the storm was so bad. There were a couple of people walking to and from work, but not many. As he hurried down the sidewalk through the driving rain, another rumble of thunder reminded him of the bombs in Vietnam.

Faces of friends and buddies flashed in his mind, but he pushed them away. Not now. There was a different war raging in his own home, and he had to deal with it now. His only mission was to find his fiancée, so he decided to take the car.

He knew where he had to go.

* * * *

Beth Ann trekked through the rain-drenched city, her vision almost totally obscured by the downpour combined with her anger, fear and disillusionment. The rain overflowed the storm drains, turning the streets into shallow canals. Wind thrashed the treetops along the sidewalk, flinging leaves in every direction and making it even harder to see. The deluge drown her feet and soaked her bellbottoms through to her skin. She stopped for a minute and took in the unfamiliar surroundings. Only a few people ventured out, some huddled under umbrellas, others ran in hooded jackets.

She passed stores and other businesses, hardly noticing them as her mind spun in circles. Most were closed because the storm knocked out the power in places. Their empty, darkened storefronts matched her mood.

Where was she, and how long had she been trudging through this flooded mess? Drivers, foolish enough to be out, struck the oily pools, causing waves to smash against the sidewalks. Finding shelter became a priority before she got washed away.

She started walking again, then stopped to find herself standing in front of a bridal boutique. Her eyes fixated on the gowns, and she once again lost track of time. Would she and Kaylob ever get married now? What if he didn't make it back home?

Seeing bridal gowns would once have filled her with hope, but now only despair filled her. So much had changed since the night they'd spent at the ocean, sitting by the fire on a private beach and talking about their future as they watched the sun come up. The next day she had watched Kaylob surf. He'd always had passion about surfing and had even taught her. What if he never had the chance to surf again or become a chef? Tears stung her eyes as she bent over, drew in some breaths, and tried to focus.

After a while, she realized where she was, although she couldn't believe she'd wandered that far from home. Somehow she had ended up right across the street from the park with the old oak tree so special to Kaylob and her.

She dashed across the street and made it without slipping in the oily puddles. The streetlights flickered on just then, making her realize just how long she'd been gone. She managed to find her way through the darkness and rain to their special tree. Even through her tears she could see the initials they'd carved on it. She fell to her knees, touching the letters.

E.A.R. & K.S.O
F+1

Elizabeth Ann Rose & Kaylob Shawn O'Brien, Forever plus a day.

The engraving mocked her now, and her tears fell faster.

She needed to find that letter. It was buried five steps back from their initials. The rain continued to drench her as she counted the steps backward. Without so much as a thought about the water, mud, and grass, she fell to her knees and began digging with her bare hands.

"We made promises in that letter," she yelled at the tree between sobs. "Why, Kaylob? How can you leave me alone again like this?"

Bent over and clawing at the dirt with the rain and her hair in her face, she didn't realize anyone was there until she felt someone touch her back.

"Baby, I found you," Kaylob said, trying to pull her up from her knees. "I knew you'd be here. Please stop this and come home with me."

"No, leave me alone." She pushed away his hands and tried to keep digging. "I have to tear it up. It doesn't mean anything now."

"Yes it does, baby. I love you, and I always will."

She kept struggling against him for a few seconds longer, then all the fight seemed to drain out of her, and all she could do was slump against him.

"Kaylob ..." Her voice was so weak she barely heard it herself. She was suddenly so tired she didn't think she could walk if she tried. She stretched her arms up to him, and he bent to pick her up, pausing to kick the mud back in place where she'd been digging.

"Baby, I was so worried," he said as he carried her to the car.

She leaned her head on his chest. "I'm sorry. I'm just so afraid. I don't want to lose you."

He pulled her closer. "You won't lose me. I promise."

He placed her in the car and wrapped his jacket around her. The drive home was silent except for the sound of the rain and the water splashing against the tires.

Once they got inside, he led her to the couch and sat down facing her. "I know we're both soaking wet, but we have to talk before we do anything else. I have to make you understand why I'm going back."

"I'm sorry I ran off, Kaylob," she said. "I won't do anything like that again, but nothing you say is going to make me understand. The best I can do is tell you I still love you no matter what."

He pulled her into his arms. "That's not good enough for me. We've always understood each other. That's why I have to make you see how I feel."

"Okay," she said. "Tell me why you decided to go back."

He took a deep breath. "You know how close Walt and I were to each other. It was more than just friendship, baby. I loved him like a brother." His voice broke and he had to stop for a second. "I tried to watch out for him, but I did a lousy job because he died in my arms. It's my fault."

Beth Ann's heart broke to hear about Walt's death. He had been such a great guy. She had even written to him a few times because he didn't have a girl back home.

"Oh, Kaylob, I'm so sorry. Why didn't you tell me he was killed?"

Kaylob closed his eyes as tears streamed down his cheeks. "I couldn't. This is the first time I've talked about it to anyone."

"It's not your fault, honey," she said. "I know you did everything you could to protect everyone in your squad. You're so brave and caring. Walt knew how much you loved him."

He opened his eyes and looked into hers. "I promised him I wouldn't let his death be for nothing, baby. I promised him I'd do my best to keep those bastards from killing any more of our buddies. That's why I have to go back and help them fight. Can you understand that? Please understand."

She put her hands on his face. "I still don't want you to go, Kaylob, but I understand you're too good of a man to break a promise you made to your dying friend. I don't like it, but I understand why you have to go."

He leaned his head into her neck, and they cried together. For a long while they just held each other, feeling the season of the wind carry away all the negative energy.

Chapter Five

After they'd both taken a shower and put on dry clothes, Kaylob sat down on the couch next to her and pulled her into his arms. "You know what? I'm starving. Want something to eat?"

"Yes, I'm hungry." She took his hand and he grinned as he pulled her up.

It didn't take him long to whip up some fantastic looking omelets. He carried both plates over to the table and set them down.

"Here you go, baby."

While they ate, she peeked across the table and watched him take a very large bite.

"Kaylob…"

"Yes?" He gave her a wink while he chewed.

"There's something I need to talk to you about too. I've been having horrible dreams. I think that's one reason I'm so terrified about you going back. In my nightmare, I'm going down this long hallway and can't get to you. I hear you calling my name and yelling that you're alive."

He reached across the table and took her hand. "They're just dreams, baby. Everything's gonna be fine."

"It still scares me." Her stomach began doing the nervous tango, and she lost her appetite.

When they finished eating, Kaylob took her by the hand and led her back to the couch. "What you did today really upset me," he said. "It's dangerous out there. Please don't ever do that again."

"I'm sorry, honey. It won't happen again." She leaned over to kiss him.

"You know, we don't really fit here in Riverside," he said. "This city feels so unsafe and unfriendly at times. To tell the truth, I'm not sure I want to fit in. It scares me to think that how you're sometimes out late by yourself. You have to remember, we're not in Novato anymore. I miss our little home town."

"Me too," she said.

He inhaled and then studied her face. "I didn't tell you this before, but when I got off the plane the other day, a couple hippies with a peace sign come up and spit in my face, yelling things I won't even repeat. There I was in my uniform, proud to be serving my country, but they treated me like I was dirt."

Beth Ann's anger boiled instantly. How dare they treat him like that.

"I'm so sorry, honey. That's horrible. It's my fault we live here because of my school and my Broadway dreams. I love you, and I'm proud of you for defending this country. You know my mom and Stanley are too. I don't like you leaving, but I am proud of you." She kissed him again then giggled. "Would you like me to show you how proud I am?"

His response was immediate and surprising. He untied her robe and placed his hand on her stomach. Everywhere he touched heated her skin. His kiss went deeper and the room started spinning. God, she wanted him so much.

"Kaylob, please make love to me," she said. "Please don't leave me again without knowing what it's like to be with you completely." She was almost crying.

"Beth Ann," he said in a breathy voice, "I want you so much it hurts, but we can't make love until we're married. I made a promise ..." He pulled back.

Tears pooled in her eyes. "That's what you always say. I'm not a little girl anymore, Kaylob. Don't you find me sexy?"

"Jesus, Beth Ann, of course I find you sexy. You're desirable, beautiful, alluring, and so much more, but..." He pulled her into an embrace. "Please don't do this to me."

She didn't push him about it again. After everything they'd been through already that day, she didn't want to cause any more upset between them.

Later that night, as she drifted off to sleep in the arms of the man she loved, she said a tiny prayer. "Please God, don't let anything bad happen to my Kaylob. Bring him back home to me and let this pain he's carrying in his heart be set free."

* * * *

The next night friends came over to see Kaylob. They played charades and had a lot of fun, but Beth Ann couldn't help wishing they would leave early so she and Kaylob could be alone. They only had seven days before he had to leave again. She knew their friends loved him too and they'd all been there for her while he was gone, so she tried not to let her impatience show.

The next morning, thunder and rain woke her. The storm was even worse than it had been the day Kaylob got home. She crawled out of bed and made her way into the bathroom. The warmth of the shower felt wonderful. After she got out, she slipped her robe on over her pink undies and matching bra.

When she made her way into the bedroom to find something to wear, she glanced into the living room and saw Kaylob sitting on the couch with his hands behind his head, staring upward. He looked so sad that she wanted to make him smile. A silly idea formed, so she tiptoed closer to him.

"Let me entertain…" she sang out in laughter as she opened her robe slightly, moving her hips to the tune of the song from Gypsy.

His attention was no longer on the ceiling. His eyes widened as he watched her continue the song and dance a few seconds more. He stood up and crossed his arms over his chest.

"Beth Ann, it's not nice to tease me like that. I should spank your bottom, young lady."

She knew he was teasing by his smile. Her hands went to her hips. "Try it, Kaylob Shawn O'Brien."

It was something they'd been doing since she was twelve. He always tried to act tough with her, but it was a very familiar game. With one step he tossed her over his shoulder and carried her over to the bed and sat down.

"Kaylob, stop it. I'm not kidding," she protested while giggling.

"Nope."

He chuckled as he placed her over his knee and pulled up her robe, pretending to spank her. When he finished, he flipped her onto the bed and started tickling her.

"Who's the boss?" he said.

"I'm the boss." She laughed, unable to catch her breath.

"Who's the boss, Beth Ann?"

He tickled her knees until she squealed. "Okay, okay. Kaylob Shawn O'Brien is the boss."

She knew what was coming next. He bent over to put his lips on her belly and blew a loud raspberry. She burst into laughter. When he finally stopped, she lay still just staring at him. He was looking away as if something was bothering him.

"What's the matter, Kaylob?" She rose to put her arms around his neck.

"Baby, you drive me crazy." He sat down again and pulled her into his arms to kiss her. He had the best lips in the world, full and luscious. What he did with his tongue sent tingles all the way through her.

"Honey," she whispered against his lips. "Please …"

She gazed into his eyes. He must have known what she was thinking.

"You know I want you, sweetheart." His voice was low and throaty, and there was no hiding how much he wanted her with just his pajama bottoms on.

She put a hand on his cheek. "Then show me how much you love me."

She felt a shiver go through him, and he stared into her eyes. "Beth Ann, you know that promise I made?"

"Yes, I know you made a promise to yourself that we'd wait, but can't you tell yourself it's okay to break it now?" She smiled and ran her hand over his chest. "I'll wait here while you go have a talk with yourself."

"No, you don't understand, baby. I made that promise to Cole at your fourteenth birthday party. He pulled me aside after we slow danced and told me I'd better not touch you until you were twenty. I promised him I wouldn't. I gave my word."

She pulled away from him in amazement. "What? My brother is running my private life? You're my fiancé and it's none of his business, and I'm almost twenty now anyway. I'm calling him right now."

"No, baby, I don't want you to do that," he said unconvincingly.

Beth Ann waved a dismissive hand. "I'm calling him now."

She got up and went to the phone. To her surprise, Kaylob didn't say another word to stop her. She dialed the number and watched as he came into the kitchen and plopped down at the table.

"Hellooo." Cole answered in his usual happy tone.

"Hi, Cole, it's me."

"Hey, Sis. Is everything okay? I was going to call, but Mom said I should give you guys time to work things out." He paused a second then jumped right into his usual over-protective role. "You need to think twice about taking off and staying away for all hours. You're not in Novato anymore. It's dangerous out there."

"I know, I know," she said. "It's not going to happen again, believe me. I was just upset. Everyone needs to stop treating me like a child."

"Then you need to stop acting like one. I know you're upset about Kaylob leaving again and you're worried about him, but he'll be fine. He's an intelligent man. He knows what he's doing."

"So, does everyone know what I did?"

He laughed. "Kaylob called Mom. You know the rest."

Everybody in the family knew that if Jean heard anything, the whole world found out seconds later. Telephone, telegraph, tellamom.

"Small wonder she didn't call the FBI." Beth Ann stared hard at Kaylob, but all he did was give her his signature grin.

"Sis, why did you call?"

"I want you to tell Kaylob you don't expect him to keep a silly promise he made to you when I was fourteen. I'm almost twenty now, and this should be our choice and no one else's. Cole, I love you but—"

"Beth Ann, wait," Cole said. "I didn't expect him to keep that promise after you two got engaged. Wow." His voice started to crack with laughter.

"Cole, this isn't funny. I want you to tell him he can break the promise right now." She lowered her voice to a whisper. "Kaylob wanted to keep the promise because he thought I was too young. Could we at least get this out of the way?"

"Going in for the kill, huh?" He started laughing again.

"Cole."

"Okay, okay," he said. "I guess I really shouldn't be surprised. Kaylob has too much integrity to ever break a promise. Still, I can't say I would have restrained myself with my girl if we were living together, let alone engaged, no matter what promise I'd made. What a trip. Put him on the phone, Sis."

She pushed the phone into Kaylob's chest and went to sit on the bed where she could listen to the one-sided conversation.

"How are things, Cole? No, I've had a little bit of a hard time but I've managed. No, she's still tossing them sometimes, but the pillows are holding up." Kaylob laughed. "She's cute without a doubt." He paused to listen a moment.

"Seven days. I will, Cole, but right now I'm in more danger from the redhead. Thanks, I appreciate that." He paused again. "Yes, she is. No kidding." Laughing again, Kaylob thanked Cole and said goodbye.

After he placed the phone back on the hook, he walked over and smiled at her. Something was very different about the way he was gazing at her now. Oh, she knew that look. Gram had told her about it. "When a man wants you, he gives you the hoochie-coochie eyes. And, honey, when he does, that means business."

Kaylob sauntered across the room, turning down lights and then turning on the radio. All of a sudden the room was scorching hot. Beth Ann thought someone must have turned up the heat. Perspiration started dripping down her back.

Uh-oh, did she even know what to do? Wait, that wasn't even a question, because she had no clue what to do. She'd read that book and ought to know, but how could she? She'd never had any type of sex. She'd read the descriptions and studied the pictures, but it hadn't prepared her for this moment.

Should she lie back on the bed? Or get up and do something? Maybe take off her robe? No, not that. How about her slippers? What had the book said? Oil, it had talked about that, but she didn't have any type of oil. Oh, wait. Kaylob had cooking oil—extra virgin like her. That should be perfect. She jumped up from the bed, dashed into the kitchen, and pulled out a bottle of olive oil.

Kaylob followed and gave her a puzzled look. "Sweetheart, what are you doing?"

"Ah, well ... I was getting some ice water. Did you turn up the heat?"

He laughed, pointing to the bottle. "That's not ice water, sweetheart." He walked over and took the oil away and then he led her back to the bed.

"I'll get us some ice water. Are you okay?"

She nodded but didn't trust herself to say anything. He went back to the kitchen and cracked open the window. A cool breeze rustled through the curtains, bringing in raindrops that spattered on the floor. Somewhere off in the distance, a low rumble of thunder sounded and a bolt of lightning lit the room, matching her electrified desires. Nothing could extinguish her flame. She wanted him and wanted him bad.

When he came back with two glasses of ice water, he set them on the nightstand and caressed her cheek. Then he leaned in for what had to be the kiss of all kisses. Practically melting, she managed to catch her breath.

"Maybe we should talk about what I'm supposed to do," she whispered. She tried to hide her nervousness, but her shaky voice tattled.

He arched an eyebrow and gave her a soft smile. "Baby, you don't have to worry about anything. I want you so much, but we'll only do what you want." He kissed her deeply again and let out a small groan. "Ah, baby, you feel so good."

A lump formed in her throat when she tried to swallow. It was clear he knew she was nervous. He tried to hide his laugh with a cough but failed.

"Kaylob, are you making fun of me?"

"Why would I do that? Just because you've been trying to seduce me since … forever, and now you're so nervous that you're getting oil instead of water?" He cracked up.

"Oh, you." She picked up the pillow and hit him with it.

He wiggled his eyebrows at her. "Well, it's true, and you know it."

She leaned up and kissed his cheek. "Only because I've always been so crazy about you."

He smiled, and the intense look returned to his eyes. When he moved his hand underneath her gown and rubbed his thumb across her nipple, it hardened at his touch. It wasn't the first time he had touched her breasts, but it was different this time because he didn't hold back.

Everything seemed to move in slow motion. She watched him unbutton his shirt and was captivated as the muscles rippled down his stomach and revealed a little patch of hair that ran from his belly button down below his pants. He was magnificent. Even the new scars she'd never seen screamed sexy.

Parts of her own body began to prepare for what was to come before she fully understood the feelings inside. She wanted to tell him how she felt, but her voice got lost, and she was sure it was somewhere between her legs.

He gave her a sexy grin, still watching her. "I'm getting in the shower. Would you like to join me?"

A note of desire came from his whisper and filled her heart with hunger. After his shirt fell to the ground, he ravished her with his eyes, and she almost passed out from his gaze. He crooked a finger at her to follow him, as he headed toward the bathroom, pausing to pull down his boxers. Heavens above, he had the best buns she had ever seen on a man. And that little birthmark on his right thigh ...

Wait a minute. When had he learned to do this whole seduction thing? She knew about his high school girlfriend and had seen them together that first summer. Was that where he'd learned it?

Then she heard the shower come on and only one thing mattered. The questions would have to wait until later.

Her robe and panties came off first, then with one quick pull her bra was history. After a nervous pause, she walked to the open doorway of the bathroom and gazed inside. The water and soapsuds trickled down his body from top to bottom, like fine art.

Her hand went to her chest. "Holy heaven, my heart will never be the same."

He turned to look at her and opened his arms. She hurried into them, their bodies fitting together perfectly. Desire ran through her when he pulled her close. To her surprise, he turned her around and began washing her hair. She leaned her head back and let him massage her scalp, his fingers moving slow and easy. Nothing in her entire life had ever felt so good as his fingers working their magic on her scalp.

When they were done, he reached for a towel and slowly dried her off.

"Jesus, Beth Ann, you're gorgeous." Tenderly, he picked her up in his arms and carried her back to the bed, kissing her deeply as he put her down.

When he started moving down her body, the feel of his tongue on her neck made her tremble. Then he moved lower. Wait, where was he ...

"Oh, Kaylob," she whispered.

All reason left as she surrendered to his touch. Anything she thought she knew about making love vanished when he showed her how deeply he loved her. She reached out to pull him up, but he wouldn't budge. The sensations continued to swell, almost pushing her over the edge. Wherever that led, she was sure it was close to heaven.

"Kaylob, please ..." she begged, feeling a deep vibration in her stomach.

Finally, he came up to kiss her lips. "You're so sweet, baby."

He explored her until she didn't think she could take any more.

"Kaylob, I want you."

"Not yet, baby." His eyes met hers as he did things she had never even imagined.

She began to tremble uncontrollably.

"Now … are you sure, sweetheart?"

Instead of saying a word, she put her arms around his neck and adjusted her body to welcome him. Their eyes locked as he moved his hips gently over hers. She knew he was worried about hurting her, but she was ready to accept all his love. Her hands pulled him toward her with more eagerness than either of them expected. Still, he eased down slowly.

"Oh, baby. I love you so much."

His words electrified her soul. She pushed her hips up to greet him, and their solid passion entered deep into the blaze of love. She realized she was crying and moaning at the same time. With one deeper push, she felt a little twinge that turned into solid heat.

Kaylob pulled back to take his weight off her. "Are you okay, sweetheart?"

"I'm so much better than okay."

He smiled and lowered his lips to kiss her as he moved completely into the core of her soul. Nothing in her imagination had ever prepared her for this. Kaylob was every love poem she had ever read. His eyes never left hers as he made love to her. With each little moan or whimper she made, he kissed her lips and whispered beautiful words to her. His total focus on her experience brought her to tears.

Why would anyone ever want casual sex when being in love feels so incredible?

Throughout that stormy September day, she called out his name many times as they found out how perfect they were together. What touched her heart even more was how they both cried in those final moments. Nobody had ever told her making love was creating love. When they both experienced heaven at the same moment, she understood the meaning behind how two could become one.

Chapter Six

When Beth woke the next morning, the sound of Kaylob's breathing let her know he was sleeping. Gingerly, she got up and tiptoed into the shower. The warmth of the inviting spray felt wonderful. Her tenderness and soreness was uncomfortable, but the elation she felt made it worth every ounce of pain.

When she finished her shower, she dried off, brushed her teeth, and slipped on Kaylob's tee-shirt. She found herself humming "Baby I'm Yours" by Barbara Lewis, their favorite song from childhood. Quietly, she opened the door and then tiptoed to the end of the bed.

"Kaylob, I'm yours. I'll be yours until the rivers all run dry."

His sexy blue eyes opened, and she melted as he reached up and pulled her into his arms. She slipped back into bed and finished their song. This man was so easy to please. You would have thought she hung the moon or bought him a new skillet.

They'd been lying in bed cuddling for about twenty minutes when Kaylob whispered in her ear. "I never knew making love would be so incredible."

Beth Ann kissed his chest, looked up at him, and arched her eyebrow. "Do you have any idea what you did to me?"

A tender smile curved the corner of his lips. "Yeah, I might just have an idea."

"Kaylob, I know why I was crying, but it surprised me to see you were crying too."

He pulled her closer. "Last night overwhelmed me. It will always be the most beautiful experience in my life."

He pushed the damp hair away from her face. "I was finally making love to my childhood sweetheart, the angel I've loved since the first day we met on the railroad tracks. You know I've always been protective of you, and I'll admit your innocence is one of the many things I've loved about you the most."

Pulling back, he looked into her eyes. "Last night, the realization that I was willfully taking that away from you overcame me. I watched you transform into a woman when you experienced passion for the first time."

She put her hand on his face. "All because of you, Kaylob. Thank you."

He smiled and kissed her. "I never thought it possible to love you more than I already did, but I was wrong. Now … I have to get into the shower before I start something all over again." He winked as he got up, and his legs wobbled slightly as he walked to the shower.

With a long, heartfelt sigh, she got up and went to the kitchen. She considered cooking breakfast, but after more thought, she decided she didn't want to burn the place down. So she made coffee and daydreamed about the best night of her life.

When she went back to the bedroom, Kaylob had finished his shower and was making the bed. "Beth Ann, are you okay?"

"Yes, I'm great, why?"

He pulled back the sheets and pointed. "Look."

She walked over to see splotches of blood.

"Sweetheart, I'm so sorry," he said with a sick look. "I thought I was careful."

"You were. I was the one pulling you harder, remember?"

"Such force for someone so little. I guess you wanted me too." He chuckled and kissed her forehead. "I would never want to hurt you though."

She waved her hand dismissively. "The book says sometimes there's blood, but it's nothing to worry about." She moved closer and kissed his neck.

"What book?"

"I bought a book before you came home from boot camp because I thought we would make love then." She giggled. "It has pictures and everything."

With an impish grin, he started searching around the room.

"Kaylob, what are you doing?"

"Looking for the book," he said, laughing.

"Oh, is that so?"

She picked up a pillow and walloped him with it. Before she knew it, he had her on the floor.

"Say it, you little redheaded pillow thrower. Say 'Kaylob is the smartest and the handsomest guy in the world.'"

"Robert Redford is—"

Her words changed to a squeal when he tickled her harder. When she couldn't take it any longer, she laughed and repeated what he wanted her to say, but it didn't stop them from playing on the floor, something they'd been doing forever. Some people might think it was cliché, but Beth Ann knew their love was a once in a lifetime love.

After all the roughhousing ended, he held out his hand to pull her to her feet. Her smile faded, replaced by a sharp pain at the sight of his uniform hanging on the door. He would be leaving again soon. Her spirit fell, and her stomach began to hurt. How in the world could she survive that again? Tears formed in her eyes, but she forced them back.

Despite her efforts, Kaylob must have sensed the change in her mood, because he turned her toward him and searched her face. "Sweetheart, what's wrong? Are you okay?"

She tried to push away the feelings of doom and force a smile. "I'm fine."

He tilted her face up to look at him. "Please tell me what's going on. Did I hurt you?"

She shook her head. She didn't want to spoil their happiness, but she couldn't stand him thinking he'd hurt her. "I was just thinking about you leaving again. I don't want you to go away and fight in that war."

"I know, baby. I'm so sorry. What can I do?"

"Besides not going, you can hold me as close as you can. Do you think you can do that?'

"Now that I can do." With one big swoop, he enveloped her in his strong arms. "I'll hold you as long as you need."

"How about forever and a day?" she whispered.

They stood there holding each other in silence for a long time. She loved gazing into his beautiful blue eyes, but she was touched when she saw his unshed tears. Oh, God, maybe he was hurting as much as she was. That had never crossed her mind until then. She needed to be strong for him.

Thinking of his pain, Beth Ann looked into her heart and found a woman emerging from within. She was a woman now because of the love they'd shared, and that woman was going to be there for him. He'd lost his best friend over there, and even though she hated him going back, she understood why he felt like he had to go.

The morning drifted into early afternoon, and they both decided they needed to get out and get some fresh air. Even though their apartment appeared dollhouse cute, 980 square feet got a bit too cozy sometimes.

They stepped outside into a spectacular day. Beth Ann wasn't sure if it seemed more beautiful because their mood enhanced everything or if her newfound womanhood made her more aware. A few clouds dotted the sky, and the air still smelled damp from all the rain. They walked down the little streets and found a quiet café. Kaylob must have caught the slight apprehension as she sat down at one of the outdoor tables, because he looked concerned.

"Worth it," she told him seductively. "So worth it."

His sexy little half smile sent a shiver into her stomach. He went in the café and came back with two cups of coffee and two oversized chocolate chip cookies. They sat in silence under the umbrella and enjoyed their drinks while all around them the sounds of cars, laughter, and city noises filled the air as they basked in their newly shared experiences.

"Penny for your thoughts," Kaylob said.

She took his hand. "It was fate that day at the train station when you were washing windows and saw me."

He let out a sly laugh as he took a bite of his cookie. "Fate and my determination to meet you."

"What? No, remember the first glance we gave each other?"

He snickered. "It was our first glance, but it wasn't the first time I saw you."

She frowned at him over her coffee cup. "How could that be? I had just gotten off the bus in Novato."

He swallowed before he answered. "I hid and watched you step off the bus. I was so smitten that I grabbed the first bucket and rag I found and hoofed it to the train station to watch you through the reflection in the window. Yup, I was a scheming little devil when I saw you. I had to see more."

She smacked his hand. "I discovered how much of an imp you were the second we met, Kaylob Shawn O'Brien. You winked and made me blush, not just once but twice. My mom thought I had a fever."

He nodded while he chewed. "I almost died laughing when I saw your mom touch your head."

"Oh, yes, Mr. O'Brien, I remember you laughing. I wanted to get out of the car and kick you."

"Or kiss me," he said with a chuckle.

A bashful grin washed across her face. "I have another question for you."

"Okay, sweetheart, what is it?"

"Was last night the best time for you?" Looking down at her hands, she felt her lips tremble. "You know you were my first. I hope I did everything okay. I know you dated that high school girl before we got together, and I heard rumors."

He got up and moved their chairs closer so he could put his arm around her shoulders. He gently lifted her chin to look in her eyes.

"Baby, you were the best. Everything you did was perfect. You were always the sexiest little thing, and, good golly Miss Molly, look how long you teased me."

They both laughed. When they were done, they tossed their empty cups into the garbage can by the curb and started to walk home. The forecast had predicted another heavy downpour, so they hoped to get back before it started. They didn't make it.

They hurried out of the rain to the little market that was catty-corner from their apartment. Fruits and vegetable were set out front with a green awning to protect everything. The smell of fresh baked goods hovered around them before they stepped inside. Kaylob said he wanted to buy some wine and pick up a loaf of French bread and goodies. The place always carried the right foods, deli meats all lined up and salads ready to go. Walking inside brought the wonderful aroma of all the different foods.

Beth Ann headed to the sandwich department to look for some turkey and cheese while Kaylob went in search of white wine. When they went to pay, the short cashier didn't ask for Kaylob's ID, which surprised Beth Ann until she thought about how he carried himself and appeared much older than most twenty-two-year-old guys. His height and body size made him look more mature, but the biggest factor had to be his personality. He could charm a honeybee out of honey, but he never acted self-important or used his appearance to get what he wanted.

Kaylob waited for the total while Beth Ann continued to admire her amazing fiancé. She remembered the time he'd helped Mrs. Jenkins upstairs, the nice lady who'd lost her husband to cancer a few years back. One day as she climbed the stairs lugging three bags of food, Kaylob went up to her and, in a charming voice, told her how lovely she looked. He'd gently taken the bags and carried them upstairs for her.

With Kaylob away at war, who was going to carry Mrs. Jenkins's things up for her, and who would cook for Beth Ann? Nobody at her house—she always burnt everything. Kaylob had always been the chef in the family. The thought sent a sharp pain through her heart. Even though she'd known of Kaylob's loss, some things still hadn't worked their way into her consciousness. She didn't want to experience the intense pain again.

Her thoughts were interrupted when the guy behind the counter spoke. "Anything else?"

Kaylob was staring at some cookies on a rack beside the cash register. Beth Ann was grateful for the giant ginger snaps because they kept him from seeing her unshed tears.

"I'd like two of those please," Kaylob said.

The clerk smiled. "Sure thing. Only two?"

Beth Ann's sweet-toothed fiancé glanced at her, but she said, "No thank you."

Kaylob leaned over to whisper, "After our exercise session, I think you could have at least one."

Heat rose to her cheeks, so she glanced at the floor.

"Make that three," Kaylob told the clerk, squeezing Beth Ann's hand meaningfully.

They headed outside to find the rain coming down harder. Puddles had already formed everywhere they looked. Kaylob took the groceries and bent down so Beth Ann could climb on for a piggyback ride, something they'd been doing for years. They ran laughing while she clung to his neck and kissed his cheek.

The wet steps up to the door were slippery, so he set her back down where she could enter the code. Inside the lobby, she stopped to collect the mail. Nothing much, just a few bills along with a letter from—oh God—Blake Tanner. Crap. She wondered if Kaylob had been paying attention and glanced over her shoulder. Thank God he was busy watching the rain come down in buckets again. With a quick move, she shoved the letter between two bills. She didn't want anything to spoil their good moods.

Kaylob and Blake had never liked each other in school, but years had gone by before she'd found out why. Kaylob had never been jealous except with Blake, which was the main reason she didn't want to deal with the letter. Not today.

After they got upstairs to the apartment, Kaylob stood behind her with the groceries while she tried to unlock the door. Why was her hand shaking so much over a dumb letter? While she fumbled with the key, the mail dropped out of her hand. Holy night, the letter landed on the ground with the addresses showing. She swooped it back up, but not before Kaylob saw the name on the return address.

His mood shifted instantly. When they went inside, he immediately headed into the kitchen and started putting away their stuff, not saying a word. Cautiously, she placed the mail in the little basket by the phone and decided to go sit on the couch, but changed her mind seconds later when she noticed the expression on his face.

* * * *

Kaylob put the turkey and cheese in the refrigerator with a lot less enthusiasm than he'd felt when he'd purchased everything. Why the hell was Blake Tanner writing to Beth Ann? He hadn't said anything, mainly because he didn't want her to know just how irritated he was.

While he sliced the bread, he knew she was watching him and probably getting nervous. She knew he didn't like Blake, but she had no idea how close he'd come to beating the hell out of the guy. Tanner had the nerve to tell him more than once that he loved Beth Ann and wanted her, and Kaylob hated him for it. If the guy ever so much as touched Beth Ann... Holy hell, he couldn't even think about that.

Beth Ann came in the kitchen and started pulling things out of the refrigerator. She always puttered when she was nervous, and he would venture to guess this was one of those times. He put down the bread knife and walked over to close the fridge.

"Feeling a little nervous are we, sweetheart?"

"Uh, no. Why would you say that?"

He pointed at the counter where she had pulled out eggs, a bowl of tuna, soy sauce, Worcestershire sauce, jam, ketchup, chocolate syrup and—good God—the baking soda. She was so darn cute.

"New recipe?" He tried to hand her a baking dish. "Do you bake it at 350, and should I alert the fire department?"

"No, you know I don't cook." She hit him with the kitchen towel and stared at the items on the counter.

"Would you like a little wine?" He picked up the bottle and laughed again.

"Just a small glass," she replied. "I guess I better put these things back. I was thinking of cleaning the refrigerator that's all.

Kaylob chuckled and nodded. "Sure you were. You know I just cleaned it." He leaned over and kissed her head.

Her puttering had lifted his mood until his thoughts drifted back to the letter. Blake Tanner was a jerk, always breaking some girl's heart. The last Kaylob had heard, he was living part-time in Texas but still spent time in Novato. He was single and rich because his parents had died when he was younger and left him a good sum of money. Kaylob felt bad about his parents, but he had a feeling Blake was up to something. For a brief moment, he regretted volunteering to go to Vietnam again.

After he poured the wine, they moved out of the kitchen and sat on the couch. He offered a toast to their time alone together and tried to ignore the shared tension, but he was aware of her still watching him warily, and it made him chuckle.

"What's so funny?" she demanded.

"You," he said with a big grin. "I know you're waiting for me to say something about it. No need for you to putter and worry. I know he sent you the letter. I'm not going to ask about it."

She giggled and got up. "You just did, in your own way. Nice to see you're a little interested."

"Elizabeth Ann Rose, you know I'm a lot interested, but it's your letter." He hated that his jealousy was showing. "I am wondering why you tried to hide it and didn't mention it from the start."

"That's simple. I didn't want to spoil the mood. We may as well get it out of the way so we can forget about it." She went over to the basket and picked up the letter. When she sat down again, he didn't hesitate to move closer so they could read it together.

Hello, Beautiful,

I heard Kaylob is home but will be leaving again in 10 days. Don't know why he would choose war instead of being home with you. I hope things turn out good for him. I couldn't imagine leaving you all alone in Riverside. I would never leave you alone there or anywhere.

I heard you're doing well with your singing and dancing. I'm going to arrange my schedule so I can make it to one of your shows soon, even though I'm spending more time in Texas right now. You're the talk of Novato, Beth Ann. I always knew you were special.

I'm going to be near Riverside in two weeks because I'm conducting business in Palm Springs and was hoping you could have dinner or lunch with me. I'd love to see your new place and spend some time catching up.

Give Kaylob my best. I'm looking forward to stealing you away for dinner soon. I'm still holding out for that kiss to congratulate you on your engagement. Kaylob's a lucky man. A very lucky man.

Love always,
Blake

The letter was bullshit. Yeah, he wanted to steal her away all right, but not for dinner. Kaylob tried to hide his irritation and feigned innocence.

"Are you going to meet him?"

Beth Ann shrugged. "I don't know. My schedule is going to be crazy. What do you think?" She moved closer and put her head on his shoulder.

Besides his unwillingness to show his jealousy, Kaylob knew better than to tell her what to do. "I would never tell you not to meet him". "I trust you, and this is something you need to decide. Forget about kissing him though. He can hold his breath waiting for a kiss. Other than that, it sounds harmless enough. Besides, it'll give you a chance to show off your engagement ring."

She smiled and lifted her hand to admire it. "I love my ring—it's so beautiful, but not as much as I love the man who gave it to me."

He gave her a gentle kiss. "So, if you were to meet him, you'd meet him for lunch instead of dinner, right?"

"Okay, honey, I'll let him know—lunch and no dinner." She let out a little chuckle.

"What's so funny?" He glanced down, arching an eyebrow.

"You're jealous."

"Good guess." He pulled her into his arms. "Maybe you should get me some pillows."

They both laughed and held on to each other.

"Kaylob, do you know that I'm crazy in love with you?"

"I love you too, baby, but crazy doesn't cut it."

He let out a low growl and realized he wanted her all over again. What she did next stunned him speechless. Yowza. She was hot and a very fast learner. He carried her back to bed, and they spent the next few hours teaching each other some more tricks.

Later while she slept, Kaylob lay awake thinking. He had never imagined anything so incredible as making love to his Beth Ann, but he couldn't forget he'd be leaving again soon. He hated the thought of her being alone. Now, more than ever, he wanted to stay with her. He'd loved her since they were kids, but now they had experienced something beautiful, connecting them for life.

What would happen to her if he didn't come back? Jesus, just thinking about that tortured him, so he tried to push it from his mind. He turned and gazed at her sleeping form. She was such a true beauty. Gorgeous couldn't even describe her.

He leaned over and tucked a piece of hair behind her ear, and her lids slowly opened. The way she stared into his eyes embraced his heart and stirred his insatiable hunger. He enveloped her, savoring every sensation and studying every inch of her. Sometimes, while he explored the wonders of her body, shyness would spread across her face, then he'd love her even harder and pleasure would take its place.

The little girl he'd treasured had become a woman. A feeling of possessiveness invaded him and left no room for trespassers. He loved knowing he was the only man who had ever touched her, and he wanted to keep it that way. If that made him chauvinistic, it couldn't be helped.

Holy Mother of God, what was she doing now?

Her lips and tongue were on his chest and moving lower. She looked up at him and smiled.

"Elizabeth Ann Rose, what are you doing?"

"Showing you something else I read in that book."

"Ohhhhhh, baby, I love that book."

His pulse surged as she showed him what she had learned. Slow and easy, until he thought he was going to lose his mind.

"Baby, you better stop."

"No." She shook her head and continued.

God, he loved her stubbornness.

Chapter Seven

After seven glorious nights, Kaylob and Beth Ann both felt as though they were a part of one another, a connection that could never be broken. Their entire last night together was spent wrapped in a passionate embrace that neither of them wanted to end.

Pain filled him when finally he had to pull away, but he had no choice. He had to get out of bed and pack. He knew putting on the uniform would break her heart, so he waited as long as he could to do it. The plane was leaving at noon, and he couldn't be late.

She sat with her knees up and her arms wrapped around them. He leaned over and kissed her shoulder.

"I love you baby, but I have to get dressed."

Without looking at him, she nodded. When he came out of the bathroom wearing his uniform, she was sitting at the kitchen table staring out the window. The pain etched across her face damn near broke him. He was so glad they would be saying goodbye in private at least. They had decided to let Frankie drive him to the airport to avoid a public scene that would be hard on both of them.

Their neighbor Jack had agreed to check on her after he left, so Kaylob called to tell him he'd be leaving soon. After he hung up, he walked over to Beth Ann and pulled her into his arms. She choked back a sob.

"My baby girl, please don't." He held her and tried not to sob with her.

After a minute or so, someone knocked on the front door. Frankie stuck in his head. "I'll be down by the car."

Kaylob nodded as he lifted Beth Ann's face so he could look at her. "I'll be back, I promise."

Damn it, that was the second time he'd said that. He should kick his own ass for making a promise he wasn't sure he could keep.

"Sweetheart, I have to go, okay?" He gave her hand a squeeze. "Frankie's waiting."

She still didn't speak, standing by the kitchen table like she was glued to the floor.

Another knock alerted them of Jack's arrival, but when he came in and saw Beth Ann's face, he backed out to give them some privacy.

"Baby, let's get you to the couch." Kaylob picked her up and carried her to it, then he squatted in front of her and held her gaze. "I love you, sweetheart. Jack's going to stay with you awhile."

She still said nothing, and Kaylob started to worry. He leaned over to kiss her forehead, inhaling her fragrance and trying to memorize it to take with him. When he tried to stand, he realized she was clinging to his jacket.

"Baby, I have to go."

A tear ran down his cheek and landed on one of her hands. Never had he imagined this much torture. Her knuckles turned white as she clutched his uniform tighter. The hardest thing he'd ever done in his life was to pry her hands loose and bring one of them up to his lips to kiss her palm.

"I'm so sorry, baby. Please say something."

"I love you, Kaylob." Her voice broke as she said his name.

"I love you too, Beth Ann. Forever and a day."

He turned to leave, but she stood and wrapped her arms around him. After one final kiss goodbye, he pulled away and she sank back to the couch.

Jack came back in and hurried over to sit beside her. Kaylob mouthed 'thank you' and backed away as Beth Ann leaned her head against Jack. Shouldering his duffel bag, Kaylob left quickly before he lost his nerve. With unfathomable pain, he moved down the stairs and tried to rein in his emotions before Frankie saw him, but he failed.

Frankie was leaning against the passenger side of the car, staring at him as he approached. He put his hand on Kaylob's shoulder and opened the car door. "You okay, buddy?"

Kaylob whisked away the tears and stowed his bag in the back. "As okay as I can be." He got in the car and shut the door.

Frankie climbed in the driver's side and glanced over. "She's going to be all right. We'll all look out for her. Try not to worry."

With a nod, Kaylob found he couldn't speak, so he stared at his plane tickets, wishing like hell someone else would take his place.

Frankie said little on the hour drive, and Kaylob knew he was giving him time to collect himself. Mostly they just listened to the radio. "Unchained Melody" played just as they pulled into the airport and parked. As Kaylob sat and listened to the words of the song, his stomach twisted in fear. No matter how much he tried to ignore the feeling, it still gnawed at him. He might never come back. Why had he promised Beth Ann that he would? Both men sat in silence until the song ended.

"Hey, buddy," Frankie said, "when you get home, you'll be marrying the redhead, and I'll throw you the biggest bachelor party this town has ever seen."

"Sure thing, Frankie."

Kaylob knew he needed to get out of the car, but his hand seemed stuck on the handle. Frankie reached over and touched his shoulder again.

"I'll keep an eye on her. Don't worry."

"Thanks, buddy. I know you'll take good care of her."

The Ontario airport was packed as usual, so they walked through the crowd and took a seat near Kaylob's gate. Frankie picked up a magazine and started thumbing through it while Kaylob tapped his plane ticket on his leg. Neither said much, yet they said everything.

Finally, Kaylob heard his flight number and stood up. "Listen, if anything happens to me—"

Frankie rose and cut him off, his voice breaking. "Nothing's gonna happen. My dad went twice. He made it and so will you."

Kaylob pulled him into a hug. "Bye, Frankie. I'll miss ya, buddy."

"I'll miss you too," Frankie said, his eyes misty. "See you soon, Kaylob."

Kaylob was fighting like hell not to cry again. He had to leave and leave now. Without looking back, he turned and walked away. He hated to say goodbye. He was leaving a lot of people he loved and would miss everyone, but not as much as his Beth Ann.

* * * *

Beth Ann had lost track of how long she'd been sitting on the unmade bed, crying her eyes out. Someone had stolen her heart, so how was it still beating? Jack had gone upstairs some time ago to take a phone call from his sister, but he'd promised to be back soon.

A knock at the door forced her to get up. She opened the door to see Jack poised with some delivery guy holding a beautiful vase of long-stemmed red roses. Jack was so cute and short, standing there with a big smile and his curly brown hair practically vibrating with excitement as he stared at the seven roses. She couldn't help thinking what an odd number that was.

Jack grabbed the card as the delivery guy gave Beth Ann the flowers. She smiled and thanked him, then she snatched the card back.

"Will you wait a second, Jack?" She rolled her eyes. "They're for me, and it's my job to read this."

Jack grinned. "Well, I see you're feeling better."

She handed the vase to Jack, and he carried it to the breakfast bar then hurried back to her side. Beth Ann stood by the front door and read aloud what was written.

To my future wife.

I love you, sweetheart. These seven roses signify our seven days of perfect love. Each rose is a symbol of our experience together. Their names are Elizabeth Ann, Enchanting, Ecstasy, Surprising, Thrilling, Captivating, and Love. Elizabeth, my rose, making love to you was enchanting. What I feel when we experience this together is ecstasy. What you did to me was surprising. Every day with you was thrilling. Watching you was captivating. My heart has total and complete love for you.

Forever and a day,
Your Kaylob

Jack's eyes got big when she finished reading. "Beth Ann, oh my God, you guys finally—"

"Yes," she said. "We made love. No words can describe how wonderful it was, more than I ever dreamed or imagined."

They walked to the couch and both sat down. She held the card, rereading Kaylob's words.

"Ah, honey, how wonderful." Jack patted her knee. "There's no doubt that you two belong together."

"I know," she said, trying not to cry again. Jack grabbed her hand to pull her up. "You, my lady, are eating dinner with Lenard and me tonight.""Jack, that's sweet, but you don't have to cook for me." She didn't really feel like socializing, but eating dinner with someone would be nice."Apparently I do, young lady, but only because I want to."

She had a wonderful dinner with Jack and Lenard. They did their best to help distract her and it worked as long as she was with them, but as soon as she entered her apartment, the sight of the unmade bed stabbed her heart with pain again. She touched the spot where Kaylob had lain last night while he made love to her, and she fell onto the bed in tears.

Sometime later, as she was wiping the tears from her eyes for the millionth time, her engagement ring caught the light and drew her attention. She stared at it and remembered the night Kaylob had given it to her eight months ago, one of the best nights of her life.

Kaylob had just came home from boot camp, and they were going out to eat. She had spent extra time doing her hair and was wearing a new dress she hoped he would like. After she put on her earrings, she checked her reflection in the mirror. Her long red hair fell down to her waist, and the skimpy black dress looked good with her skin tone and petite figure. She was being daring and hadn't put on a bra. She hadn't burned it, but tonight the bra was history.

She walked out to the living room where Kaylob was reading one of his favorite magazines, Cooking to Perfection. She cleared her throat and she saw the exact second he noticed her, because his eyes popped out and his mouth fell open.

Groovy, her honey was scoping her out, but why didn't he look happy? In fact, she could see the wrinkles forming across his forehead. Maybe he was in physical pain because he wanted her so bad. She sure hoped so. They'd been waiting so long to go all the way because he said they had to wait until they were married, and she hoped it was finally starting to get to him.

He stood, his eyes moving from her head to her toes. "Beth Ann, you can't be serious about wearing that dress."

What did he just say to her? She had bought the dress for him.

"Yes, I'm very serious." She twirled around to give him the full effect. "Don't you like it?"

"Uh ... well, yeah, if we're alone, but not going out in public. Come on, look how tight it is. Please, baby, go change."

Her temper flared. "Kaylob Shawn O'Brien, I like it and I'm wearing it out."

"Please go find something else to wear," he said. "It's too damn revealing."

Her hands went on her hips, and she gave him the redheaded 'I-dare-you-to-say-it-again' stare. "Who do you think you are?"

"Last time I checked, I was your boyfriend, and I don't want you wearing that out in public." He folded his arms across his chest and frowned at her.

"You can't boss me around like that. This is the seventies." She could feel her face turning red. "You know I'm right."

He shook his head slowly. "Well, of course you're right. You always are."

She walked over and put her hands around his waist, smiling at him. "I'm glad you came to your senses. I don't want to fight with you, honey. I've missed you so much." She gazed up into his beautiful blue eyes. "Are you ready to go?"

"Not yet, but it won't take me long. I'll change and be right out."

All right, out of sight. She'd won this battle. She picked up his boring magazine and sat on the sofa, wondering how anyone could enjoy cooking or, even worse, want to read about it. Still, she wished with all her heart that he could follow his dream and become a chef instead of being in the army. He was so talented at everything he did, and his cooking was out of this world. She just hoped the next two years would go by fast.

A few minutes later, Kaylob walked out and put his hands out to her. "Let's go, sweetheart."

Holy night. She stood and took a double take. He had on skin-tight leather pants, a tank top that exposed most of his chest, and there was a cocky smile across his handsome face. How dare he try to go out wearing something like that. His muscular build got too much attention from the ladies already.

He took her hand and kissed her palm. "I made reservations. We don't want to be late."

Flames burned from her eyes as she smacked his hands away. "Cheater."

"What are you talking about?" He tried to appear innocent. "How am I a cheater?"

She stomped off into the bedroom, stepped into the closet and grabbed her pink dress. Her entire outfit had to be changed, even her shoes. When she finished changing, she went back out to the living room where Kaylob was buttoning his white shirt over black slacks. He still looked handsome but she was too mad to appreciate it, especially when he tried to conceal a chuckle.

His eyes skimmed over her. "Wow. You decided to change, too. You look beautiful." He lifted both eyebrows, trying to flirt. "Really good choice, sweetheart."

"Kaylob, you cheated. I hate your guts." She crossed her arms and stuck her nose up in the air.

"Aw, baby." He walked over and tilted her chin up to look at him. "You don't hate my guts. You love my guts."

His grin was so darn adorable. How in the world could she stay mad at him?

He gathered her into his arms and nibbled on her neck. "You take my breath away, baby. You're so stunning and sexy, and you smell so good."

What in the world was she going to do with him? He was a charmer with a capital C.

A few minutes later, when they stepped outside holding hands, a light breeze lifted her hair and blew it around her shoulders. A shiver went through her like something really good was about to happen. The moon was luminous as dusk approached. Never had she felt such intoxication. She held Kaylob's hand while they walked and enjoyed the sunset. It didn't take long for them to arrive at the restaurant.

Once inside, the scent of garlic along with a hint of cinnamon and apples filled the air. The smell reminded Beth Ann's stomach that it was empty. Kaylob gave the hostess their names, and she led them to a table where they sat side by side. The place was elegant and romantic, with candles that cast a delicate light across the walls.

They were seated in an area that allowed them to hear the piano music. The night seemed dreamy as they swayed to the music and laughed together. She gave him a tender smile as he held her gaze. The way he looked at her always made her feel beautiful, and she loved how the pervading light of their love seemed to touch the hearts of others.

The waiter came over and brought menus and lemon water. After he left, Beth Ann hummed to the music and touched Kaylob's hand.

"I love all this, Kaylob. Thank you for bringing me here."

"I'm glad you like it, baby. I looked for someplace special for us." He ran his finger down her cheek to her neck. The simple touch left a trail of heat.

"It's all so nice." She looked around. "But being with you anywhere is special."

He grinned and gave her a lingering kiss, the first of many until the food arrived and interrupted his sweet lips.

After the scrumptious dinner, they decided on coffee and dessert. While they waited for it to come, Beth Ann heard one of their songs, "Can't Take My Eyes Off of You."

She sang along with the next line, wiggled her eyebrows, and blushed.

Kaylob smiled at her as he stood, sank down on one knee, and took her hands in his. Her eyes filled with tears, and everything in the restaurant went silent. Her heart pounded so loud she almost couldn't hear. Oh God, was this the moment she had dreamed about all her life?

Kaylob's expression displayed complete adoration and love. She blinked back the tears while she waited for his words.

"Elizabeth Ann Rose, I've loved you since the day I saw you get off that bus in Novato. I knew you were the angel I would be with forever and a day. I adore you with every bit of my heart and soul. I want to spend my life with you. Will you make me the happiest man in the world and marry me?"

Her voice was stuck in a lump in her throat.

"Baby, do you want to marry me?"

Finally, she managed to swallow. "Yes. Oh God yes, I want to marry you." Her arms went around his neck.

The people at the tables close by whistled and applauded when Kaylob slipped the ring on her finger, a diamond in the center cut like a rose with the other diamonds shaped like leaves. It was incredible and perfect, and she loved it almost as much as she loved him.

"It was my grandmother's ring," he said. "I had it changed for you to look like a rose."

"Oh, Kaylob. It's perfect. I love it and I love you." She held up her hand and gazed at the ring, then she kissed him and everything around them vanished.

Now, lying on the bed they'd shared for seven love-filled nights, Beth Ann kissed her ring and savored the precious memory. At least she had plenty of other wonderful memories of their times together to get her through until her Kaylob came back home to her again.

She decided to stick to her usual routine because she had to get up early for school the next morning. When she walked into the bathroom, she saw one of Kaylob's shirts in the hamper. Lifting it to her face, she inhaled his fragrance. It was just what she needed to help her rest soundly.

Wrapped in Kaylob's shirt and wishing it was his arms, sleep came faster than she expected. She hadn't realized she'd drifted off until the phone startled her awake. She needed to turn that thing down. She glanced at the clock and saw it was midnight.

"Hello," she said into the phone.

"Beth Ann, you sound sleepy," Kaylob said. "I woke you."

"Oh, Kaylob, I miss you so much. I'm sorry I acted the way I did. Can you forgive me?"

"No, never." He laughed. "My sleeping beauty, there's nothing to forgive. I should be the one asking you to forgive me."

"I want you to come home to me like you promised," she said, twisting the cord. Her eyes caught a glimpse of the flowers in the window. "The roses you sent are amazing. You're incredible. Do you know that?" Her voice started to break. "I love you… "

"Ah, my baby girl, please don't cry. I love you too."

They talked until he ran out of change for the phone, Afterwards, Beth Ann drifted back to sleep, dreaming of the day he would be her husband.

* * * *

After taking off in Ontario, Kaylob went to San Francisco where he spent hours getting briefed and cleared by the liaison to make sure he was okay to go back after losing his best friend. The itinerary had him waiting for a flight to Hawaii then onto another aircraft until he would finally arrive in South Vietnam. He made his way to the military service desk to board the plane to Hawaii. While he was checking his bag, he recognized a buddy through the sea of fresh faces boarding the plane. Patterson had been in the same barracks as Kaylob in boot camp. "Hey, O'Brien," Patterson said as they sat beside each other on the plane. "Didn't know you would be on this flight."

"Yeah, back to the front to run through the jungle," Kaylob said.

"Yeah, same here. My first tour in 'Nam. Had to leave my girl behind again. She's pissed at me, pissed at Nixon, pissed at commies. Hell, she's pissed off at everything."

"I hear ya," Kaylob said. "I left my fiancée behind too. She was one upset little redhead when I told her I was going back."

"Redhead, huh? Hear they have tempers, those redheads."

"Yeah, she's got one all right, but she's got a lot of other wonderful things too. Here, let me show you a picture of her."

Kaylob pulled it out of his wallet and handed it to Patterson. The photo showed Beth Ann standing by a creek when they'd gone camping. She had on pink shorts and a matching swim top. The photo showed her laughing at a dog that was fetching a Frisbee. Kaylob loved that memory, but it made him miss her even more.

Patterson arched an eyebrow. "Wow, you scored. She's a fox. How long have you two been together?"

"Since we were kids. Hell, I was thirteen when she first knocked my socks off."

Patterson laughed and pulled out a picture of his own. "Here, take a look at my girlfriend. We've been together for about a year."

"Pretty girl, Patterson. You gonna marry her?"

"Not sure if I'm ready for that step, but I have to admit this girl got to me."

Kaylob nodded. "When you find the right person, it makes it easier to settle down."

They both smiled. Kaylob leaned back and allowed his mind to drift to his fiancée with his eyes closed. He already missed her so much and couldn't wait to be home with her again. Guys like Patterson reminded him of why he'd returned to the war. It was important to do the right thing.

Chapter Eight

The next morning, Beth Ann started her week off as usual, only without Kaylob. She ran around getting ready before Carol arrived to pick her up. When she answered the knock on the front door, she exclaimed in delight over Carol's much shorter afro. Along with her mocha skin, it really enhanced her beauty and perfect body.

"Carol, your hair looks groovy."

"Thanks, I love it, and it'll be a lot easier to manage for rehearsal." Carol winked. "Ready to go?"

Before they could get out the door, the phone rang and Beth Ann ran to pick it up.

"Hey, baby, it's me."

"Kaylob. You called me. You weren't sure if you could."

"Of course I called. I miss you."

Her tears were already building. "I hate this. I miss you so much my body hurts."

"Aw, baby, me too, but I'll be home again in no time."

"Where are you?" A long pause made her wonder if they'd lost the connection. "Kaylob?"

"Hawaii, baby, but we're leaving here in a few hours."

"You're in Hawaii? You better walk around with your eyes closed." She giggled.

He laughed. "Oh, sweetheart, nobody can compare to you. You know what though?"

"What?"

"I would love to marry you here. This place makes me want you even more."

"Our wedding in Hawaii? Wow, I like that thought."

"Miss Rose, how about a Hawaiian wedding when I get back home?"

"That sounds wonderful." Despite her joy, her voice broke. "I love you, honey."

"I love you too, my baby girl," Kaylob said.

She stood for a minute after they said goodbye before she placed the phone back in the cradle. Carol came over and put an arm around her.

"Aw, honey, he'll be home soon. God will bring him back to you safe."

"I hope you're right, Carol. I just hope you're right."

* * * *

The first week went by fast thanks to work, but no letters from Kaylob. Beth Ann was getting a little anxious until she remembered that it took a long time to get letters the first time. Working out and training helped to relieve some of her stress.

The next week was harder still when no letters came. Beth Ann's anxiety shifted into gloom. Her insides clenched each time she found the mailbox empty, and she longed to read his words through the folded pages. While she rehearsed the time flew by, but the moment she stopped, the hours stretched into centuries.

Friday finally arrived, and Beth Ann woke to the sound of the phone's ridiculously loud shrill.

"Hey, beautiful," Blake Tanner said. "I'm in town this weekend. How about that dinner you promised me? Can I come and see you this evening?"

Beth Ann was surprised to hear his voice, but even more surprising was the southern drawl he must have picked up in Texas.

"Sure thing, cowboy," she said, "but can we make it lunch?"

"Still have your sense of humor, little lady." He laughed. "How about six pm? That's the only time I have, and I'd hate to miss out on seeing you."

"Well, okay, if that's the only time you can do it. I'll see you then." She knew Kaylob would not be happy, but she'd explain it to him. She gave him directions to her apartment, then they said goodbye.

After work that evening, Carol parked her car and followed Beth Ann upstairs. When they entered, Carol glanced around and shook her head.

"Your place is a mess. Mr. Neat would have a fit."

"I've been bummed out," Beth Ann replied. "Still no letters."

"They'll be here soon, don't worry. Do you want me to stay and help you clean?"

"No thanks. It gives me something to do." She walked over to the counter and started putting dishes in the dishwasher. "I can't stand it, Carol. I miss him so much."

Carol picked up the dishrag and started wiping the counters. "He's going to be fine, honey, and he'll be home soon. Want me to stay and keep you company for a bit? I have a meeting later, and my friend from Washington State is coming down to stay with me."

Beth Ann snagged the cloth from her hand. "Get going to your meeting. You don't need to be late."

Carol kissed her cheek. "All right then, if you're sure. I can stay longer if you need me."

She pushed Carol to the door. "Go, I'm fine. I have an old friend coming to take me to dinner."

"Really? Who?"

"Later." Beth Ann laughed, pushing her out the door.

She continued cleaning until everything sparkled, and then dashed into the bathroom to get ready. When she came out, she admired how nice the place looked. Her kitchen was small, but it had beautiful avocado green counter tops with white cabinets and matching green carpet. She loved the breakfast bar and remembered when she and Kaylob had found the bar stools with seats that matched perfectly counter top. Their dining room table overlooked the street, reminding her of how much they always loved to watch the activities below.

A rap on the door startled her from her daydream. She answered it to see Blake standing in the archway with a bottle of wine and a smile showing off his twin dimples. She had always thought he was one handsome guy with blond hair like Kaylob's and comforting blue eyes. He wasn't as tall as Kaylob, but he had big muscles and was four years older than she was. She wondered if he would be Carol's type. Besides Kaylob, Blake Tanner was the best-looking guy she'd ever seen.

His eyes surveyed her from head down to toe, and he whistled. "Kaylob is one lucky man."

"Hello, Blake." Heat rolled up her cheeks. Damn, she hated blushing. She turned and put the bottle of wine on the kitchen counter, hoping the blush would be gone when she looked at him again.

He stepped into the apartment and glanced around. "Very cute place."

"Thanks, it's a nice place to live, and I love it. Let me grab my purse and we can go." She could feel his eyes following her.

When she came back to the living room with her purse, he took her hand and they headed out for the evening.

They reminisced and enjoyed the food at the Sea Food Café. Afterward, they walked down the empty streets and shared more stories. Blake seemed so much more mature than she remembered. He also seemed brave and protective, pulling her close if a strange man passed them on the street. Someday he'd make someone a great boyfriend or husband.

When they got back to her apartment, Blake stood at the front door and gave her a sweet kiss on the cheek. She told him goodbye and watched him start to leave, but he turned back.

"My wish is for you to have a very happy life, Beth Ann. Will you be inviting me to the wedding?"

She noted a little sadness in his voice. "Of course we'll invite you, Blake. You're a friend."

Not more than thirty seconds after he left, there was a knock on the door. She half expected it to be Blake, but instead she found Jack beaming.

"Guess what," he said while holding his hands behind his back.

"You're pregnant?" She moved and let him enter.

"How'd you guess? And it's yours."

They both laughed, then he stuck his hands out and showed her two envelopes. "You got letters from Kaylob." "The mailman put them in Betsy's mailbox by mistake, and she's been gone for a week. She came up to see you twice tonight. Since you weren't home, she brought them to me."

Beth Ann squealed as she hugged Jack and took the letters.

"Hold on, young lady," he said. "Who was that guy I saw leaving?"

"Blake Tanner, the one I told you about. My old friend from Novato."

"Ah, right. What a hunk."

She laughed. "Jack, don't let Lenard hear you say that. You're already pregnant by someone else." She sat down and focused on the letters. "Let's open these up. Can you please get me a Tab?"

"Sure thing."

When Jack was sitting beside her, she opened the first letter.

Hello my sweetheart,

I love you and miss you so very much. I can't stop thinking of our seven days together. I want to feel you in my arms again. I was thinking that maybe we could get married as soon as I get back home instead of waiting like we planned. Maybe you could start planning a Hawaii wedding. It's up to you, baby, whatever you want. I just want to make you my wife and be together as Mr. and Mrs. O'Brien forever. If we continue to save, we could do Hawaii and see if our friends and family could buy their own tickets. I wish we didn't have to be on such a budget, but I really want to marry you in Hawaii.

Love, forever and a day,
Your Kaylob.

"Very sweet," Jack said. "Open the other one."
"Okay." Beth Ann tore open the second envelope.

Hello Sweetheart,

I was hoping to hear back from you by now. I hope you are well and everything's okay. I miss you. Please write to me soon. Did you meet up with Blake? I hope it was lunch. I know there weren't any kisses. I miss you, baby, and need to hear from you. Maybe these letters are taking longer than before. Just know that you are my baby. Remember that last night we were together, all night? We didn't talk about that much, but I think that is a rare thing. I miss you so much. I miss all of you, the way you smell, the way you taste. Hell, I just miss you.

Love, forever and a day,
Your Kaylob.

Jack arched an eyebrow. "All night, huh?"
"Yeah." She blushed. "Honestly, Jack, the entire seven days surpassed amazing."
Giving her a soft smile, Jack patted her arm and stood up. "He'll be home soon."
She held the letters against her heart and nodded. "I just miss him so much. I've started having those nightmares again."
"He's gonna be fine, honey. You had those nightmares before he got home last time, remember?"

49

"What if they mean something?" A pit formed in the bottom her stomach. Jack waved his hand. "Think positive, okay?"

"You're right. I'm going to push those thoughts out of my head." She stood and hugged him. "Thank you, Jack. What would I do without you?"

Placing his hands on his hips, he gave her a sly grin. "Starve to death."

They both cracked up.

After Jack left, Beth Ann wrote Kaylob three letters explaining what happened. She told him Blake Tanner had behaved like a perfect gentleman and delicately explained that his schedule hadn't allowed lunch. He'd only pecked her cheek goodnight. Lastly, she said yes, yes, yes, of course she would marry him yesterday if possible.

Getting those letters helped the next few days pass with much less stress. On Friday, Carol called her at school during rehearsal and said she wanted to come over after work to hang out. Seeing Carol would help a lot too.

After she got home from work, Beth Ann ran into her apartment and jumped in the shower, leaving the door unlocked so Carol could come in since she should be there any minute. It was pouring down rain again, and Beth Ann was soaked through to her skin.

After she finished her shower, she picked up the blow dryer to dry her hair. Over the roar, she heard the front door open and the TV come on.

"Soda's in the fridge." she yelled over the hair dryer. "Help yourself."

Before she got dressed, she decided on a whim that she would show Carol how toned she was getting. Carol's workouts always encouraged her to push harder. The one thing Beth Ann had learned from school with the female dancers was that nobody was modest. It was no big deal to compare body parts. With her head down, she rewrapped her still damp hair and stepped out into the living room.

"Look at my muscles. Can you believe this—" She spun around to flaunt her body when she heard male laughter.

"Oh yeah, not bad. Not bad at all."

"Frankie, turn around," she screamed, but he continued to gawk. Holy shit, he'd never seen her naked before.

"Okay, now turn around and touch your toes," he teased.

In a move that would have made a ballerina proud, she pulled the towel off her head, wrapped it around her body and ran into the bathroom. Still in disbelief, she put on her robe and went back out, drying her hair with the towel.

"Frankie, what the heck are you doing here? I was expecting Carol, not you."

He grinned. "Yeah, I can see that. I can see all of that."

She walked over and hit him with her towel. He shook his head, looking as innocent as a boy with a key to the girls' locker room.

"Well, hell, I didn't do anything. You came out here and flashed me." He put his arm across his face. "Oh, my virgin eyes."

She poked her finger into his chest. "A gentleman would have said something."

"A gentleman did say something. I said not bad, not bad at all. Besides, I didn't see all that much. Just the front, the back and, oh yeah, the sides. Nice caboose by the way." His impudent grin showed off his dimple, a characteristic he often referred to as a chick magnet.

They both turned as the door opened and Carol walked in, shaking out her umbrella. When she saw Frankie, she gave him a flirtatious wink and got a dazzling smile in return. She glanced at Beth Ann and pointed to her rain-soaked, frizzy hair.

"Hey, can I use your shower? I didn't have time to take one, so I'm sweaty as well as drenched. Lord, it's pouring out there." She was dripping water all over the floor, and Frankie took a giant step closer to her.

"I can dry you off." He wiggled his brows.

Carol shook her head. "Frankie, shut up. I'm in no mood."

He chuckled. "Hey, you can yell at me, even beat me if you want. I'm Italian. I'm used to passion. You can get mad and explode, then we can make up by taking a shower together."

Carol and Beth Ann looked at each other and laughed.

"In your dreams, Russo," Carol said.

The evening turned out fun even after the flashing incident. Carol enjoyed the story and called Beth Ann the flashing redhead. They ordered pizza and spent the evening watching "It's a Mad, Mad, Mad, Mad World," laughing endlessly. Beth Ann had a great time, but it also made her miss Kaylob more. He should be there with her and their friends.

The days turned into weeks and the weeks into months as Christmas knocked on the door. October had come and gone, and she'd had a small celebration for turning twenty. Without Kaylob, her birthday meant nothing. She didn't get many more letters from him, although he had handmade the most beautiful birthday card with seven roses, all sketched and colored red. The letters she did receive said the war was pretty intense and how hard things were over there. He promised he would write her a longer letter soon. The thing she cared about most was his safety. Every night she spent time praying to God that Kaylob would be safe and come home soon.

Time away from him seemed harder during the holidays. Beth Ann avoided the news, or at least she tried. Every once in a while if she watched TV, they would announce how many soldiers had been killed. This made the nightmares even worse. She'd dream of Kaylob calling out to her and not being able to find him, and it caused her nothing but worry.

A few days before Christmas, she made plans with Carol to come over for the evening. Beth Ann hoped that keeping busy wrapping gifts would help her feel better. After they finished decorating the small tree and started on the gifts, Carol must have sensed something because out of the blue she popped up and went into the kitchen. She came back a few minutes later with two eggnogs spiked with brandy that she had brought over.

Carol smiled. "Stand up, Beth Ann. I have a toast before I go to jail for contributing to the delinquency of a minor."

Beth Ann got up and tried to return the smile. Carol handed her the glass and then raised hers in the air.

"A toast to you and Kaylob. May his journey be short, and may love lead him home to you very soon."

Tears instantly filled Beth Ann's eyes. To her surprise, Carol pulled her into a big hug and started trying to sing "O Holy Night." Beth Ann joined in, if for no other reason than to save a perfectly good song.

Chapter Nine

The morning sun found Kaylob sitting in the tent, thinking about his last letter to Beth Ann. Outside the guys yelled while tossing around a football in an attempt to break up the boredom in between the chaos of patrols. Over and over he wished he hadn't said so much about the war, aware he might have made her worry even more. Mailing letters to her this time was harder since Bravo Company had made its way deeper into the dense jungle. Kaylob wasn't sure how long he'd be gone, another reason why sending her letter was important.

He was back with his group, yet nothing felt the same. Walt was dead and everything sucked without him. The memory of his death made Kaylob's heart heavy, he needed to call Walt's family and wished he had done that while he was home. He replayed the day his best friend had taken his last breath. He'd died so fast—no time to say any last words to each other. Kaylob came back to the moment when he heard a shuffle behind him.

"Hey, O'Brien," Patterson said. "Let's go gook huntin'. We're leaving in twenty minutes."

Kaylob nodded and held up his photo of Beth Ann. "I don't leave home without my girl."

Patterson laughed. "Man, buddy, you got it bad."

Kaylob picked up his hat, placed the dirty thing on his head and tucked the picture where it would be safe. They walked out into the sunlight and experienced a warm day for December.

Patterson elbowed Kaylob in the ribs. "Personally, I think she'd like me better, O'Brien."

Kaylob playfully pushed him just before they caught the sounds of Hueys coming toward them. The wind from the blades blew fiercely as the helicopters landed. Kaylob had to get everyone lined up, but needed to wait until the copters cut their engines so his orders could be heard.

Patterson and Kaylob checked all their equipment. Kaylob had been issued an M-60, a bulky machine gun with a metal ammo box to carry the five-inch ammunition. Good thing he was in such good shape since the stuff weighed around twenty-three pounds unloaded.

"Okay," Kaylob shouted, trying to get everyone's attention. "All you little guys line up." He chuckled as he passed out clips.

"Hey, O'Brien, you're not so tough," Donavan yelled back.

"I don't see any muscles, O'Brien," Johnston added.

Most of the men started laughing and giving Kaylob a hard time. He smiled before flexing one of his biceps.

"Yeah, my redhead thinks I'm big and strong, and she's always right. Just ask her."

That busted up everyone. They needed humor to lighten the mood and ease the stress.

Patterson continued getting the M-16's ready—the standard weapon given to each soldier. Besides carrying their tools of war, everyone brought along pictures and trinkets that gave them peace of mind, even if for only a short while. They all had enough room to carry darkened memories along with fear.

Kaylob observed the look on many of their faces and understood what he saw in their eyes. They knew this mission would be tough. Many soldiers had been killed or missing in that area.

After loading everything on the Hueys, the men climbed aboard and Kaylob followed. Sweat dripped from his entire body, and a conglomeration of lumps formed in the pit of his stomach. He couldn't shake the unease he felt from knowing that Bravo would be dropped two klicks south of Hill 375, an area both sides wanted for its strategic position. Rumor had it that many of the GI's had been captured in the area. Worse still, it wasn't far from where Walt had died.

The lieutenant had said they'd be in the field for forty-eight hours, but Kaylob had been through that before and knew the estimate was as useless as any other intel provided by the higher ups.

He plunked down on the jump seat, but his mind kept returning to Beth Ann and how much he regretted his decision to return. No way in hell would he come back to fight in this war again. He was done. All he wanted was to get home and marry her.

The short flight would take about ten minutes give or take. Kaylob scanned the area below as they took off. Amazing how the landscape tricked you with its beauty. There was nothing pretty about war. Before he could blink, the Hueys landed in a small clearing. They set up a perimeter about half a klick west of the drop off. The mission was called Operation Hornet's Nest, and their orders were to secure the hill and to kill as many Viet Cong as possible.

Everything was up and finished in two hours. By mid-afternoon, they moved out and headed toward the dense bush. When they stepped into the jungle, it was as though the sun had been turned off. Layer upon layer of dense foliage blocked daylight like a blindfold while the incessant insect and bird sounds assaulted their eardrums.

The humidity and heat engulfed the men without mercy. Christ, they couldn't tell when the day turned into night, which meant how in the hell would they see the Cong? Kaylob had fear deep in his gut—what if? Goddamn stinking worry plagued his mind. He needed to shake off this shit and stay focused on the mission.

After hours of walking and trying to find the right direction, Patterson tried joking and talking about their girls back home to no avail. Something felt off, as if the group simultaneously sensed a shift. The tension became as thick as the jungle. All thirty-five guys were drenched in sweat and almost silent. Kaylob heard whispers and some choice words while they trudged through the jungle. The bugs were swarming, the heat horrid. Kaylob could feel something but wasn't sure what.

One thing they all understood was that the Cong had way more knowledge of the area than they did. So far, the point man hadn't spotted any sign of the enemy. They had just moved south a little more when Kaylob noticed one of his boots loose. He glanced down at it and then looked at Patterson.

"Damn boot's untied. Signal to Kos to keep moving. I'll catch up in a sec." Patterson nodded and continued ahead.

While Kaylob struggled with his boot, he sensed a succession of unusual clicking sounds around him. With all the noises of the jungle, he could only guess what the sounds were. Patterson halted and lifted his hand squeezed into a fist, the signal to stop. The medic and one of the new guys missed the signal and ran ahead.

Kaylob was still trying to retie his boot when the firing started. It sounded like every weapon in the world was being fired at once. Instinctively, he dove to the right and felt his boot come off, but he couldn't bother with it now. Deafening shots came from everywhere. A split second later, Patterson barked orders then Kaylob saw him and another man drop to the ground. Not dead, but shot.

Hell no. He wouldn't let those commie dicks kill any more of his guys.

The screams of injured men came from all directions. Kaylob's skin poured sweat, and his heart went wild. He rushed out ahead of them, firing his M-60 even though he didn't know where the enemy fire was coming from. Up ahead, he saw the point man caught in a booby trap, dead, but with no Cong anywhere in sight.

Quickly, Kaylob backtracked to pull Patterson and two other guys to safety before surging ahead to find the enemy. He squatted down, trying to see the Cong, but still not seeing them. Where the hell were they?

Shots zipped all around him. Everything was chaotic and tilted. It made him heave from nausea. He stayed low and crawled over to another soldier, not sure who the man was because of all the blood covering his face. Jesus Christ, it was gushing from his mouth.

Kaylob pulled him into the bush and tried to reassure him. "You'll be okay."

He did his best to wipe the blood and memories of Shaffer away. He pulled weeds along with bush and tried to cover the unknown soldier, hoping like hell the Cong wouldn't find him.

The minute he stood, he saw the assholes. Shit, Congs in the top of the trees. Goddamn. No wonder they'd killed so many.

"They're in the trees at ten and two o'clock." he yelled. "Fall back."

He took cover while scanning for a target above. Looking around, he caught sight of blood coming from several of his comrades.

"Payback's a bitch," he muttered as he opened fire toward the tree canopy, no idea if he was hitting any of them.

A bullet ripped into his side, followed by another through his arm. Oh God, he was shot. He fell against a tree, crippled from the blow. He fired again, hoping to kill at least one of the bastards. He slid to the ground, as if no longer in his body. Another shot blasted his leg, and he hit the jungle floor.

Where was his picture? He needed to get his picture of Beth Ann..

His Beth Ann, the love of his life. Her touch and the way she smelled—those were the things he had to remember. His last thoughts had to be of her.

Darkness called his name and the shadow of death blinded him, making things hard to see. Somehow, someway, he knew the Cong was surrounding him. They held up his boot then tossed it aside and ripped his dog tags from around his neck. He'd given up everything to fight this war, to save his brothers.

"Please forgive me, baby," he whispered with his last conscious thought. "Live for me. I'm so sorry. I love—"

Chapter Ten

Beth Ann felt excited because her friends Denny and Lisa were coming for Christmas. She'd met them the same year she moved to Novato, and the three of them had become inseparable, sharing secrets about love, boys and life. Lisa had lived further away, so she and Beth Ann hadn't spent every day together, but a bond had grown stronger between the two that exceeded all others.

Lisa and Kaylob had also been best friends since they were toddlers. Beth Ann could've easily been jealous of Lisa with her dark skin and those stunning blue eyes, not to mention a figure guys drooled over. Beth Ann had known from the beginning the relationship between Lisa and Kaylob was platonic, like a brother and sister. Denny was a cutie too with her funny girl attitude, not to mention she was a Sally Field look-alike.

That morning as she dressed to go to the airport, she admired the small tree she and Carol had decorated the night before. A chill suddenly went down her spine, making her shiver. Kaylob's face popped into her head and she heard him whisper "I'm sorry, Beth Ann."

The bad dreams must be doing strange things. Now she was hearing his voice while she was awake. The stress was killing her. That was one of the reasons she was so excited about her friends coming down from Novato.

After breakfast, she left and drove to the Ontario Airport. Riverside was fraught with holiday traffic, but she finally arrived. She spotted them immediately along with many guys who ogled them from head to toe.

The drive back to her apartment was even worse, and they were all elated when they finally made it. When they entered the building, Beth Ann stopped to checked the mail and found a letter from Kaylob. She went upstairs, helping Denny and Lisa carry their luggage.

While the other two put away their stuff and snooped through her closet, Beth Ann opened the letter. Denny and Lisa's voices faded as she unfolded the pages.

A spasm of emptiness tore through her when she held the letter to her heart and heard Kaylob's voice come out of nowhere, calling her name. Although she knew he wasn't really there, she couldn't help scanning the room. Why was she hearing him?

She sat on the couch and started to read.

Hello Sweetheart,

Sorry I haven't been able to write more often. We finally got done with the first operation and I had a little more time to write a longer letter. Things here are getting worse by the day. We were supposed to be in the bush for 7 days but ended up there for 2 weeks. We didn't have enough water, and the sun seems so damn hot here, even more for December. I'm thankful to be leaving here soon and coming home to your arms. I'll be home in three months, and I can't wait.

I miss home so much that it's hard to tell you in words. I miss your smile, the scent of you. When we're not fighting the Cong, all I can think about is holding you in my arms and making love to you again and again. You are my shining light leading me through this war. When I do sleep, I dream about you.

The idea of having our wedding in Hawaii sounds good. I can't wait to see you, sweetheart. Have I told you that you are the love of my life? I won't ever be coming back to this war. I feel so much older than twenty two. I think this war has taken a toll on me even more than before. The only direction I will be heading when I leave this hell is the direction of home and you.

Changing the subject now, young lady. I want to talk about the one letter you wrote me back in October. I know it's been a while, but I know you were rambling, so I knew right off the bat that you thought you were in trouble. You're so damn cute. I'm glad you were able to visit with Blake, Okay scratch that, I won't lie. I didn't like it at all, even more since it was dinner. No, I'm not mad at you, and you're not in trouble. Please don't do it again, and no more kisses until our wedding day, okay?

I guess Blake has always been my weak point. I knew as a kid that he was in love with you, and I'm sure you had a little crush on him too. I'm glad he didn't try to kiss you on the lips (or did he?) I'm sure you would have told him those lips belong to me. I guess you might say I had a tiny bit of jealousy. Really tiny, very tiny. Okay, bigger than tiny. I know you're smiling right now thinking about me being jealous. So go ahead and smile, because it's true. I don't want any other man touching you.

You are the love of my life and the most beautiful woman I know inside and out. You're soon to be my wife, Elizabeth Ann O'Brien. The name sounds like enchanted singing to my ears. I want to be there with you right now. Sometimes I worry about my decision to come back to this war and leave you behind again, but I know you have a lot of people taking good care of you. So no matter what, I know you're safe.

I love you so much, sweetheart. Always remember that. My love for you will never fade and never die. Tonight at midnight (your time) go look at the stars. I will be thinking of you then even though the time zones are different. You'll see one star that will twinkle even brighter than the others, because that's me sending you love. I will do that until I come home.

Love forever and a day,
Kaylob

Three months to plan her wedding. The thought made Beth Ann happy, but tears burned her eyes because she missed him so deeply. Lisa and Denny came and sat beside her.

"Don't cry, sweetie," Lisa said. "He'll be home before you know it."

They both hugged her. "Hey," Denny said, "I know what we need to do. Let's go look at wedding dresses."

Between the two of them, they talked her into it. She knew their motive—to cheer her up. The three girls headed out and went to many shops, spending hours looking. They only found one dress Beth Ann liked, but it was still a cheery day out, all of them giggling like back in junior high. Throughout the day, Beth Ann couldn't shake an uneasiness that invaded her.

After their day of shopping and lunch at a little café, they bustled through the door to the ringing phone.

"Hello, bride-to-be speaking." Beth Ann announced, laughing.

Denny and Lisa looked up from where they sat on the living room floor and laughed with her.

"Beth Ann?" It was Kaylob's mom.

"Oh, hi, Jackie. We were just out shopping for my wedding dress and—"

"Beth Ann, who's with you?"

Her smile faded. "Denny and Lisa. Why?"

"Could you put Lisa on the phone please? I've called your mom. She's on her way down to see you. We've been trying to call you all day."

"What's going on?" Beth Ann's stomach took a dive.

"Please, Beth Ann. Put Lisa on the phone."

Denny and Lisa stopped laughing and got up to come stand beside her. Beth Ann handed the phone to Lisa and watched her face as she spoke.

Whatever Jackie said caused Lisa to turn as pale as powder while her hands twisted the cord.

"Are they sure?" Lisa said and then listened. "Is there any chance they could be wrong?" She paused again. "Yes, of course. We won't leave her side." She swallowed and looked sick. "Oh my God, Jackie, I'm so sorry."

After Lisa hung up, a long silent moment filled the room. Taking a deep breath, Lisa moved to the living room where Beth Ann had retreated. Beth Ann tried to smile, but her lips quivered. All she wanted to do was find a place to hide. When she looked at Lisa, she saw tears building in her eyes.

Beth Ann turned abruptly, ignoring what had just taken place. She walked into the kitchen and opened the refrigerator, then she started pulling things out.

"Would you guys like a glass of lemonade or soda? I still have some here. You know Kaylob loves soda, but not as much as he loves cookies and milk." She laughed, but tears spilled down her cheeks.

Silence filled the place, except for the clock that chimed. Beth Ann knew they were watching her, so she did her best to ignore their stares.

"The Army's full of shit," she said as she swiped away the tears.

Lisa stepped into the kitchen and moved closer. "Beth Ann, I'm so sorry."

She wheeled around. "What are you sorry about? I don't want you to be sorry." She inched away from Lisa and picked up the cookie jar. "We bought this cookie jar because it holds so many cookies. My Kaylob is the Cookie Monster, you know."

Beth Ann set the jar down and started filling the glasses with lemonade. Lisa and Denny huddled closer to her. She handed Denny one of the glasses.

"Kaylob loves my lemonade."

Denny nodded and whispered, "I'm sure he does, honey."

Lisa took her glass of lemonade, but set it back on the counter. She gently held Beth Ann by the elbow and turned her around. "Beth Ann, they think Kaylob was killed. They found his tags covered in blood along with one of his boots, and it was his blood type. There was a fierce fight. A lot of our guys were killed." She inhaled deeply. "When the patrol got back there, they … they didn't find anyone else. The Army is calling him MIA—missing in action but presumed dead."

Beth Ann glared at her. "They found his boot, and they will find him."

Tracks of tears stained Denny's face.

"He's okay, Denny," Beth Ann said. "Don't cry. He's coming home."

Lisa placed her hands on Beth Ann's shoulders. "They found his dog tags covered in blood, honey. It was his blood type. They think he's dead. This was days ago, and nobody has found him."

Beth Ann slapped Lisa's hand off her shoulder. "He's not dead, they're wrong. I would know if he was dead because my heart would feel it."

Lisa shook her head. "No, honey, I don't think they're wrong."

"Lisa, it's a mistake." Beth Ann ran to the couch, picked up the letter and waved it in the air. "See, I have his letter."

She picked up the envelope and looked at the date. A hush fell as she slumped onto the couch, still holding the letter.

"It can't be true. I would know. You guys are just giving up on him. I know he's out there. Maybe he's lost, but he's still alive." She got up, walked over to the phone and dialed the operator. "How do I get in touch with the Army?"

Lisa and Denny both stood close by her side while she was on the phone. At one point Lisa got a chair for Beth Ann to sit in, but she would only stand.

What seemed like hours of runaround finally led Beth Ann to a Captain Jared Long, a soft-spoken man who explained to her about Kaylob and the definition of missing in action and presumed dead. He also explained how the classification of MIA was just a temporary formality due to the paperwork and red tape. He made it clear that they had no doubt that Kaylob had died and was soon to be declared dead and a hero.

Beth Ann yelled into the phone, "How can you give up on him? He's out there."

Sobs shook her body as she tried to convince the captain that Kaylob was alive, telling him that she would have felt him die, but he wouldn't listen. She was fed up with all of them.

Lisa gently took the phone away. Her voice soft and calm, she thanked Captain Long for taking time to speak to Beth Ann and asked if there might be a mistake. She listened and thanked him again before placing the phone back on the holder.

The sound of the clock signaled the afternoon had faded into evening. Beth Ann was exhausted, overcome by the storm of emotions.

"This is a mistake," she insisted. "He's not dead."

The front door opened and Beth Ann's parents stepped into the apartment. She ran into her mom's arms.

"Mommy, they're giving up on him. Tell everyone he's not dead."

Jean looked at her daughter, her eyes full of sadness. Beth Ann didn't want them sorry for her.

"Stop looking so sad. He's not dead."

The emotion became too much for her. The room faded and she crumbled. The last thing she remembered was Stanley lifting her into his arms. She leaned her head on his shoulder and noticed tears in his sad green eyes. She wept as the obscurity of darkness captured her.

Chapter Eleven

Beth Ann's memories after that were all a blur with no difference between day and night. When she did wake, she wondered how she had gotten into bed. Over the next few days, her mom would wake her periodically and make her take sips of soup. Her life became a black abyss, a void, welcoming her to escape from the hell that was now her life.

Her family and friends kept vigils, making sure she moved around. Her mom and Carol had to walk her into the shower, bathing her like an infant. She hated being so weak, but she couldn't help it. She wanted Kaylob to come home now.

She vaguely heard voices coaxing her to return to her friends and family. "We're here, honey. We love you. Please come back."

She didn't know who spoke, nor did she care. There was only one thing she cared about—Kaylob. Sometimes a man, probably a doctor, would stick her with a needle and take her into numbness.

Days later, she awoke to see her grandmother sitting in the rocker by her bed, humming her old Christian songs. Beth Ann's lip quivered and she held out her arms. Gram lifted her onto her lap and cradled her as she had done many times when Beth Ann was little. Those moments were the most tranquil ones she experienced since the heartbreaking news. She needed Gram more than anyone else in the world, except Kaylob. Gram rocked her.

"He's not dead, Gram," Beth Ann whispered "They've given up on him and I need him so bad. I love him."

"I know, sweetie. Oh Lord, how Gram knows."

Beth Ann noticed the moisture in Gram's blue eyes. "Don't cry, Gram. We'll find him."

She reached up, laid her gentle fingers on her grandmother's tears and swabbed them away. Beth Ann felt the vibration of Gram's weeping before the medicine carried her away again.

* * * *

63

Days went by, maybe weeks. Beth Ann had no concept of time. One morning as she lay in bed, she overheard her mom crying while she spoke on the phone. Beth Ann knew she was talking to Gram.

"We can't put her on the phone. She still won't talk to anyone and hasn't said anything since you left. Honestly, she had the most response to you, and it's been two months."

Two months? Beth Ann couldn't believe that much time had passed since Kaylob was lost. She wondered where he had gone. She strained to hear what her mom was whispering into the phone.

"We're going to pack up her things and make arrangements to have her transported to Novato. She needs to go home."

No. Beth Ann would not go home. She had to wait for Kaylob. She wanted to get up and move on her own, but she couldn't seem to get her body to move, as though she were paralyzed from the pain and the loss. There was no way she'd let them imprison her in the numbing darkness again.

"Gram, can I call you back? Beth Ann is getting up... Yes, I'll call."

Beth Ann's weak legs protested as she rose to her feet, trying to catch her balance.

"Mom, I'm going to take a shower." She wheezed, discovering her voice almost gone.

She tried to ignore her parents' pained and helpless looks, Stanley at the breakfast bar drinking coffee and her mom at the kitchen table. Her mom's jet black hair that was normally perfect, now looked a mess. When Beth Ann entered the bathroom, she shut and locked the door. A few seconds went by, then whispers told her that Carol, Frankie, and Jack had arrived.

Her first look in the full-length mirror made her gasp. Who was that stranger? She couldn't believe the skeletal, sunken image staring back at her, so gaunt and pale. With a deep breath, she lifted her pajama top to reveal her ribs and collar bone. Then she dropped her clothes on the floor and turned on the shower.

The water hit her like needles, stinging memories into her lethargic mind. Those last seven days with Kaylob were all there. Heartbreak overcame her as she leaned against the tile then slid down to the floor and sobbed. Without Kaylob, she felt empty and alone. The physical anguish caused her stomach to clench, and she vomited. When she was done, her hand went across her mouth while she sobbed.

"Kaylob, please come home. Where are you? How do I continue?"

After sitting—for how long she hadn't a clue—the warm water ran out. She turned off the shower and stood in front of the mirror, examining her mangled hair. Kaylob had always told her how beautiful her hair was.

She glared at the stranger in the reflection and watched the tears slide down her face. After a few seconds, she opened the bathroom drawer and calmly took out the scissors, then she began cutting her hair one strand at a time.

An ominous silence swept through the room as she sliced off her hair and jabbed her scalp. With the silence came a wave of pain. The only love she had ever known had been gone for two months. In that moment, she realized all her dreams had to be abandoned. From the ashes of war, her love might never return. Pandemonium slammed through her while she hacked off more of her hair. Blood flowed down her face, but she didn't give a damn.

"I want it gone. I want it off." she screamed. "I hate you. I hate God. Kaylob, why did you leave me alone? You promised me."

Outside the bathroom, she heard alarmed voices that sounded miles away.

"Beth Ann, let me in," her mom pleaded. "Beth Ann, please."

The voices grew louder. "Beth Ann," Frankie shouted. "Open this goddamn door."

"Honey, please open the door," Jack's voice cajoled.

Beth Ann stood like a weather-beaten statue, naked and dead. She had become a freak. Distorted images twisted and shifted in the mirror. She stared at her image and started screaming. The jiggling of the doorknob couldn't stop her uncontrolled agony.

The door finally flung open, and her mom cried when she saw her. "Oh my God, Beth Ann. What have you done?"

Beth Ann shivered and convulsed. She sensed everyone's eyes on her nakedness. The floor was littered with hair, water and blood.

Jean grabbed the robe and covered her while examining her to find the source of the blood. Tears rolled down her mother's face full of pain unlike anything Beth Ann had ever seen. Her mother's hands clutched her arms.

"Beth Ann," she said in a demanding whisper, "you are not dead. This has to stop." She reached for a rag and held it to her daughter's scalp to stop the bleeding.

Beth Ann pulled back. "Kaylob made me promise to keep living when he left. Why can't I break that promise? He broke his about coming home."

"You can't, Beth Ann. You're alive. Kaylob would want you to live for you and for him."

"Screw what Kaylob would want. He didn't care what I wanted, and he went and got himself ... disappeared." She refused to say dead. She was furious with him, but she still believed he was alive and couldn't understand why everyone had given up on him.

As she listened to her mother, Kaylob's words shadowed her plea. She sank down to the ground, pulled her knees up to her chest and covered her face with her hands.

"Oh, Kaylob, please come home."

Except for the dripping of the shower, everything fell silent. Beth Ann looked up at her mom, clouds of heartache and lost hope forming her mother's features. The truth lived in her mom's brown eyes, the little girl who brought color into the world existed no more. The storms of war had stolen Beth Ann's love, but the enormity of her emotions carried the life away from her mother.

Everyone clustered around the doorway, except her mom who remained beside her. She recognized the emotion on their faces—grief. They must feel she'd had lost her mind, and so did she. She had battled through hell's bleakest pain of an epic love gone. Missing. Lost.

"Beth Ann, please," Stanley begged.

Her love might be gone, but just like Kaylob, it wasn't dead. At that moment, Beth Ann understood she had to stand up and had to do it alone.

Taking a deep, cleansing breath, she fought back the tears and wiped her face with the sleeve of her robe. Like a foal standing for the first time, she started pushing up off the floor. Her mom and Stanley stepped over to help, but Beth Ann's hand shot up for them to step back.

Jack waved at them. "Let her do this on her own."

With a new inner strength, she found the ability to stand. They all stood back as she headed out to the closet to find some clothes, but Carol moved quickly to close the closet door and step in front of her.

"Beth Ann, please let me get you something to wear."

Beth Ann started to argue, then she understood why. All of Kaylob's things still hung in the closet waiting for him. She nodded and went back into the bathroom and sat on the hamper. Her eyes scanned the mess she had made, and her hand went to her hair—gone, like Kaylob.

Her mom came in with cleaning supplies and opened the shower door. Beth Ann hated for her mom to have to clean the vomit along with the blood and hair.

Jack stepped in and leaned down close to her face. "Would you like to eat something, honey?"

A tiny yes was all she could manage. A few minutes later, the smell of eggs and bacon made its way to her senses and her stomach growled. Beth Ann moved in front of the bathroom mirror, cleaned the blood off her face and examined a few areas she had gouged.

A few minutes later Carol came in and brought her pink top and white sweats along with panties and a bra. She helped her get into her clothes, now many sizes too big. When Beth Ann finished dressing, she turned to examine herself.

"Did you know pink is Kaylob's favorite color on me?" she said, her voice almost a whisper.

"Oh, shit, I'm sorry," Carol said. "You want me to get you something else?"

"No, this is perfect. I have to honor him until he comes home."

Carol embraced Beth Ann while they cried and then she attempted to fix her whacked off hair. Afterward, they went into the dining area where Jack was finishing up breakfast. Vain hope filled their faces as Jack handed her a plate of food.

In the end, she got down one egg, one piece of bacon, a few bites of toast, and a full glass of orange juice. The food gave her marginally renewed strength. The morning hours slipped into early afternoon. Beth Ann sat on the couch with Frankie, her head resting on his shoulder. Anyone who witnessed them together had enough insight to see he was not going to leave her side. The TV had been on all day, but Beth Ann had no clue what programs had aired. All her thoughts were on Kaylob.

Jack and Lenard cooked spaghetti for dinner along with a homemade chocolate cake. Everyone seemed to exhale when Beth Ann finished eating. Her mom's eyes flickered with hope as she saw her daughter coming back to life.

* * * *

The next morning, after Beth Ann ate breakfast, she turned to Frankie. "I need to get out of here. I need some fresh air." Then she remembered that her hair looked like a bad accident. "I can't go out like this. I need some help with my hair."

Her mom's face lit up. "Honey, I can take you to get a new style."

"No, Mom. I want you and Stanley to go home and get your life back."

"No," her mom said in a way only a mother could say.

Despite the refusal, Beth Ann insisted. "Please, Mom. Stanley." She stepped closer. "I'm going to live again, I promise. You guys have been gone for two months. You need to go home and sleep in your own bed, be in your own home. Please, for me?"

Frankie walked over. "I'm not leaving her side. I'll stay as long as she needs me." He glanced back at Beth Ann. "I love her and won't let anything happen to her. Kaylob asked me to watch out for her before he left, and I won't break my word."

Beth Ann could see her mom relax at Frankie's words. The love Frankie felt for Beth Ann didn't hide in those moments.

Beth Ann took her mom's hand. "I'm sorry for putting you through this, but I need to get back to school. I'm going to be all right. Kaylob wanted me to live, and I want me to live."

Jean nodded and tears filled her eyes. Beth Ann gave her mom a warm hug.

"I love you, Mom. Thank you both for all you've done."

Jean turned to Stanley. "Did you hear that, dear? We're being kicked out."

Chapter Twelve

After Jean and Stanley packed up what little stuff they had brought, they headed back to Novato. Beth Ann had to start life all over again. She couldn't believe two months had passed, but the fact remained that Kaylob was not dead. After a few hours of doing nothing, the apartment started closing in on her.

She left Frankie on the couch alone and Carol on the recliner trying to stay awake by doing the funky chicken. Beth Ann felt their eyes following her into the bathroom. With trepidation, she had to gauge how badly she looked, so she gazed into the mirror. Just as she thought, she was now a freak.

Whispers came from the other room. Carol had been reading *One Flew Over the Cuckoo's Nest*, and Beth Ann couldn't help but wonder if she'd chosen to read that book because her very good friend was a little cuckoo. A few seconds later, she sensed a presence standing in the doorway and turned to see Frankie.

She held up a piece of her hair and pouted at him. "Nada, absolutely nothing can fix this."

Frankie gave her a tender smile and stepped out. The next thing she overheard was him on the phone. "Jack, hey, buddy. Can you help our girl out? With her hair."

Beth Ann strolled out of the bathroom just as Frankie placed the telephone back on the holder. He winked at her, and a feeling of love rushed into her heart.

She wrapped her arms around him. "I love you, Frankie. Thank you."

He held her tightly and took in a deep breath. As she glanced up into his eyes, she saw tears in them and realized how bad he must be hurting. To witness her meltdown had to have been horrific for him, especially on top of the sadness he experienced from losing Kaylob. Yet as much as she wanted to help him, she didn't have the strength to do that right now. She had to take one step at a time into a new world, a world without Kaylob. She had no idea how to do it, but she knew she had to try.

A few minutes later, someone knocked at the door. Before anyone could answer, Jack rushed into the room smiling.

"Okay, my little chickadee, we are about to make the hall of fame makeover."

He moved the dining chair into the kitchen and waved his hand. Beth Ann walked over and slumped down in the chair, wondering if it was even possible for anyone to fix the mess she'd made.

Jack looked down at her and seemed to read her mind. "We can fix that up, sweetie. Happy hair will make a happier girl." He leaned down and gave her a kiss on the top of her head. "I'm going to be gentle with your scalp. Honey, we're going to get through this, I promise."

She managed a forced smile because she knew he wanted to make her feel better. Luckily, he was fantastic with hair and had owned his own shop once.

"I hope so," she said. "I look like a freak."

"Not for long." Jack started spraying water on her head, and it dripped down her face. Frankie went into the kitchen, grabbed a towel and handed it to her while Carol pulled up another chair. A warm glow radiated from the three friends Beth Ann was so glad to have.

Jack started snipping like there was no problem, going on about how everyone had been growing their hair out these days, making most styles good for both guys and gals.

"I'm still old-fashioned though," he said. "I want guys to have short hair because it makes it much easier to tell them from behind." He quickly covered his mouth. "Just don't tattle on me to Lenard."

He cut and snipped here and there, humming a tune Beth Ann didn't recognize. After about thirty minutes, he ended with a not-so-subtle flair of his hand. "Okay, Beth Ann," he exclaimed. "Now that's adorable, plus your natural curls really enhance this style. No looking yet until we do your makeup."

He opened a box filled with all different kinds of goodies and started on her face. When he finished, he smiled at his handiwork and winked at her.

"Beautiful once again. Okay, go look."

With uncertainty, she stood up and headed to the bathroom mirror. She had to admit that the eyes staring back at her showed a smidgen of life. Her hair was cut shorter than it had ever been, but she liked the style. Thank goodness no evidence of her own handiwork showed.

With concern, she climbed on the scales and gasped. Oh Lord, ninety-three pounds. While she was still trying to process her weight loss, Carol entered.

"What, sweetie?"

"Oh, Carol. I only weigh ninety-three pounds. I have to start eating again."

Carol winced. "Yeah, we're gonna have to fatten you up."

70

Beth Ann's emotions swung wildly between being alive and the walking dead. Kaylob would be back—nobody could tell her anything different. She missed him badly and worried that he was hurt, but she had to try to live as normally as possible. He'd want her to do that.

She went into the kitchen. "Thank you, Jack. I almost look human."

He hugged her. "Honey, you're beautiful."

Frankie clutched her hand and kissed it gently. "You're a fox again. Would you like to go out and get some lunch?"

She nodded. "I need that. I don't even weigh a hundred pounds."

Frankie's eyebrows furrowed in deep thought. "Where would you like to go?"

"Anywhere but here."

Carol gathered a few things while Jack swept up the hair. Beth Ann asked them both if they wanted to tag along with her and Frankie.

Carol hugged her. "I need to go clean up my apartment and spend some time with my cats. You two go ahead, but call me if you need me. I'll be back soon."

Jack waved his hand as he headed out. "You two have a lovely time. Lenard and I are going to have a fight about who took out the garbage last night, or maybe who made the bed. I'll think of something good."

Beth Ann looked puzzled.

Jack laughed. "Never mind, honey. I'll explain later."

When Frankie and Beth Ann went downstairs, they saw Mrs. Jenkins in the lobby. She glanced up at Beth Ann with sorrow in her eyes. Now Beth Ann understood why she had hardly ever left her apartment that first year after her husband died. The widow had lost everything because of his cancer—their home, the business, and then she'd lost her husband.

Mrs. Jenkins walked up to Beth Ann and put her arms around her. "I'm so sorry for your loss. What a wonderful young man he was. I understand how hard this must be. You come up and visit me soon and we can talk, okay?"

Beth Ann nodded. "I'll come see you soon."

"Good. Oh, Beth Ann, I have to tell you this hairstyle is adorable on you."

"Thank you, Mrs. Jenkins."

They said goodbye, then Frankie took her hand and stepped outside the building. They waited a minute to let Beth Ann's eyes adjust to the sunlight before making their way down the stairs to the sidewalk. The sounds of traffic, laughter, and life carrying on greeted her like a frigid blast of awareness. The same food stands lined the streets, the smells floating through the air, but nothing seemed right. The city was alive, but she still felt lifeless.

A man walked down the street with his golden retriever. He had to stop when the dog spotted Beth Ann. She removed her hand from Frankie's so she could bend down to pet the beautiful golden creature. The pup licked her cheek and wagged her tail as though she sensed Beth Ann's sadness. Someday, she hoped to have a Golden Retriever. She and Kaylob had talked about it many times.

Beth Ann and Frankie watched as the man led the dog around the corner and out of sight. Frankie took her hand again, and they walked to a little Italian restaurant called Café Savilla. The meal tasted wonderful, and Beth Ann was proud of herself for eating everything on her plate.

By the time they left, dusk had settled over Riverside, and as much as she disliked it, she knew they needed to go back. She dreaded going home because of the memories there waiting for her.

Over the next few weeks, she and Frankie accomplished many outings together but made sure to avoid the park her and Kaylob had visited. She'd promised herself she would not go back there until he came home. The end of March had always been beautiful in Riverside. The sunsets cast many colors over the landscape and buildings. For Beth Ann, just saying the month seemed strange. Three months had passed since the news about Kaylob, and she had no words to describe how much she missed him.

The wind of the season brought wonderful memories of whispers and gentle kisses.

* * * *

The first week of April, Beth Ann dressed and made a decision to make it her independence day. She announced to Carol and Frankie she needed to go out alone. It would be her first trip outside without Frankie beside her holding her hand. Her protective friends stood up as she headed toward the door.

"I'm okay," she said. "I'll be fine. I need to do this."

Frankie and Carol looked at each other and then at her with concern on their faces.

Beth Ann smiled. "Don't worry. I'll be back in about an hour."

She left and went cautiously down the staircase. She had tried to be brave in front of them, but she couldn't hide her shaky legs from herself. Today would mark the first day of her new freedom, and the thought gave her the courage to step outside into the morning light.

The sidewalks thrived with the normal hustle and bustle. Great, the first thing she noticed just had to be Mr. Tattooed Guy from the corner market who smiled and winked at her. All around her, the city pulsed with routine life, so her mission would be to perform for everyone as though she was normal too. People stepped out of stores with their bags of treasures, laughing and looking happily at their companions. A couple holding hands kissed lightly when they hailed a taxi. Another lady caught her eye with the way she pulled her little dog on a short leash, unaware the pup had a hard time keeping up.

Suddenly, Kaylob's voice echoed in her mind. "What do you want to eat, baby?"

She turned quickly in a circle, trying to find him.

Again his voice slammed her. "Beth Ann, I'm here."

Oh, Lord, she had lost her mind for real. She needed to find a place more private. Down the road to the south she came to a four-way stop. She needed to catch her breath and calm down, so she took a right turn.

The area appeared quiet. She'd never been there before, but there seemed to be a magnet drawing her to the vicinity. An old abandoned building came into view right across the street from a beautiful hotel. When she approached the old place, she peered through the windows and felt as if she shared a connection with it, maybe because it was alone and abandoned like her.

Tears sprang to her eyes and added to the bewilderment she felt at what she saw next. Kaylob appeared carrying boxes that he placed on a very large bar. Chills like she'd never experienced ran through her as she watched him throw back his head in laughter at a little blonde girl skipping toward him.

"Daddy, Daddy, come look." The child wrapped her arms around Kaylob's leg.

Oh my God ...

Beth Ann watched herself walk over to Kaylob and the child, a beautiful golden dog following her. She saw herself sweep the tiny girl up in her arms with nothing but love in her eyes for the child. As fast as the vision came, it faded away.

Tears stung her eyes again. Don't let this happen, not now. She couldn't lose her mind. Although dizziness jostled her, she knew she needed to move away. She ran to the main street as if summoned and almost ran into Frankie. He must have decided to check on her.

"I'm taking you home, sweetheart." He swept her into his arms.

She leaned into him and wanted the ground to swallow her.

Okay, her first attempt had failed, but tomorrow she'd try again. Or so she thought, because her overprotective best friend wouldn't even consider it. After a few more days, she had to try again, but she would stay away from the haunted building.

Once she'd succeeded going out for a few days, she started shopping at the corner market and walked a little further each day. Kaylob's words pushed her to keep on living, and she had the odd feeling that he was holding her to that promise.

When she walked in her apartment the following Sunday afternoon, she found Carol and Frankie arguing about the TV and who would get the couch or the floor. Frankie had Carol on his lap, trying to convince her they needed to share the foldout.

Beth Ann stood watching them in amusement, then suddenly everything changed. Strange noises echoed through her mind. She heard the sounds of a jungle along with a dog barking.

Frankie's voice pulled her back into her living room. What the hell was going on?

"Come on, Carol," Frankie said. "You know I'd treat you right." He kissed her neck and raised his eyebrows.

"Russo, let me up, you brat."

"Okay, okay. Can't blame a guy for trying."

He released her, then she bent down and kissed his head. Carol looked over and made eye contact with Beth Ann. A tilt of her head let Beth Ann know she needed to laugh and act normal, so she chuckled while she went into the bathroom to get on the scale. Groovy, she weighed one hundred and two pounds. Yet when she glanced in the mirror, her dull, lifeless eyes reflected sadness. No longer did they shine.

Carol and Frankie were still horsing around when she went back to the living room, so Beth Ann cleared her throat. "You're both going home tonight. Maybe you can work out better sleeping arrangements, and I need my space. Besides, you guys have given up enough to babysit me."

They stopped their antics and stared at her. Frankie began to shake his head no and started to protest, but Beth Ann cut him off.

"I'm going back to school next week and need some time to prepare," she insisted. "You two have been my rock. I love you and can't thank you enough, but I'm better now."

Frankie glanced at Carol. "She's kicking us out? I guess you're coming home with me tonight."

"In your dreams, hot stuff," Carol said. "To think we've only eaten her out of house and home, hogged her TV, and left popcorn under all the furniture."

"Scoot, you two." Beth Ann found herself really laughing, which surprised her.

They both got their things and headed off, but Frankie stopped and reminded her that he lived only ten minutes away.

When her friends were gone, Beth Ann stared at the closed door for a couple of minutes. After three months, it was her first time alone in the apartment. The thought briefly crossed her mind about moving out, away from the memories, but she couldn't leave because she had to wait for Kaylob.

Chapter Thirteen

The rest of the day Beth Ann spent sprucing up her home and keeping herself busy. Much to her surprise, she managed to sleep restfully that night even after hearing Kaylob's voice calling out to her.

The sound of the phone's shrill ring woke her later that night. Carol was bursting with excitement because a call had come in from an agent who wanted to talk to Beth Ann concerning the role in a Broadway show. He had a huge production and asked to see them both.

Beth Ann panicked. "Am I ready? What about my hair?"

"Beth Ann, a lot of women have short hair. Look at mine."

Carol's excitement eventually persuaded Beth Ann to agree to go. The next morning, Carol showed up bright and early. They headed out for the audition in Orange County. Their preplanning prepared them for the horrendous traffic on Highway 91, so they arrived just in time for the tryouts. The job of finding a parking place took longer than the commute.

When they walked into the cavernous, poorly lit theater, the light from the outside projected a beam directly to the stage where a peculiar, whisper-thin gentleman with a stain of a mustache continued moving his head, tracking several dancers. He glanced up at them and gave Carol an approving smile and a wink.

"Hey, gorgeous. Glad to see you. This must be Beth Ann."

"Yes I am." Beth Ann moved toward him and shook his hand. "Nice to meet you."

"I'm Mitch. Carol has told me you're quite a singer and a good actress too."

"I've sung in a few plays in school and the Belleview Studio productions in San Rafael. I did some acting too."

Mitch scanned them up and down and nodded. "So, Carol, I hear your dancing is better than ever. Want to show me what you got?"

Carol winked at him. "You know I don't swing that way."

Mitch shook his head while Carol pulled off her jacket with a smile. She moved to the center of the stage as Beth Ann and Mitch stepped to the side to observe.

"Ready when you are, big boy."

Mitch motioned for someone to start the music, and Carol started to move. Her dancing made Beth Ann's ability seem weak. Carol's body moved like smoldering smoke on glass one minute and a deer through a forest the next. Her long legs and flexibility would put a feline to shame.

"More graceful than the morning fog rolling off the ocean," Mitch whispered as he leaned closer.

Carol stopped when the music ended, not breaking a sweat. Several of the dancers who had paused to watch restarted their exercises, nervously acting as if they'd just witnessed a dancing thesis.

Carol pranced over. "Your turn, honey."

Beth Ann waved her hand. "Even in my wildest dreams, I don't have those moves."

Before she said anything else, Mitch smiled. "Okay, let me hear you sing then. We can train you to move later."

Mitch brought out his piano player, and they picked "Somewhere Over the Rainbow" because it was one of the songs in the production.

Beth Ann hadn't sung since Kaylob had ... left. She hadn't even hummed and felt her stomach take a nosedive. She swallowed hard and shot a look at Carol who nodded and winked. The pianist motioned for her to start, but her nerves got the best of her.

Carol went over to Beth Ann and put her arm around her shoulders. "Honey, you can do this. Just imagine that you're singing to Kaylob."

Carol moved back by Mitch and leaned over to whisper in his ear. Beth Ann wondered if Carol was telling him about Kaylob.

She closed her eyes and imagined him there with her. The music started and she found her voice.

"Somewhere ..."

After only halfway through, Mitch told the pianist to stop.

"Superb, young lady. The job is yours if you want it. Both of you."

The girls hugged and let out a little squeal.

Mitch gave them a second before continuing. "If we make it through opening night, we'll hit the road for six months. Any problems with that?"

"Not for me," Beth Ann announced, grinning broadly.

Carol's face wore a defeated expression. "I'm sorry, Mitch. That would be an issue for me. I can't be gone that long. Sorry about that."

Mitch sighed. "Are you sure, Carol? We really need your talent in this production. Half these kids can't walk let alone dance."

Carol walked over and picked up her purse and jacket. "I'm positive. Sorry, Mitch."

Obviously disappointed, Mitch released a deep breath. "Well, how about doing some training with these kids? I'll make the effort worth your while."

"Sure, Mitch. I'd love to help out."

He turned to Beth Ann and told her what she'd be making. Beth Ann ran up and hugged him.

"Yes, yes, a thousand times yes."

He let out a laugh. "You may want to hold off on celebrating. This work ain't easy. Trust me, you'll be earning every dime. Be here tomorrow at nine a.m. sharp."

* * * *

Beth Ann couldn't believe she had just landed a lead role as an actress and singer in a real Broadway play. She'd be on the road if they lived through opening night. Broadway had been her dream since she was a young girl, and now the dream had come true. She wished Carol would be going with her, but she knew Carol didn't want the travel because of her cats and important Women's Rights rallies.

The traveling would give Beth Ann time on her own and a necessary distraction from the residual pain. Maybe she could go more than ten minutes without thinking about Kaylob and how much pain he must have gone through when he … went missing. Had he been thinking of her?

She had to push those thoughts out of her head. All they did was cause deeper anguish. Tonight she would go out and look at the sky and wait for the brightest star. That would be Kaylob thinking of her even though they had time differences. That was another secret she hadn't told anyone. Every evening when the sky was clear, she would go down by the pool and wait for that one special star that would twinkle more than any of the others. Tonight, she wanted to send Kaylob a special message about her Broadway role. He would be so very proud.

* * * *

The training for Broadway made the days roll by faster, but she was glad to have Friday night off and the chance to sleep in the next morning. Unfortunately, she didn't get much rest because of the same recurring nightmare.

A long hallway stood before her, dingy and dark. A smell filled the air. What was that? Bamboo layered the ground, and the horrid odor made her stomach turn. Before she had the chance to cover her nose, the smell was gone. Then she was standing in front of the old abandoned building, the one where she had seen the vision. Did she want to peek inside? The desire pulled at her heart strings. She must.

The minute she put her face to the glass, the scene unfolded. The little girl was playing with the golden dog. Oh God, Kaylob was holding Beth Ann and throwing his head back in laughter. She opened her mouth to call out to him, but a lump formed in her throat so big that she couldn't even mumble.

Her mind screamed out to him and made her wake up. The dream faded and she lay in bed alone. How in the world could she ever be happy again?

The words 'Kaylob, please come home' echoed in her mind as she drifted back to sleep.

* * * *

Kaylob didn't know how long he had been in the hellhole. From what little he had heard from the other American POWs, it had been months. The Cong kept him isolated for the most part, but the other prisoners were teaching him to communicate by the code they tapped to each other. Someone had dug out his bullets when he first arrived here. Kaylob knew he had developed an infection and been given penicillin injections. He wondered why they bothered to save him. Maybe it was because they wanted another POW to torture or get confessions of war crimes by beating it out of him.

It would be nice to know where the hell he was. All he knew was that he was in a POW camp in South Vietnam. He lay on a dirty cot in a bamboo hut not big enough for standing. He had managed to grab a bamboo stick to keep the rats away. He heard them at night when he slept as they scurried by his bed, looking for something to eat. One time they had chewed on his toe because it was infected. After that, he slept with his ears open and the stick in his hand.

Of course, he had more than rats to be concerned about. The Cong started to thrash him every chance they got. In the beginning, they hadn't beaten on him, maybe because he was barely hanging onto life. Now, however, they seemed to enjoy the torture by dragging him outside and beating him black and blue. They used anything and everything—kicking him, hitting him with bamboo sticks and some type of club to break his bones. He had broken bones all over his body, his elbow and two fingers were the latest. He wished he could get a weapon and shoot the assholes, but that wasn't likely considering his injuries and lack of strength.

The only bathrooms they had were holes they dug in the ground. They had to squat over them with no way to clean themselves. Many of the guys were dying from jungle disease. Kaylob was bad off, but he knew he had to stay alive. He had to get home to Beth Ann.

As if out of nowhere, a figure appeared in front of him. Why hadn't he seen him coming? It was one of the Cong—the one the prisoners had nicknamed the pig's ass. Actually, a pig's ass was a whole lot nicer than this idiot.

"Get up now or we drag you," he yelled at Kaylob. "You bury one of your own today."

Kaylob wanted to punch the asshole in the mouth. Damn, how he wished he could escape this insanity. Yet to stay alive and make it back home, he would do what they told him. He had buried a few guys already and tried like hell to mark the areas.

"Get up now." The Cong kicked him hard.

Kaylob stood up as much as he could since the room was not high enough for him to stand straight. He glared at the Cong just as two other scumbags came around the corner. As he walked ahead of them down the bamboo hall, they hit his back with something.

"Go faster before we break you back."

The pain ripped through his shoulders and down his spine. "Screw you, bastards," he said through gritted teeth.

When he got outside, the sun almost blinded him, and he wished it had. Jesus Christ, he had to look at more dead bodies. Almost daily more of the prisoners died. It tore at his heart, and he knew he'd fight to stay alive, he'd do what he had to do.

"Pick him up." the Cong yelled.

Whack.

They hit him again, trying to kill him like they had so many of the other soldiers. Many had died with broken legs, arms, and ribs. A few had their heads bashed in.

Gritting his teeth against the pain radiating through his shoulders, Kaylob shifted his position and bent over. The smell of the fallen soldier was horrid, so he tried to hold his breath. Tears stung his eyes as he looked at the young man's face. This was someone's son, brother, best friend, maybe husband. Kaylob's gut clenched, and he knew he was going to vomit. It came up and there was nothing he could do.

"Pick him up now or we shoot you, and this time we no make it better."

It took every bit of strength Kaylob had to pick up the soldier and carry him. He tried his best to be gentle with him and do it with respect.

On the way to the burial place, they passed another soldier lying on the ground. More tears burned Kaylob's eyes as the young man pleaded with him.

"Please help me. Don't let me die." He was lying in his own waste, and vomit ran out of his mouth.

The Cong laughed and mimicked the soldier. "Oh, don't let me die." They spit on him and left him lying there. The American soldier looked at Kaylob and begged him with his eyes, but there was nothing he could do.

His legs went weak. "Goddamn this place, this war, and these assholes from hell," he muttered.

He had to focus on something else before he lost it. Once they made it up the hill, he started digging the hole on the hillside for the brave soldier. After it was done, the Cong kicked the dead man inside the hole with a mocking laugh. They made Kaylob use his hands to throw dirt over him. He had never thought he could hate the way he hated these bastards.

He vowed inside his heart to Beth Ann that this would not be his fate. "Baby, I'm coming home," he whispered, "and I will keep my promise to you."

Chapter Fourteen

The first few weeks of rehearsals helped Beth Ann get through the days without Kaylob. She was glad to stay busy, but she rarely had time to spend with Frankie and missed him a lot. At least she still got to see Carol since they commuted and worked together.

Day after day danced by. Lisa and Denny frequently called to check on her, and her mom and Stanley came back to visit, happy to find her looking healthy and eating again. Cole called her often, and Gram called her weekly, which Beth Ann loved. She looked better and better and acted normal, but deep inside she hid a secret. She was out of her mind and had to be careful not to let anyone know.

One day she picked up the phone to call Frankie but froze when Kaylob's voice echoed through her mind and she heard him talking to her. "Baby, I'm coming home."

Yes, Kaylob would be coming home. When he did, she would tell everyone how wrong they'd been.

She still needed to call Frankie, so she shook it off and dialed his number. She heard a woman's giggle in the background when he answered.

"Hi, Frankie."

"Hey, stranger. I've missed you something awful."

"I miss you too, but it sounds like you have company. I can call back."

"No, don't you dare hang up. Are you busy this weekend? I want to see you."

"Are you sure, because I don't want to pull you away from anything important or … you know."

He was at her door thirty minutes later, bearing gifts of fruit, cheese, and wine. They stayed in and watched movies, played cards, and spent time together. Beth Ann didn't remember falling asleep, nor did she remember getting into bed. Around midnight, she woke and glanced at the clock on the wall, then adjusted her pillows, and drifted back to sleep.

The same long white hallway stretched in front of her, and she could hear Kaylob calling her name. She frantically raced down the hall to reach him, but when she got to the doors at the end of the hallway, they wouldn't budge. Kaylob's voice was so clear and desperate.

"Kaylob, open the door," she yelled. "Please open the door." She pushed and tugged but instead of the door opening, she felt an arm pulling at her.

Frankie gathered her into his arms. "It's okay, honey. I'm here, I've got ya."

Her terror retreated as he comforted her, so she was able to sleep peacefully the rest of the night. The next morning when she woke, her heart swelled when she saw her best friend fighting to stay awake.

"Frankie, you're the best."

A weak smile formed across his lips. "I'm glad you got some sleep. Now it's my turn."

"The bed is all yours, sleepyhead." She got up and covered him with a blanket as she kissed his cheek. He passed out before she walked into the bathroom.

While Frankie slept, she sneaked out and spent time with Mrs. Jenkins. They shared a cup of coffee, and Mrs. Jenkins told her about her struggles after her husband died. They too had been childhood sweethearts.

Beth Ann wanted to ask Mrs. Jenkins a question, but had to find the courage. After a few minutes of sipping coffee, she glanced over at the older woman.

"Did you feel him die?"

Mrs. Jenkins stared at her and then set down her coffee cup. "Feel him die?"

"Your husband. Did you feel he was gone in your heart?"

Mrs. Jenkins took another sip of her coffee. "Well, I suppose I did. He died in my arms, so I felt a deep loss. Why do you ask?"

Beth Ann looked down at her hands. "I never felt Kaylob die. Sometimes I still hear his voice calling out to me."

Mrs. Jenkins took Beth Ann's hands in hers. "Honey, I still hear my husband calling me too."

"But I hear it out loud," Beth Ann said. "It startles me."

"Dear, have you spoken to anyone about this?" The old lady patted her hand. "Grief counseling can help."

"No, I'm dealing with it. But what if he's not dead? What if he's still alive like those guys who're caught and held by the enemy?"

Mrs. Jenkins' eyes slid into sadness. "Oh, honey, he's been gone for a long time. They would know by now if he was a prisoner of war. They have special intelligence that knows these things."

Beth Ann nodded and said nothing. She still couldn't help worrying that Kaylob was still alive. What if he was hurt and calling out to her? What if he was crippled on the ground, eating bugs, frogs, and other things to stay alive?

She put down her cup and stood. "Thank you for talking to me, Mrs. Jenkins."

A slight smile tugged at the lady's lips. "Things will better, sweetheart. You're young and have a whole life ahead of you." She wrapped her arms around Beth Ann. "I'm going to miss you, my dear. Promise me you'll write and let me know how you're doing."

Beth Ann agreed and hugged her back. Mrs. Jenkins would be moving soon, her daughter had built a little cottage for her on her property. Beth Ann was glad Mrs. Jenkins wouldn't have to be alone anymore.

Throughout the weekend, Frankie and Beth Ann got to behave like kids on summer vacation. The end of May approached and temperatures warmed, so they took advantage of it by going to parks, taking long walks through the beautiful trails, and letting their minds wander with the summer breeze. The time away gave her a chance to recharge, refocus, and reconnect with her lifelong friend.

Sunday afternoon, Frankie held her hand as they strolled through the park. Beth Ann stopped when she spied a hot dog vendor.

"I'll buy if you fly," she offered.

"Hey, I'm not turning down free food."

Beth Ann handed him a five with a chuckle. "Don't spend it all in one place."

She got comfortable on the park bench while she waited for Frankie, enjoying the beautiful day. The sun sparkled its way through the green trees. People walked their dogs as children ran and played on a nearby jungle gym. The sweetness of the cut grass tickled her nose.

Movement caught her attention as a guy came over and sat down next to her with a smile. Not feeling a hundred percent comfortable, she did her best to smile back. He seemed normal enough with brown hair and a nice smile, but then he moved closer,

"Hi, I'm Richard. I'm a Leo and you know what that means. I could really groove on you."

When he finished his pick-up line, Beth Ann noticed Frankie standing behind him with hot dogs in his hands. He stepped over to face the guy and handed Beth Ann her hot dog.

"Hi, my name's Frankie and my sign is son of a bitch," he said in a voice Beth Ann had never heard before. "Believe me, you'll be meeting him soon if you don't get your ass out of here now."

Mr. Leo made a hasty retreat and did not look back.

Beth Ann was shocked at Frankie's words, but let out a small giggle as she gazed at him sweetly. She loved him being protective.

"My hero." She rubbed his muscles while they ate their hot dogs.

Chapter Fifteen

The next few weeks, her health continued to improve. The scale showed she had gained weight along with muscle and tone. Once again she enjoyed looking in the mirror at life returning. Thank God insanity didn't show.

One night when Carol and Frankie came over for the evening, they were all watching TV in her living room. When Beth Ann came back from the bathroom, she inhaled, her heart melting at the sight of her dear friends. They had been with her and supported her for months. Frankie was never far away and was always putting her first.

"Look at you, Beth Ann," Carol said. "I should start taking you to some NOW rallies."

Frankie shot a stern expression Carol's way and pointed his finger at her. "One crazy bra burner is enough in this family."

Beth Ann smiled at the two of them, but couldn't help feeling sad. She and Kaylob had always loved watching Frankie and Carol banter.

Carol got up from the couch to glower mockingly at him. "Yeah, there's nothing worse than a bunch of crazy braless women with access to fire, right?"

Frankie laughed and arched his eyebrow, "Actually, some of them are quite a treat to look at without those bolder holders. What do you gals do at all those meetings? Swap recipes? Talk about knitting? Ways to please your man?"

Carol hit the top of Frankie's head with a pillow. "Maybe if you came, you might find out."

Frankie paused for a second, trying unsuccessfully not to smirk. "I just might do that. I'd love to come … and find out."

Carol looked shocked. Beth Ann heard a loud whoomph as a pillow bounced hard on his head. "Frankie, you're bad to the bone." Carol shook her head and picked up another pillow, threatening to smack him again.

He smiled sheepishly. "Hey, what'd I say? I'm just agreeing with you." He grabbed her wrist and was raising his eyebrows. "I just want to come, that's all. Right, Beth Ann?"

Beth Ann had no idea why Carol had hit him when all he'd said was that he wanted to go to one of her rallies. She crossed her arms over her chest and glared at both of them.

"Why would that make him bad to the bone? He said he just wanted to come."

Carol and Frankie looked at her then turned to each other and started laughing again, this time at her. When she stomped off toward the bathroom, she turned to find them still cracking themselves up.

"Beth Ann, you are so cute," Frankie commented, and Carol nodded in agreement.

What in the world had just happened? Beth Ann shook her head and gave up on understanding them. When she came out of the bathroom, they were fighting over popcorn. Frankie would throw some at Carol, and she'd use her mouth to catch and eat the pieces.

Since they were acting crazy, Beth Ann decided to call their newly discovered condition "popcorn drunk," something that happens to a couple of loonies combined with too much popcorn. Add more nuts, stir, and ignore. They ended the weekend with laughter and fun.

* * * *

Kaylob's ghostly presence had begun to rattle Beth Ann, so throwing herself into the production made things a bit better. Frankie made a spare key to her place, and many times she would come home to find dinner cooked and a clean house. He was almost living there with her, but it was strictly platonic no matter what people thought.

She and Frankie decided to see a movie on one of her few weekends off, although watching Cabaret was almost like she was still working. Frankie had to endure her critique practically throughout the whole show. During the walk home, they talked more about the movie, or rather Beth Ann talked about the movie, because all Frankie did was go on about Liza Minnelli's legs. When they arrived back at the apartment, they were both tired so Frankie pulled out some blankets to sleep on the couch.

Beth Ann glanced at him and then at the blankets as she stood by her bed. It was getting so she hated going to sleep because she was so afraid the dreams would come back to haunt her.

"Frankie, instead of sleeping on the couch, can you hold me tonight?"

He got a serious expression and shook his head. "No, not a good idea."

"We're friends. I trust you," she said.

"Yes, true, but I'm still human."

"We've been friends since the sixth grade. Nothing's going to happen. I miss Kaylob and need someone's arms around me tonight." She gave him a very cute pout that usually got her what she wanted.

When he sighed deeply, she knew the reluctance had just melted away. It was replaced with a nervous smile. "Okay, I'm sorry he's not here to hold you, so I'll be his stand-in. Hell, I'll hold you."

They took turns in the bathroom. Beth Ann finished first and then waited in bed. Frankie was taking his time, and she had a feeling he wanted her to be asleep when he came out. Finally the door opened and Frankie walked over to the bed. She smiled and threw back the blankets, but he wouldn't climb in. His hesitance brought up memories of how many times Kaylob had refused to get under the covers with her.

For a short time while Frankie held her, she almost forgot her misery. However, she couldn't forget the voices haunting her day and night. She knew she was using Frankie's arms to pretend that Kaylob was holding her.

"If I ever fall in love," Frankie had once said, "I want it to be what you and Kaylob have, the real thing. I won't settle for anything less."

When morning came, she opened her eyes and realized she had slept through the night with no dreams and no voices. She was surprised to find Frankie gone, but she sat up and spotted a note on the pillow beside her.

Good Morning Sleepy head,

I had to dart home to take care of a couple of things. You were out of it, so I didn't want to wake you. I'll be back around noon.

Love you,
Frankie

* * * *

Frankie entered his apartment and headed for the bedroom. There was one thing he knew after sleeping in bed with his best friend all night, he had to stop. Sure, he'd loved her since childhood, but he also loved being her best friend. Nevertheless, he had not slept well with the turbulent emotions welling inside him at having her so close to him like that.

No, he couldn't sleep in bed with her anymore. The temptation was too great. He needed to take a shower to wash out his brain. After he took off his clothes, he turned on the shower and jumped in, not giving a shit if it was cold. He needed that.

After he got dressed again, he made a pot of coffee and poured himself a cup. He decided now would be a good time to call Carol and bounce his feelings off her. He dialed her number and let it ring three times. Almost ready to hang up, he heard her answer.

"Hey, sexy. It's me."

"Oh, Frankie. How's everything?"

"Carol, she had me sleep in the bed with her last night and ... well, shit. It was hard."

"Oh, really. How hard was it? Really hard or semi?"

"Very funny, Carol. You know what I mean."

"Well, I tried to talk to you about this before and you didn't want to discuss it. Come on, I know how much you love her. Don't do that anymore unless you want to take things to the next level. Whatever, think about it. Maybe you're what she needs."

"I can't do that." He ran a hand through his hair. "She'll always love Kaylob. Anyone who falls in love with her will never own her heart like he did. Besides, I don't want to screw up and lose our friendship. Should I just refuse next time and not give her a reason?"

"That's up to you. Give her credit, she's a big girl."

"You know how childlike she is though. If I say the wrong thing, it'll hurt her feelings. I can't lose her as my best friend."

"You're not going to lose her, but if you keep sleeping in bed with her, shit's gonna happen. Just tell her no."

"Easier said than done. Did you see how she sits on me? Carol, the girl drives me insane and doesn't even know it."

"Yeah she needs to stop that. I saw your face last time I was there and she had her little PJs on. How long did you stay in that cold shower?"

"Long enough. Okay, I have to get back over there. Hopefully she won't ask me to sleep with her again."

"Good luck, Frankie. Call me later."

"Okay. Hey, how are things with you? Is she there?" Frankie asked.

"Yeah, she's here. It's getting pretty serious. We're talking about her moving in with me."

"You're going to have to spill the truth soon. I'm happy for you. She seems like a good lady."

"Looks like we're both gonna have to do some spilling. Thanks, Frankie. You've been so supportive. I love ya, you nitwit."

"Yeah, I know. Love ya too. Bye."

He hung up and stood at the breakfast bar, thinking about Beth Ann. He needed to have a heart-to-heart talk with his best friend, and he needed to do it soon. Real soon.

* * * *

Beth Ann settled at the dining table and thought about how needy she'd been ever since the Army had declared Kaylob MIA. Today she planned on doing something special for Frankie because she had asked so much of him lately. She decided she would take him out to dinner that evening and let him choose where they went. Everyone had been doing everything she wanted and tiptoeing around her, including Kaylob's family. They hadn't even had a service for Kaylob yet because she wasn't ready. She still refused to accept that Kaylob had died in Vietnam, and everyone knew that was how she felt.

She decided to call Kaylob's mom and check in with her. She picked up the phone and dialed the number, but even doing that hurt. Besides, she could tell how depressed Jackie was just by the sound of her hello.

"Hi, Jackie. It's me, Beth Ann." A pregnant pause prompted her to speak. "Jackie, are you okay?"

"Yes and no. I've been afraid to call you, but I know it's time to tell you something."

Beth Ann immediately felt lightheaded and had to inhale deeply. "What is it, Jackie?"

"The Army officially declared Kaylob dead. We need to hold a service for him."

"When did you find that out?" Beth Ann did her best to sound calm.

"Oh, honey, they called us a few weeks ago. We were wrong not to call you right away, but we were afraid the news would set you back again. They said he died a hero and saved many guys."

The news that Kaylob was a hero didn't surprise Beth Ann at all, but they were all wrong about the rest. He had not died over there, and she knew it. Jackie wanted to give him a full military funeral including a medal ceremony, but Beth Ann knew she couldn't attend. While she understood his family needed closure, they didn't understand that she needed Kaylob. She explained it to his mom the best she could.

"Okay," Jackie said, "but do you want anything from his room? We just can't have it here anymore. We're donating everything to good causes."

"No," Beth Ann answered quickly. "I can't take anything. That would be too painful. I'm sorry, Jackie." She couldn't even think about going through his stuff.

"Beth Ann, we all love you. I understand you can't do this right now. I know how much you loved Kaylob. You made my son very happy."

Tears drowned Beth Ann's eyes as she tried to stay strong. "Thank you. I'll be okay. Are you okay?"

"Yes, my sweet girl. I'm taking it one day at a time."

After they hung up, Beth Ann made her way into the bedroom and went to the closet. All Kaylob's clothes still hung there like a placid shrine. She picked up the jewelry box Kaylob had made for her and tucked it away.

The sense of emptiness overwhelmed her. Kaylob was her rock, her anchor to life. They were meant to be, their souls linked from a very young age. How did anyone unlink a love like that? She drifted out to her bedroom, eased down on her bed, pulled a pillow across her chest, and wept.

The door opened and Frankie hurried over to her. She tried to hide her face, but didn't succeed.

"Beth Ann, what is it?"

She peered up at him and cried. "They declared him dead, Frankie, but I can't feel him gone."

He sat down next to her and drew her close. "I'm so sorry, honey. You didn't feel him die because you're in denial." He turned her shoulders to face him. "Don't you dare leave us again, do you hear me? We love you. I love you. Beth Ann, I can't lose you again."

"I won't leave again, Frankie. I promise." She put her head on his chest and let him comfort her.

That night, Frankie stayed and held her. Sleep came, but it came in numbing fits. She woke in between awake and asleep and saw Frankie watching her serenely. His eyes showed understanding, and his arms were so warm. A part of her wondered if she and Frankie would be good together, in a way other than friends. That thought stayed on her mind as she drifted off to sleep.

The next morning, she and Frankie sat at the kitchen table having coffee. "I'll be glad when Kaylob gets home and cooks me breakfast again."

Frankie appeared shocked as he reached over and pulled her chair closer. "Beth Ann, Kaylob is gone. You have to accept it. You can't keep doing this. He's not going to return to you. I know what you think, and it's wrong. Don't be naïve, and don't spend your life in limbo. Say it, sweetheart. Allow yourself to say that Kaylob is gone and never coming back."

She couldn't do that, even though she knew it would make everyone feel better if she did. To hell with that. She wasn't going to voice something she didn't believe.

Chapter Sixteen

As time marched on Kaylob was more alert about his surroundings, and knew he was deep in the jungle. He lay on the dirt floor with his arms tied behind him, intolerable pain shooting all the way through his body. The Cong fed the Americans small amounts of rice, and then they were forced by the sick bastards to gather manioc. It was a potato-type food poisoned with Agent Orange by the U.S. spray planes. The Cong was fully aware of what the food did because many of the guys got sicker by the day, and death hovered like a black fog. Since he'd been there the sick pricks left the dead bodies on the ground for torture, telling the rest of them that this was their fate.

The only good thing about the misery was that it reminded Kaylob he was still alive. He had been hearing Beth Ann calling out to him, crying to him. Oh God, the heartache of not being able to go to her. He still had no clue of his exact location, but knew he was in hell. He wondered about Patterson and the other guys in the mission. Were they alive or dead? Cobwebs still befuddled his head, and he was trying to piece together what he remembered.

If only he knew how long he'd been a prisoner. He thought maybe eight months. Even with his brain still fuzzy, he remembered the Cong had been up in the trees.

He was still in a dirty room with dirt floors, bamboo walls, and no windows. Not even a touch of sunlight. The bastards had even taken his cot so he had resorted to gathering bamboo leaves for his bedding, although right now he had nothing, except the filthy rats they left behind.

He decided he would try and gather more bedding today. At least the leaves gave him a little comfort. Suddenly, he caught sound of footsteps coming toward him.

Only one guard this time. The idiot stood there looking at him like he was nothing more than a rotting corpse. His smirk made Kaylob want to knock the shit out of him. Unfortunately, the prisoners were too outnumbered to fight back.

The short little Cong with bad skin stepped inside the room and stood over Kaylob. "You Beth Ann is with many men," he crooned. "She make them all happy. She forget you."

"Twisted little skunk," Kaylob said. "You don't know her. She wouldn't do that."

"She with dozen men. She have one, two every day. We see this."

A sharp pain went into Kaylob side as the pig kicked him again and again. Kaylob yelled, but he laughed too, trying to keep his spirits high and not let them break him. He closed his eyes against the beating and started to fade out.

There she stood, his Beth Ann, running and laughing with the wind blowing in her hair. She turned to smile at him, holding her arms open. The sight of her standing on a green hillside with the ocean all around took his breath away.

"Kaylob, come home." she called out. "Please, Kaylob, don't go."

He tried to yell back to her, but his voice would not work. Then, with every piece of strength he had, he pushed it out. "Beth Ann, I love you. Here I am, please hear me, baby."

At least the sky had sunshine today that brought him warmth. He wanted to send Beth Ann a song, so he started to sing.

"... I hunger for ..."

They kicked him again, so he got louder.

"... still mine ... Godspeed ... me."

Tears mixed with the crud on his face as they kept beating him mercilessly.

For the first time in his life, Kaylob understood hate. He had once thought he hated Blake Tanner for loving his girl, but that had been nothing compared to this.

Now he knew what true hate.

* * * *

Beth Ann found even the frantic pace of rehearsals couldn't stop the agony of missing Kaylob. She wondered if the longing would ever go away, along with the nightmares and hearing him call her name.

A few days earlier while she was on break from rehearsal, she had walked downtown to get something to eat and swore she recognized Kaylob from behind. She ran up calling his name, but when the man turned around, she realized she had made a mistake. The guy appeared perplexed as she fumbled an apology and retreated.

Not only was she crazy, she'd started acting insane. She had slowly walked back to rehearsal, no longer in the mood for food. The rest of the day, she hadn't been able to get through the songs and kept missing her cues. Finally, Mitch told her to go home and get some sleep.

Frankie said she needed to accept Kaylob's death. How the heck could she do that when she kept hearing him calling out to her? Now she was looking in the eyes of strangers and wondering if they knew where he had gone. She'd have to fight even harder to hide her idiotic behavior from her friends and family. She had to become a very good actress, not just in her Broadway show but in her daily life.

As opening night approached, she looked forward more and more to the premiere. Maybe it would help her be a little more sane.

For the first time, Beth Ann experienced exhaustion not only from work but from the emotional drain of all the nightmares and voices. She moved over to the bed and sat down, reminiscing about the day Kaylob had asked her to be his girl. What a special time that had been. She settled down on the bed and put her face in the pillow.

"Kaylob, please come back home. You were supposed to be here when I did my first Broadway play."

After what seemed like endless hours, she drifted off to sleep. Sometime during the night, Kaylob's voice called out to her and woke her. She shoved the pillow over her head and forced herself to fall back to asleep.

The next morning, she woke to the sun filtering through her tiny apartment and the sound of the clock ticking along with muffled noises from the street. They all sounded the same, some things never changed. As she walked to the kitchen, a knock startled her. She opened the door to see Frankie with muffins and hot coffee.

"How sweet." She threw her arms around him while snagging a muffin.

"That's me—always sweet, and like this coffee, always hot." He laughed as he tried not to spill the coffee.

She knew he had come to spend the day with her to show his support and to ease her jitters. "Frankie, have I told you how special you are?"

He nodded and winked. "Yeah, but I don't mind hearing it again."

It was just what she needed. Her Frankie, the guy she trusted with her life.

Her excitement grew as the day went on, and she could hardly believe that opening night had finally arrived. Everyone had worked long hours rehearsing for the premiere, but there was still more to do, so they spent the whole afternoon preparing. Things like costume modification, last-minute lighting instructions, sound cues, and getting the systems checked and double checked.

Beth Ann's head was spinning as she was pulled in so many directions. She had meetings with people she had never seen before. Everyone had been coming and going with measuring tapes and clipboards. The cast members scurried about like cats following the sound of a can opener. Thank goodness her outfits were ready to go. All she needed help with was her makeup and hair.

She decided to take a break and walk outside to see the marquee lit up with The Chorus Years, A Musical Review of Times. Her heart skipped beat and tears glistened her eyes when she read the next line 'Introducing singer actress Elizabeth Ann Rose.'

Seeing her name up in lights felt surreal. She would truly be stepping into her dream. The sky was clear, and off to the west she saw some twinkling stars. She looked at her watch, and her eyes filled with more tears as she gazed up into the sky.

"Kaylob, look at my name up there," she whispered. "I wish you were here to see this with me. I miss you so much. Please hurry home." She found the most brilliant star in the sky and knew that somewhere, maybe over the rainbow, Kaylob was watching her perform tonight.

She had to finish getting ready, so she walked back through the stage entrance and down a long hallway. People were going in every direction with the sounds of laughter all around. She went back into her dressing room—small but with her name on the door—and sat in front of the mirror to put on the final touches of her makeup.

A knock made her jump. No way was it time to go on yet. She glanced at her watch as she opened the door. Surprise hit when she saw Carol and Frankie, but the sight of Blake Tanner standing there with roses stunned her speechless. Her cheeks heated immediately at the way his blue eyes skimmed over her.

Carol reached out and touched Beth Ann's shoulders. "You look amazing, Beth Ann, or should I say Elizabeth Ann Rose? Did you see your name up in lights?"

Beth Ann nodded. Holy cow, she couldn't believe how her face burned every time she glanced at Blake. He smiled, showing off his twin dimples, then he handed her the flowers.

"You're stunning," he said.

"Thank you." It was all she could manage to reply.

Frankie stepped up to hug her. "I'm so proud to call you my best friend. As a matter of fact, I'm just damn proud of you."

She smiled and returned his hug, glad to direct her attention somewhere other than Blake.

Carol laughed and told her to break a leg just before they all turned to leave. She stared at Blake as he walked away, unable to take her eyes off the way his pants fit. His derriere looked extra fine. Just as she started to close the door, Blake turned and saw her staring at him. Holy night, she was busted. A slow smile crossed his lips and left no doubt that she had been caught.

She stepped inside and closed the door fast. How the heck could she think of Kaylob one minute and check out Blake Tanner the next?

Another knock at the door almost gave her a heart attack, but this time it was Mitch. He stepped in and smiled at her.

"Hey, kid. You okay? You look a little flushed."

She nodded. "I'm nervous, Mitch."

He moved closer. "You're gonna be fine. You've got five minutes to pull yourself together, then someone will give you a final knock. Hey, don't forget to invite your friends and family to the party afterwards. It'll be in the big room downstairs—food and beverages to celebrate."

He gave her a swift hug. "Don't worry. I know you'll do a wonderful job."

Her nerves danced in her stomach as she waited for the final knock. One more time, she looked into full-length mirror. The elegant dress had white sheer mesh with a one-shoulder overlay and was lined with silver sparkles from front to back. Her tights matched her skin, giving an illusion of nudity. The outfit showed her firm, toned body, the result of working so hard learning how to dance. She had trouble with one song more than all the others—the one she'd auditioned with, "Somewhere Over the Rainbow." She prayed tonight she would be okay.

Another knock on the door summoned her and promptly scared the million butterflies in her stomach into erratic flights of fancy. She took a deep breath and headed out. Trying to calm her nerves, she waited in the area offstage for her cue. Within minutes, the music announced it was show time. Her dancing partner, a handsome guy named Danny with strawberry blond hair, gave her a big smile from across the way.

She stepped out onto the stage and crossed the floor to meet Danny. Right on cue, he lifted her into the air and then let her slide down his body. Everything went flawlessly as they moved with grace and skill to Mancini and Mercer's "Moon River." Beth Ann loved singing with Danny because they harmonized so beautifully. She almost felt like her idol, Grace Kelly.

The frequent sound of enthusiastic applause gave her chills as she and Danny sang and acted out the love story, told through songs from musical reviews. The show was spectacular, and the audience clearly agreed. Everyone cast member gave an outstanding performance.

Then it was time for Beth Ann to close out the show with the last song of the night, "Somewhere over the Rainbow." She had to push away the pain in her heart so she could sing the song the way she needed to do it.

The cue came, and she paused, gazing up toward the sky. In a soft voice, she said, "This song is for Kaylob Shawn O'Brien. You will always be my hero."

The audience grew quiet, and she caught the sound of a few coughs. Then the music started.

"Somewhere over…"

Her voice hit every peak perfectly and sounded better than she'd ever sung before. She knew from the faces of people in the audience that they liked it too. They were clapping even before the song ended, and many people dabbed their eyes with handkerchiefs. As the final note faded, the crowd rose for a standing ovation, and Beth Ann's heart swelled.

Mitch joined her on the stage and took a bow. Danny introduced him as the guy who'd put the show together. Twice the curtains opened and closed for more bows as flowers were tossed onto the stage. Beth Ann couldn't have asked for her first show to go any better. Everyone began to hug her and tell her how wonderful she'd sounded.

Mitch pulled out his handkerchief and wiped off Beth Ann's tears. "You've made a name for yourself, kiddo."

She kissed his cheek and gave him a big hug, too overwhelmed to speak. Despite the fact that she embraced her happiness, she couldn't forget the unfathomable heartache that still held her captive. Without Kaylob there beside her, things weren't the same. This had been her lifelong dream, one he had supported since they were children. He should be there with her to celebrate her success.

Chapter Seventeen

Beth Ann drifted back from the crowd as two of the girls from the show—Margo and Julia—called out her name over the noise.

"Elizabeth, you have a bunch of people waiting for you in the party room." They both hurried over to her. "Come on, you can't miss out on the fun."

Beth Ann decided she would wring the happiness out of herself if she had to, even if only for a moment. There had been no happiness for so long, and God knew she deserved some.

When she entered the party room, she tried not to notice Blake, but knew she hadn't succeeded when the butterflies in her stomach returned. Trying to hide her apprehension, she moved to greet her mom and Stanley. The place was filled with people she knew, along with her cute little Gram whose old eyes brimmed with delight when she gazed at Beth Ann. No one had ever squeezed her heart like Gram's hugs.

So many of her friends and family were there—Lisa, Denny, Carol, Frankie, Jack, Lenard, her two brothers, and of course Blake. He was the one person she tried to avoid, but it didn't take a psychic for her to know he couldn't take his eyes off of her.

Overall, the party was going well and she was having fun, which surprised her. Lisa kept catching her attention as if she wanted to tell her something, but too much was going on for them to get a chance to talk. Finally, Lisa motioned her head toward the door and Beth Ann nodded as they headed outside. Beth Ann paused on the way out and glanced at Mr. Dimples.

Once they were outside, Lisa grabbed her hand with tears in her eyes. "Terry and I are trying to get pregnant."

Beth Ann couldn't speak, so she swallowed instead. "A baby?"

"No a tadpole. Of course a baby, silly." Lisa laughed. "I know how you feel about kids." She mimicked Beth Ann: "They're great for breakfast, lunch, dinner, or even a midnight snack."

She was right. Kaylob had wanted children, but had pushed away his desire for them because he knew how Beth Ann felt. The memory hurt. Damn, she didn't want to cry, not now. She wanted this night to be free from stress. Just one night of fun before she went back to her daily sadness.

"Hey, you okay?" Lisa looked concerned.

Not trusting her voice, Beth Ann nodded. The next thing she knew, Lisa was guiding her back to the party. Just before they got inside, Lisa stopped.

"Beth Ann, please tell me you're happy for us."

A commotion across the room saved Beth Ann from having to reply. Mitch stood in the doorway, smiling broadly.

"They loved the play. And they loved you too, kid." He started reading from the review. "Those of you fortunate enough to see The Chorus Years, watched the birth of a new star. Elizabeth Ann Rose was pitch perfect. She took "Somewhere Over the Rainbow" past the rainbow and into the stratosphere. Judy Garland would be proud of the rendition. The entire show is a 10-star hit. Theater goers, we're talking incredible talent all around. Expect 'The Chorus Years' to be on the short list for a Tony."

Everyone else in the room broke into applause, but for Beth Ann it was bittersweet. The joy of success was wonderful, yet the sadness of not sharing the news with Kaylob caused her heart to ache.

"Pack your bags," Mitch shouted. "We're hittin' the road."

She had been waiting for that news. Traveling was just what she needed. Because she had a home back in Riverside, it wouldn't be like the traveling with her parents when she was a kid—never having a home and living in hotels or in the car.

Before things got too crazy, she turned to Lisa and hugged her. "If having a baby is what you want, then I want it for you."

"Thanks, honey." Lisa hugged her for a second before all the yelling started. "Give them a speech, Elizabeth."

Frankie moved next to her, and she reached for his hand. Beth Ann saw Blake's expression change to something she couldn't quite read. Her friendship with Frankie had never been a secret, and everyone knew they were best friends. She noticed Gram's eyes lighting up, full of pride for her granddaughter.

Beth Ann cleared her throat and addressed the crowded room. "This last year has been hard without Kaylob. Thanks to all of you for your support. Your letters of love and encouragement meant the world to me. I've survived, and I know now I can go on. If Kaylob were here tonight, you know what he would say."

Frankie laughed and held up a toast. "Let the party begin."

That was so true. Kaylob had always said that at any special event.

The party went on into the wee hours before the crowd and cast started thinning out. Beth Ann stood by the door, giving everyone hugs, shaking hands, laughing, and telling a few jokes. At last, the room was almost empty.

Lisa and Denny had to catch a two a.m. flight, so Cole gave them a lift to the airport. The rest of the family had gotten hotel rooms because they knew the size of Beth Ann's apartment, but she made plans to have breakfast with them in the morning. Her mom and Stanley had driven all the way up to Salem to pick up Gram and bring her. She had the best family in the world.

After avoiding Blake for most of the night, she thought she'd dodged that particular dimpled bullet, but on her way out she found him leaning against the wall by the door. Holy Broadway, he was sexy. He walked toward her and she felt the heat creep from her neck to her face.

"Hey, can I talk to you?" he said.

Her heart skipped a beat and guilt rippled through her when she thought about Kaylob.

He must've sensed her reluctance because he touched her elbow. "Please, Beth Ann. Can we talk?"

Frankie and Carol walked over, both of them looking at Blake suspiciously.

"Everything okay?" Frankie said. "Ready to go?"

Beth Ann nodded. "Just let me grab my stuff out of the dressing room, and I'll be out in a minute. Blake is going to walk me out."

Frankie acted like he wanted to say something, but Carol grabbed his arm and pulled him away.

"Okay, we'll wait for you in the car," Carol said, although she also looked as if she wanted to keep an eye on them.

Blake took her hand and walked down the hallway in silence. When they were inside her dressing room, he turned to face her with another expression she wasn't sure how to read.

"I'm proud of you, Beth Ann."

She grinned. "You're sweet, Blake. Thank you so much for coming. I'm sorry I didn't get to talk to you more tonight."

"I'm glad to be here. I didn't know if you would want to see me, and I'm still not sure. It looked like you were avoiding me all night."

He stepped closer and ran his hand down her arm. A tingle tiptoed every place he touched her.

"Don't be silly. I wasn't avoiding you." A nervous laugh escaped and Beth Ann tried to lighten things. "Hey, where are all the girls on your arms?"

He winked. "I gave that up before the end of high school. Something happened in my life that made me want to be a better person. I still date, but I don't need three or four girls hanging off my arms anymore."

She moved away and crossed the room to gather her stuff. "That's very mature of you." She turned to smile at him. "So you narrowed it down to two?"

He walked over and put his hands on her arms, his blue eyes boring into hers. "No, not even two. Listen, I heard you almost died or at least wanted to die last year. It sounded bad, and I'm so sorry you had to go through that, but, honey, you look beautiful now."

"I still hear his voice," she whispered, her voice trembling.

A tear spilled and ran down her cheek, but she didn't try to hide her emotions from him. She heard compassion in his voice and felt it when he wiped her cheeks and put his arms around her.

"I know what it's like to experience such a horrible loss," he said. "I still hear my parents' voices too. The other day, I picked up the phone and dialed their old number. I forgot for a minute they were gone. So don't beat yourself up. It might take years for your mind to accept that he's gone. It's been years for me, and I still try to call them sometimes."

How could she have forgotten that he'd lost his parents in a horrible car accident—hit head on by a drunk driver. She remembered hearing that he had fallen apart after they died.

"Thank you for understanding, Blake. Sometimes I feel like I'm going crazy. It's good to have someone to talk to who knows what I'm going through." She really meant it, but she couldn't tell him everything of course.

His arms around her were warm and comforting. Jack held her that way too, but this was different. Like something she didn't know she needed. They stood there in each other's arms longer than she expected until he gently lifted her chin and looked into her eyes.

"Would it be rude for me to ask for that kiss now? I've waited about nine years, give or take." He paused. "If it's too hard for you, I can wait. I do hope someday to give you that kiss and ..."

He cleared his throat and started to move away, but she pulled him back and kissed him. His eyes opened wide, his astonishment plain. She almost had to stop kissing him to chuckle at the playboy acting shocked.

Slowly he began to respond more deeply. His breath smelled sweet like coffee and pastry, and it sent her head into a whirlwind. It was a good thing Frankie and Carol were waiting for her, because, oh God, she didn't want the kiss to ever end. Finally, she forced herself to move away from him.

"Beth Ann," he whispered and pulled her back for more, which she obliged. His tongue danced gently across her lips.

Oh God, she had to catch her breath. She pulled her mouth away. "I have to get going. I need to get ready for this trip."

He held her a few seconds longer, immersing his nose in her neck and taking a deep breath. When he finally released her, he smiled.

"That was definitely worth the wait."

He took her hand and walked her out to the car. When they hugged goodbye, he wore a gentle smile that almost melted her on the spot. She had always loved his smile, nothing new about that. When his twin dimples flashed, she heard Gram's voice warning her: "Those dimples are the devil's work."

He stepped away and gave her a cute wink. "Good luck. No, wait—break a leg."

"Thanks. See you around, Blake,"

"Oh, yeah. You'll see me around for sure."

He swaggered away and then stopped in front of a limo parked nearby. He turned and gazed at her. Holy hot peppers, his look was spicy with a dash of come-hither. She waved and watched him get in the limo. As the car drove away, she touched her lips and remembered his kiss. The memory caused a sudden pain to stab at her heart, and she knew it was guilt. How could she be in tears over Kaylob one minute and kissing Blake the next?

Suddenly, the answer came to her. It must be because she was mad at Kaylob. She'd begged him not to return to the war, but he'd done it anyway. She loved him with all her heart and missed him terribly, but she also felt betrayed because he'd left her again.

Someone nearby cleared their throat and made her jump. She turned to see Carol and Frankie leaning against Frankie's car a few feet away, looking at her intently.

"Oh my gosh," she said. "I didn't see you standing there."

"Clearly." Frankie glowered at her. He opened the passenger door and motioned for her to get inside.

She avoided his eyes and walked around him to climb in the back seat because she wanted more time to daydream about kissing Blake. Frankie and Carol both sighed, then they got in the front seat. Nobody said anything for several minutes, then Beth Ann broke the tension.

"I'm going to miss you both so much while I'm away."

"Yeah, maybe I can get a few more dates with you gone," Frankie responded.

Beth Ann reached up and hit his shoulder. "Have I stopped you from dating, Frankie?"

"It's a little hard to explain to another woman when you're going over to spend the night at your best friend's place," he said. "Especially when she happens to be a beautiful, single, sexy theater star. Ranks pretty low as a pickup line."

Carol giggled. "Yeah, so what'll your excuse be when they don't come on to you now?"

Frankie turned and tickled Carol under her arm. "Women always come on to me."

Beth Ann sighed. "Well, why don't you guys hook up?"

Frankie shot a look at Beth Ann through the rearview mirror, then he smiled at Carol. "Yeah, I wish we'd get together, then apart, then together, then—"

Carol hit him as if they had some inside joke.

"I'm serious," Beth Ann said. "You'd make a great couple. Look at the two of you"

Frankie laughed. "I thought so too, but I found out I'm not Carol's type. I don't own any neutered cats, I won't eat mac and cheese, plus I never show up on the second date with a U-haul."

Carol smacked him again. "Shut up, Russo."

Beth Ann sighed again. "Frankie, Carol doesn't eat mac and cheese, plus she has neutered cats so you wouldn't have to own any yourself."

Carol and Frankie howled in laughter while Beth Ann just shook her head.

"You two need to stop eating popcorn."

"Let It Be" came on the radio, and they all sang along with the Beatles about times of trouble and Mother Mary. Beth Ann was glad she had these two good friends in her own times of trouble.

Chapter Eighteen

The next day Frankie helped her pack her clothes to get ready for the road trip. He promised he'd come by while she was away to water her two little plants and keep the place company. She was really going to miss him, and they wanted to spend her last few nights together.

While she pulled some more clothes from her closet, Frankie sat on the bed looking oddly at her kitty cat shirt.

"You gotta be kidding," he said. "You're not taking this, are you?"

She snatched the shirt from his hand. "Frankie, that took me hours to pick out."

He shook his head. "No wonder your friends draw straws to see who has to go shopping with you."

"For your information, Lisa liked this shirt and begged me to buy it."

"Oh, that's the shirt. She told me about that. She said she would have agreed to anything to get out of that store." He fell over onto the bed laughing.

Beth Ann rolled her eyes and went back to the closet. "Frankie, were you serious about what you said in the car last night? Have I really kept you from dating?"

He sat up again. "No, I've dated plenty. You've been rehearsing a lot lately, remember?"

"So have you been serious with someone?" she asked playfully.

"I've been with someone, but it never got serious."

She turned to look at him. "Really? Did you go all the way?"

"You're impossible," he said. "I don't kiss and tell."

"Come on, Frankie. Have you ever … you know?"

He shook his head and sighed. "Yes, Beth Ann. I've been with several someones. What did ya think, I'm a virgin?"

"No. Well, I didn't know what to think. Does Carol know? Maybe she'd get jealous and come after you."

"If you must know, Carol introduced me to one of the ladies I've been out with. She was pretty, but she acted it. To top it off, she treated the waitress rudely when I took her out to dinner. It was a total turn off."

"Okay, I'll stop worrying about your love life. Let's have some fun tonight. I want to get a bottle of wine, watch some old movies, and have a good dinner."

He smiled at her. "Whatever you want, Beth Ann."

They finished packing her clothes and spent the rest of the day cleaning her apartment. Since Frankie had already turned twenty-one, he went out and bought a bottle of wine and some Chinese food. After they finished watching Gidget Grows Up, Beth Ann had a large glass of wine which made her more than a little tipsy. When she asked Frankie for more, he poured it reluctantly.

"Be careful," he said. "You're not used to drinking, and that glass was enormous."

She was feeling dizzy and giggly and almost lost her balance when she stood to go the bathroom. Frankie jumped up and caught her, then he proceeded to take away her wine.

"Looks like you've had your limit, young lady."

She frowned at him and headed to the bathroom to change. When she went back to the living room wearing her PJs, Frankie was sitting on the couch reading one of his law books. She took his book away and plopped down on his lap.

"I love you, Frankie. I'm going to miss you."

"Ah, you're so cute. How much did you eat before you drank the wine?"

"A couple of egg rolls and some of the poo poo platter." She giggled. "Poo poo."

He chuckled, then she felt him tense, and his face sobered. "You know, you really need to stop sitting on my lap all the time. We're not kids anymore." He stood and pulled her up with him. "No more wine for you, missy. You're going to bed."

Her lip fell into a pout. "Frankie, you're my best friend. Why do I need to stop sitting on your lap? I can kiss you if I want to. We kissed before. Remember when we kissed?"

"Of course I do. I don't think you'll remember much about tonight. It's bedtime."

"No, kiss me, Frankie." She put her arms around his neck. "Kiss me once before I leave. Please?"

He glanced down at her and sighed. "Okay." He quickly kissed her lips. "There you go." He pulled her toward the bedroom, mumbling something about her kissing Blake.

"I must not be very appealing if my own best friend won't kiss me the right way." An even bigger pout formed on her lips. "Yes, I kissed Blake, but that was different. He's not my best friend, but he kissed me like I wanna be ki … kissed."

"Stop this and go to bed." He pointed at the bed and looked at her sternly.

"Okay, find ... I mean fine." She walked over to the bed and stood there.

Frankie kept pointing to the bed. "I am never buying wine for you again."

"Frankie ... Franklin ... Fr-Frank." She paused to giggle. "Will you hold me tonight?" She pulled on his shirt and looked up at him with a coaxing smile.

"No way," he said. "Not with you acting like this."

"But … but you're my best friend in the whole wide world. Don't you trust me and luff me?"

He put his hands on her shoulders and moved her away from him. "Beth Ann, I'm only going to say this once. I'm your best friend who happens to be a man. If you think I don't notice your body or the way you walk into a room, think again. I've seen all of you, remember? I had to pry you out of my mind with a crowbar. It wasn't easy, and to be honest, the image is still lodged in there tight. You're beautiful, sexy, and you happen to be my very best friend. Please remember, I'm only human. Hu-MAN. With man taking the lead."

She plopped down on the bed, trying to get her tipsy mind to process what he had just said. Frankie pushed her back and pulled up the blankets to cover her, but she sat up again and looked at him.

"But I need to ask you one thing then I won't ash ... I mean ask anything else, okay?"

He let out a huge sigh, giving in to the inevitable. "What? You're slurring your words."

"I just wanna know how you kiss before I leave."

"That's a bad idea," he said, but he sat down on the far edge of the bed.

She couldn't see very well in the dim light, and the wine had her head all fuzzy, but she could see how conflicted he was about kissing her. He was such a good friend, and it made her heart swell.

"Please, Frankie." She pulled on his shirt to get him closer.

"Fine." He got up and sat beside her. "But I'm only doing this because you're my best friend in the world."

He put his arms around her and moved his lips across hers for a few seconds, then he kissed her deeply. He was definitely not lacking in the kissing department. He could be called a superb kisser. Heck, maybe even better than Blake. Yet as much as she liked Frankie's kiss, it didn't do the same thing to her that Blake's had done.

When the kiss ended, Frankie grinned. "There, happy?"

She could tell he was watching closely for her reaction, so she tried to smile even though she felt dazed. "Very."

She lay down and let him finish covering her with the blanket. She watched as he walked into the living room and turned on the TV.

* * * *

The next morning, Beth Ann opened her eyes to see Frankie sitting at the kitchen table, looking out at a partly cloudy and gloomy day. His expression appeared tense. She got up from bed and slipped on her robe.

She didn't remember falling asleep, and she was glad she didn't remember any dreams, because there was no telling what they might have been.

"Hey, Frankie. Good morning."

He glanced at her and then turned away, still staring outside without saying a word. Beth Ann shuffled over to where he sat and looked down at him.

"Are you mad at me about last night?"

He didn't look at her. "A little, yes, and I've got a monster hangover."

She sat down on his lap and put her arms around his neck. Normally, that was okay. Today he lifted her off, placed her on the chair, and shook his head.

"Beth Ann, do you remember what I said to you on the hill that day when we were kids?"

"You said you loved me, and you'd come back to see me when you turned eighteen. And you did."

"No, the other part."

She paused, not really sure what he meant.

He took her hand in his. "I told you I wanted to go steady with you, and the only reason I didn't ask you was because of Kaylob. I knew you both loved each other."

"But, we were just kids."

"Why do you think I could handle being your best friend?"

"Because you love me. I'm your best friend, and I'm sweet and nice and—" She stopped when she saw the solemn look he was giving her. She folded her hands on her lap, trying to be serious and struggling against a sudden feeling of sadness.

Frankie lifted her chin. "Yes, I love you and you're my best friend, but has it ever occurred to you that maybe I could love you differently if the circumstances changed just a little bit?"

"No, not really," she answered. "I'm sorry."

An ache simmered in her heart at the thought that she'd hurt him. Had one glass of wine caused her to lose her best friend in the world? Had her desire to see how he kissed strained their friendship? She tried to swallow the tears, but a few skimmed down her cheeks.

He put his arms around her and pressed his face into her hair. "Oh, God, don't cry. I can't stand for you to cry. Beth Ann, please don't ask me to kiss you like that again unless you want more. Because I'd take all you'd give me, and I might lose you as my best friend in the process. It's too late to have it both ways."

"Do you love me as more than a friend, Frankie? Because I'd do anything you wanted me to do. I love you that much. If you want to be with me, we can try when I get back. Or you could make love to me now. Frankie, I love you so much."

He drew back and looked at her a moment, and she could tell he was fighting with himself over how to answer her. Then he sighed and shook his head.

"No, I can't even let myself think of you as more." He squeezed her hand and then kissed it. "You're my very best and dearest friend. Yes, it could have been more at one time. Hell, you have no idea how close it came to being more last night. You are damn hard to resist. I think we both know that your love for Kaylob is where your heart is. If I had you, I know I couldn't settle for half your heart. I'd want all of it, all of you. We both know that can never happen. So I'd rather have all your heart as my best friend than half your heart as my girlfriend."

She pressed her hand to her heart. "Frankie, that's the sweetest thing you've ever said to me." She paused a second and then smiled at him, trying to look sexy. "So I'm hard to resist?"

"You're a brat, Miss Rose." They both laughed.

"Seriously, you and Kaylob showed me what I want someday when I fall in love. I've witnessed what real love looks like, and I don't want to settle for less."

She threw her arms around his neck, giving him a complete friendship hug. Frankie didn't have to explain what he meant, because she fully understood. He was so right. She'd never be able to give anyone her whole heart, because it belonged to Kaylob. Suddenly, things around her started to change.

Oh no, not now. Not in front of Frankie …

As the room faded, she grew more and more aware that she was surrounded by dense jungle and was no longer standing in her tiny apartment. This was it, her mind had finally slipped.

Just as suddenly as the jungle had appeared, Frankie's loud voice brought her back.

"Beth Ann, hello." He shook her shoulders roughly. "What's wrong?"

She stared at Frankie, her eyes wide and his face full of questions.

"Beth Ann, what the hell just happened? It's like you weren't even here."

"I'm fine, Frankie. Just nervous over this whole tour thing." She moved over to her bed and started fumbling with her clothes.

"I don't know if I believe you. I called your name five or six times and was talking to you. I snapped my fingers in front of your face and you didn't even blink. It's like you were in a trance. Has this been happening a lot?"

Beth Ann shook her head. "I'm just stressed about this tour."

"Maybe it's too soon for you to be traveling."

"No, I need this, Frankie. I need to get out of this apartment for a while and away from all the memories. How can I move forward when I'm surrounded by them every day?" She tried to force a smile but got nothing from him in return.

"Okay," he said, his tone stern. "I want you to check in with me weekly, if not more. You clear?"

"Yes, dear." She leaned over and pecked him on the cheek.

They finished getting ready and left for the tour bus. They remained silent during the drive, although she kept seeing Frankie stealing glances at her. She had a pretty good idea what he was thinking about. The man had always been a worrywart. Actually, she had a little anxiety about leaving Frankie, but the trip made her feel sadder than she expected.

"You're my best friend," he whispered in her ear when they kissed goodbye. "The very best friend in the world, and I love you."

"I love you too, Frankie."

She was going to miss him terribly, almost as much as their just lost innocence. Once again, Beth Ann grew up a little more.

She hoped this trip would be the perfect time for her to mature, and maybe the tour would be the very thing to bring her back to rational behavior. Until Kaylob came back, she had no intention of spending a lot of time at home. She'd made up her mind she would work until she was too old to perform anymore.

Soon after Frankie left, Mitch came walking out with a clipboard and told everyone which bus they were on. Beth Ann was on Bus A with the main singers, actresses and actors. There would be a total of eight cast members plus Mitch all living together for six months, so they'd really get to know each other.

The other two buses held the rest of the dancers and singers. Even though there were whispers about how they had the cream of the crop, she couldn't imagine sleeping, bathing and all the other behind-the-scene happenings in such tight quarters aboard their bus. The little bunk beds were made from red velvet, four on each side with curtains that closed for some privacy. Mitch had a bigger area in the very back. There were two bathrooms, one for the girls and another for the guys. Some of the seating had tables and some didn't. She had never seen a bus like that before, with so many comforts of home. They even had a TV, fridge, and a little built-in stovetop with storage for snacks and food.

The six-month tour began.

Chapter Nineteen

Monday turned to Friday, and the weeks began to whisk by. Mitch acted like Beth Ann's second dad, or perhaps her third. How many dads did one girl need? Her birth dad had written to her but had never come for a visit, even when she had her meltdown. If truth be known, that had been hurtful. However, she refused to be mad at him. She loved her dad no matter what.

Travel became her escape from Kaylob's haunting cries, jungle sounds, and the crippling sadness that still popped in for unpredictable visits. Whenever she felt homesick, she'd reminisce about her childhood and made sure to phone Gram once or twice a week. That always seemed to make Gram happy, and she said she also loved getting the reviews Beth Ann sent.

She had received a few cards from Blake. He said he was hoping to catch her on tour, and she couldn't deny that she was hoping for that too. The kiss they'd shared was a lovely memory, and she wanted him to come to see her soon. She felt flattered that he often had little cards waiting for her at some of the cities where they were doing the shows, which meant he must be tracking the tour.

The next time they stopped to eat at a restaurant, she wanted to call Frankie and Carol to see how they were doing. The last stop she had called her parents, but she needed to talk to her best friends. When the buses came to a halt, she climbed out and found the nearest payphone. The booth had a strange odor, but she stepped inside, deposited her coin, and dialed Frankie's number.

"Frankie, it's me," she said when he answered.

"Is this the little redhead who used to love me but seems to have forgotten about me since she became a big star?"

"Oh, Frankie, you know that's not true. I miss you so much."

"Likewise, sweetie. You have no idea."

He filled her in on life in Riverside and all his classes. Just the sound of his voice made her homesick for him. She told him about her shows.

Next, she called Carol. She was still teaching dance and was of course still very involved with her rallies. Beth Ann missed everyone back home so much.

It was hard to say goodbye, but she had to get going since everyone was already loading up. Reluctantly, she hung up and made her way slowly back to the bus.

It was hard for her to believe mid-November was approaching and they'd been touring five months. Another birthday had come and gone. What astonished her was that she had turned twenty-one on the road. Kaylob had been missing for almost one full year. December twenty-second would mark the anniversary—only a few weeks to go.

She tried to push the memory away. Christmas shouldn't be a sad time. Until Kaylob came home, she had to at least try to have some holiday spirit.

She tried daydreaming about happy Christmases in the past, and just as she thought things were better, the sound of Kaylob's voice cried out to her and almost made her jump. She tried to be still so nobody would notice. Oh, God, he was calling her name, repeating that he loved and missed her. She felt as if she was being sucked through a dingy, dark tunnel.

She stood in the middle of a jungle. Where was this place? Off in the distance she saw four trees and a wide river in the background. The sound of a dog barking drew her attention, but she couldn't tell where it came from. He sounded frantic, and she wanted to go to the poor doggie, but her feet would not move. Weeds and bamboo covered the ground. Oppressive heat parched her. A revolting smell assaulted her nose. What was that? Her stomach turned and she thought she would vomit.

The sound of Mitch's voice called her back. When she opened her eyes, he and three cast members stood staring down at her with concern.

"Hey, kid, you okay?" Mitch said, sitting beside her. "We were calling you, and you didn't seem to hear."

She nodded. "I was just spacing out."

Mitch took her hand. "I've never seen someone space out that hard. You scared the hell out of us. Look at you, you're all sweaty. You sure you're feeling okay?"

She nodded and forced a smile. "I was just deep in thought about home." She didn't like lying, but no way could she tell them she had been deep in a jungle smelling shit or something.

Mitch told everyone to go sit back down and then turned back to Beth Ann. "Sweetie, you'd tell me if something was going on with you, right?" His forehead crinkled with concern.

She leaned her head on his shoulder. "Of course I'd tell you."

He stayed with her until she dozed off, and she awoke to find a blanket thrown over her and Danny sitting next to her reading a magazine. She had begun to think of all eight members on the bus as family. Every one of them knew about her breakdown and about Kaylob, yet they had never spoken of him. They endured her nightmares that interrupted her sleep along with everyone else's, and they never complained.

The tour had become a bigger success than any of them had dreamed, with dates being added in every location. They made stops in many cities and received rave reviews and standing ovations in even the biggest ones. Blake had begun sending her flowers and asked her to call him.

The next time she got to a phone, she chewed her lip, swallowed hard, and dialed his number. Unfortunately, he wasn't in and his housekeeper, who seemed very sweet, took a message. Actually, Beth Ann was both disappointed and relieved. She hadn't forgotten their kiss and really wanted to talk to him, but she had no idea what she would say to him.

The flowers continued, and they were always beautiful. The last time there had been chocolates and flowers. He was so thoughtful, and somehow he knew where they would be stopping. Each time she got to her dressing room, something from Blake was there waiting for her. She couldn't deny he was making an impact on her with his sweet words.

Mitch said their biggest tests would be in New York and Chicago. He did his best Sinatra imitation as he told everyone: "If we can make it there ..." The entire cast joined in unison and finished the famous line chorus. Beth Ann loved these people, but she still yearned for her friends at home.

They rolled into Denver on December 22nd for a one-night show, or at least that was the plan. Often they ended up doing two or three nights. As they drove down the long driveway to the theater, she noticed the picturesque beauty of the vibrant city with lights framed by mammoth white-capped mountains.

When they got off the buses, they were surprised by the brisk chill. It was a lot colder than they expected. Almost everyone had to turn around and grab coats. Beth Ann put on a heavy wool sweater then once again stepped out into the chill air. Laughter and excitement danced all around, but her heart was heavy. She tried to hide the urge she felt to cry and scream, because exactly one year ago today she had been told that Kaylob was missing.

All the Christmas decorations made the memory even more pronounced. Tears flooded her eyes as she stood staring at the nighttime sky, searching for that one special star that shined the brightest. Off to the east, she saw the one most brilliant twinkling star and knew Kaylob was sending her a message of love.

"Hey, beautiful, it's cold out here. Let's get you inside."

She jumped when Danny touched her shoulder. He was such a good guy, and she really liked him. He took her arm and guided her toward the stage entrance. She tried hard to blink away the tears, but a few slipped by. Danny must have seen them because he stopped and turned her to face him.

"Elizabeth, are you feeling okay?"

"It's just so cold out here." She was getting way too good at lying. She was going to Hell on a greased slide without a doubt.

"Okay, let's go." He put his arm around her and they headed inside.

That December evening on the stage in Colorado, they put on a flawless show, and Beth Ann thanked God for the distraction. When time came for "Somewhere Over the Rainbow" to close the show, she got a string of standing ovations. No matter how many she got, though, they never failed to cause a tear or two. Such an outpouring of appreciation truly touched her.

They had two long curtain calls that gave a sensation of filling you up yet draining your energy at the same time. Walking off the stage, Beth Ann's eyes fixated on an unexpected sight at stage right. Looking every bit like a proud yet anxious parent stood her birth dad, a nervous smile spread across his face.

She'd never seen him look that way before, and all she could do was look at him for a moment. The fact that he had come on this of all days filled her with emotion, and she ran to him. He held out his arms to her and embraced her.

"Dad, I had no idea you were coming." She looked up into his face. Her dad had always been handsome with his strawberry-blond hair, blue eyes, and tall, lean build.

"You brought the house down, Beth Ann." He picked her up and swung her around, making her giggle. "You're amazing. I am so very proud." His smile moved into his eyes.

"When did you get here?"

"Yesterday. I wanted to be sure to get here in time. Can we spend some time together?"

"Sure, we're not leaving until the morning."

She hurried to change, then she knocked on Mitch's door to tell him she was leaving with her dad.

"Go have fun, kid," Mitch said, waving her off.

Her dad suggested they get a bite to eat at a little diner down the street. He mentioned that he'd found the place on one of his travels and thought she would like it because he knew she loved trains. When they stepped inside, Beth Ann was instantly charmed. It appeared just like a train, with old-time booths and music boxes on each table. The delicious aroma of food smelled yummy, making her stomach growl right on cue.

A loud smash of dishes made everyone turn and look toward the kitchen, but laughter filled the air seconds later. After Beth Ann and her dad were seated and ordered drinks, she flipped through the songs on the table while her dad sipped his beer. A song popped out at her immediately.

Her dad must have noticed, because he said, "Honey, what is it?"

"That's our song." She pointed at "Baby I'm Yours" by Barbara Lewis. "Mine and Kaylob's. I just realized I haven't heard it since he ..." She paused to swallow. "Since he left."

Her dad's face displayed embarrassment. "I'm sorry I wasn't there for you, and uh ... I thought maybe my being here today might help."

"Is that why you came? You remembered the date?"

He surprised her when his eyelashes became misty. "Yes, I remembered the date, but that's not the only reason I came. I wanted to see you in your show, and I knew today might be hard for you. And, well ... I also missed you."

She paused to give herself a chance to take in all he'd said. Her mouth opened then closed again, because she really didn't know how to respond.

"I have something I need to say, and it's important," He said slowly, watching her.

"Okay." She folded her hands in front of her. "Go ahead."

"I know I haven't been a good father. You don't have to pretend, because we both know the truth." He sighed. "I've always loved you. I'm sorry for your childhood. Before your mom married Stanley, I know your life was hard. I dragged you guys with me while I tried to fulfill my dreams. I just wanted you to know that I'm sorry. I hope you can find it in your heart someday to forgive me."

She gazed into his eyes and started to speak, but the waitress came over just then to take their orders. Beth Ann was amused when they ordered the same thing—burgers well done and French fries with no salt. The tiny waitress appeared about eighteen. She was adorable, with pretty blonde hair, dark eyes, and a beautiful smile. Her name tag read Amy.

After the waitress left, Beth Ann realized her dad seemed nervous about what she would say about his apology. She reached out and touched his hand.

"Now about my forgiving you, Dad. Yes, my childhood was hard, but some of it was fun too." She leaned forward. "I did miss having a home, and I didn't like—no, I hated living on the road and never having a best friend. Heck, I never had a friend period. I loved being with my family, our singing, playing, and laughing together. Yeah, we were poor, but we were rich in so many ways. I think I turned out pretty okay, and look at Cole and James—both great guys."

She paused and looked at their hands a second before continuing. "I lost the love of my life this last year and almost died. I didn't want to live anymore, but here I am. I found out I'm stronger than I knew I was. You're a part of who I am, so don't beat yourself up. I'm delighted to have you as my dad. I love you, and I'm touched that you chose today to show up."

His lip trembled, and a tear slid down his cheek. He stood up and excused himself, and she knew he was embarrassed by his emotions. Her dad had always been a big goofball, never serious. She had never seen him cry before, not even when her mom had left him.

The waitress brought their food before he came back. "I hope everything's good. If you need anything else, just let me know."

Beth Ann nodded and noticed her dad making his way back. He sat down in the booth, his eyes red from crying.

"You're a wonderful young lady, Beth Ann. Thank you for saying all those loving words. I don't deserve your forgiveness and understanding, but I'm grateful for them. I love you, honey."

She leaned across the table and put a hand on his cheek. "I love you too, Daddy."

He touched his heart and almost choked up again. "You haven't called me Daddy in years."

Beth Ann smiled. "A girl is never too old to call her daddy Daddy."

Something good happened that night as her dad stood under the stars in Colorado, hugging her goodbye. A new bond was forged between father and daughter. That was the night their relationship changed, and she had a feeling that somehow Kaylob knew.

Chapter Twenty

Chicago was three days away, with shows scheduled every day in between. Beth Ann started to crave her own bed and a little more privacy. Attempting to sleep on the bus wore her down, and the lack of solitude didn't improve her overall mood. Some in the group were getting as cranky as Lenard did without coffee. If Cindy, one of the dancers, didn't get her cup, everyone including Mitch ran for cover.

Fortunately, they'd get four days off once they hit Chicago so the stagehands could improve the production, props, lighting etc. The company paid for the cast to stay in one of the finest hotels in the city while the work was being done. Mitch said they would each get a suite. Beth Ann had heard Chicago was an exciting town to explore and couldn't wait to get there.

When they were still three days out, Mitch called her over to sit by him on the bus. She got up from her very comfortable seat and plopped down next to him.

"How are ya, kid?"

"Good," she answered. "I miss my friends, my family, and my bed. A little peace and quiet and better food would be nice. Other than that I'm peachy."

He took off his reading glasses and closed the magazine he'd been reading, his left eyebrow raised questioningly. "Speaking of friends, I got a call about you from some kid named Blake Tanner. He caught me right when we were leaving the show the night you went with your dad. I got sidetracked with that little backstage spat and forgot to tell you."

"That's okay. It's easy to forget when you have a couple of people fighting. Did he tell you what he wanted?" She tried to sound casual. "By the way, he's not a kid. He's twenty-five."

"Oh, well okay. The old man said he wants to meet up with you. You haven't had any visitors besides your dad since we hit the road. I think it'd be good for you to spend some time with a friend. He seemed very excited to see you."

She nodded. "Yeah, it would be nice to see someone from home."

"Was this guy an old boyfriend or something?" Mitch raised both eyebrows this time.

"No, Kaylob was the only boyfriend I ever had."

"You're kidding. Really, kid?"

She shrugged, a little embarrassed. "Kaylob was the only guy I ever dated because we fell in love almost at first sight when we were just kids. Blake Tanner ... well, I did have a crush on him, but my heart belonged to Kaylob."

She felt a shadow cross over her after her comment. Looking out the window, she thought about the jungle and Kaylob's voice. Then she thought about Blake, the all-American boy, so handsome and rich. He'd been a star football player that all the girls had loved. Yet none of them had known the truth about Mr. Tanner, the secrets he'd shared with no one. If only he would have let her help him back then. She had tried more than once. She couldn't remember him ever having one close friend or even a steady girl.

Mitch cleared his throat. "Hey, kid, where'd ya go?"

"I was thinking about Kaylob," she answered guiltily.

Mitch took her hand. "Remember, you need to move on. I bet Kaylob would want that."

She nodded. "I know he would." He wasn't here, because he just had to go back to Vietnam to help his brothers.

"It will be nice to spend some time with Blake," she said and meant it. Remembering his kiss made her touch her lips.

"Great." Mitch gave her Blake's phone number along with his room number. "His hotel is right around the corner from us, and it's one of the swankiest places around. The guy must be loaded."

Beth Ann lifted her shoulder in a half shrug. "Yes, he's very successful."

Mitch winked and gave her a hug. "Well, good. I'm glad you're going to see him. I hope it'll help with those nightmares you keep having."

"I'm sorry, Mitch. I know I wake up you and everyone else screaming like that."

"Look, kid, nobody cares about that. We only care about you."

"Hey, I care." someone shouted from three rows back. "I could at least get to comfort her if I have to get up."

"Shuddup, Roscoe," Mitch fired back.

Beth Ann giggled. Roscoe flirted with all the girls and was full of hot air. She stood and leaned over to kiss Mitch's cheek. "Aw, thanks, boss."

"It's okay. You're too beautiful not to let another guy get a crack at ya. Just ask Danny. He'd sure like that chance."

Danny whipped his head around to shoot Mitch a glare. For the next dozen miles, everyone teased poor Danny about having a crush on Beth Ann.

Later, Mitch stood up and got everyone's attention. "Well, gang, we'll be hitting Chicago in three days. When we get there, you'll get four days off to play."

The entire cast started talking and sharing what they were going to do. Beth Ann couldn't help feeling excited about seeing Blake and how much fun that might be. However, she didn't want to appear too eager, so she decided she'd wait and call him after being in town for a couple of days.

As she gazed out the window, her eyes captured the blue sky with white puffy clouds that looked as if they formed a bridge, maybe leading to Heaven. With no beginning or end, thoughts of Kaylob swept through her. His arms had always been like being covered in her favorite blanket, making her feel safe and protected. She pulled her shawl over her shoulders and continued daydreaming.

As she watched the sky and listened to the voices lulling her, a sudden shift hit her. A long tunnel filled her vision, pulling her away, and Kaylob's voice was the only one she heard. "Beth Ann ... Beth Ann, please."

Again she stood in a dense jungle near a river. Sunlight beamed through the thick foliage, and a smokescreen covered the area as though trying to hide something. Where in the world was she? The ground was swampy, the air humid, and the heat almost burned her body. What the heck was that foul, rotten stench?

Gradually, she grew aware she saw someone off in the distance sitting by a tree. A man with a beard. He appeared long and skinny, nobody she recognized. The poor guy cried out in agony and she instinctively tried to go to him.

Then the familiar sounds of laughter brought her back to the tour bus.

What had just happened? Great, now she'd lost her mind completely. Sweat dripped down her face and dampened her shirt. She reached up and tried to wipe it off with her fingers just as Danny came over. He sat down next to her, and she tried her best to act normal.

"Beth Ann, you don't look well." He gazed at her with concern. "I've never seen you sweat, not even when we're rehearsing or dancing hard."

She threw off the blanket. "Oh, I guess I just got too hot."

He sat there for a minute, then a slow smile spread across his face. "I thought I could take you out sometime since you're not dating anyone." His face reddened despite the smile.

"Sure, why not? We could go to dinner or lunch sometime. I'd like that." She liked Danny as a friend and had to make sure not to lead him on.

He lit up like a pinball machine, this time from excitement. Although he wasn't her type, he seemed like a good guy. Perhaps she might be able to steer him toward Michelle, the understudy for Juliet.

After Danny left, her thoughts returned to the jungle scene, and the memory gave her chills and mystified her. Before she could form any theory regarding what she'd seen, everyone began singing "Chicago" and of course she had to join them.

Nervous excitement accompanied the whole gang on the bus the last night before they hit Chicago. Crawling into her sleeping area, she closed her little curtains for an illusion of privacy. Sleep came fast, but it brought no rest. Instead she had the disturbing, recurring dream and heard Kaylob's voice.

"Beth Ann, I'm here. I love you."

Doors continued to block her. Desperately, she pulled at the knobs, kicking and screaming. Sobs ripped through her.

"Kaylob. Please open the door."

A sudden shake brought her back, and she opened her eyes to see Mitch leaning over her. He climbed onto her bed, holding and rocking her. Periodically, several cast members came to check on her. Danny brought a glass of water and gave her a tender smile. All of them had been so kind after being awakened so many times.

Mitch held her until she calmed. "Kiddo, I think you need to see someone about these dreams." He motioned for the cast to head back to bed, then he hummed her to sleep.

* * * *

Finally, they rolled into Chicago. The contrast between the miles leading up to the Windy City took her breath away. She'd never seen so many bright lights and bustling activity. How exciting the next four days would be. She'd get rest, room service, and pampering.

Everyone piled off the bus and ran up to the front desk, yapping like terriers for the keys to their rooms. Beth Ann stepped through the hotel entrance and admired the architecture. Almost immediately, she sensed someone staring at her as she took in the nuances of her surroundings.

She turned and saw Blake Tanner leaning against the wall, his hands in the pockets of a black suit with a pink tie that made him look like a movie star. How odd for a guy to wear that color, but somehow he made it look stylish. She caught a glimpse of quite a few women checking him out. When he grinned, showing off his twin dimples, several of the ladies from the cast giggled with delight.

A girl named Misty from Bus B came up beside her and nodded in Blake's direction. "Hey, you know that guy?"

Beth Ann smiled. "Yes I do."

No mistaking Misty's look of disappointment. "Damn, I was hoping he was available. Look at that body and those dimples. Why does he look so familiar? Is he an actor?"

Beth Ann almost laughed. "No, he's in real estate."

Blake had always strived to succeed. Maybes he worked so hard because he was adopted. More likely it was because of his adopted parents' inability to show love. His home had always been frigid, but in school he had been wild and free, ever the playboy with girls fighting over him. Despite all that, he had grown into what seemed like a good man.

Blake started walking toward her with his customary strut, and every female in the place took notice. While she turned to sign some papers for her room, the band of marching butterflies played drums in her stomach, which told her Blake was standing right behind her. She turned to see him very much in her personal space.

"Blake, what are you doing here? The show isn't for another four nights."

He chuckled. "You're a sight for sore eyes." He picked her up and swung her around then set her back down. "Mitch told me you have four days off. I was hoping you'd want some company, maybe check out some of the sights here in Chi-Town. I know my way around."

"Yes, I'd love some company." Beth Ann said, trying to keep her face from flushing.

With that, he picked up her bags, and they both walked over to get on the elevator. While they waited, the unexpected sound of Kaylob's voice calling her name shook her foundation. Oh, God, not now. Not in front of Blake. With all the strength she could muster, she pushed his voice away.

Blake glanced over at her and said, "You okay?"

"I think I'm starving."

His dimples appeared. "Well, darlin, I just happen to know the perfect place to take you for dinner."

"Blake, your Southern accent is cute."

"What Southern accent?" he said then added, "You really think it's cute?"

Beth Ann laughed, and once again she heard Kaylob's voice. That was the first time she suspected it was a guilty conscience making her hear things.

Chapter Twenty-One

Kaylob's mood matched his dark dank prison. The air reeked of goddamn fresh rotting death since so many had died. Now they were burning the corpses and smoke from the bodies permeated the air. Skeletal, he trudged outside his hovel and down the humid bamboo halls. As he stepped out into the open air, he flinched at the sunshine.

He hated the sight of the bodies littering both sides of the trail. Some of the guys had been buried with just their heads exposed, trying to eat their maggot-ridden food. It made him goddamn mad. Chris, one of Kaylob's fellow prisoners, had told him he'd been there for over a year. All he wanted to do was kill the bastards and get the hell out.

His memory of the day he'd been captured had become clearer. Before any patrol, it was crucial to gather intelligence and outline the plan. That day they had screwed the pooch, and something had gone horribly wrong. Many of the guys in the platoon were caught in an ambush. They'd fought them off the best they could, but they had been grossly outnumbered and hadn't seen the enemy in the trees until it was too late. Kaylob had been shot trying to pull the guys to safety. He remembered a sharp pain hitting him before he'd blacked out. He still wondered if Patterson had survived and knew he'd probably never know.

The Viet Cong tried their best to stop any type of communication between the GI's, so they had countered with code. The idiots tried to intercept their tapping, but they could never get the rhythm of "Shave and a Haircut." Kaylob hated the pricks and thought about all the ways he would like to torture them. He came up with some mighty good plans, but he was too weak to follow through.

Frequently, he looked at the torn and weathered photo that was his most treasured possession. He knew now they'd let him keep it as part of their torture plan. He missed and longed to hear Beth Ann's voice. If only she knew he was alive, even though he might not be much longer. If she found out he had lived and then died as a POW, that might be worse for her.

At least his captors had stopped talking about her sleeping with many guys like they'd done in the beginning. They must have thought his responses weren't good enough anymore. Sadistic chumpstains. Beth Ann would never do that regardless.

His existence was worse than an animal held for slaughter. He wouldn't want to see animals living under such filthy, starving conditions. Death constantly taunted him with its embrace, coaxing him to join those who had departed the hellhole. The Cong would force the survivors to carry out some of the bodies and bury them just outside the camp. Other corpses were left to rot on the ground, covered in feces because they had been too weak to move before they died. Those were burned.

Other times, Kaylob screamed through his clenched jaws from the pain of his arms tied behind his back, pulled so hard they were yanked out of their sockets. He knew he had internal parasites from the food and water. Sometimes he couldn't keep anything in his stomach. Vomit rolled down the long beard layered over his face.

The one thing that comforted him was remembering all the funny things about Beth Ann. The memories helped keep his spirits up. He longed to feel her lips, touch her hair, and to be with her again.

These beasts could take everything else from him, but they couldn't take his memories.

Usually, consciousness would surface only long enough to endure the beatings. He had no doubt his ribs were shattered. After hours of torment, the slime balls would dump him in the hovel and leave him for dead. He would crawl with his hands tied behind his back to the plate of maggot-ridden rice and force himself to eat the shit.

Tonight they'd left him alone by four evergreen trees. The weather was cold but not freezing. One could live outside after dark. The thought of escaping remained tempting, but with no shoes or shirt and just a ragged remnant of uniform pants, he stood no chance of surviving. Others who'd tried had been killed by the bastards.

Faintly, he heard the far-off sounds of a dog barking, and it took him back home to his wonderful little town of Novato. Would he ever see home again? Would he ever see Beth Ann? He loved the town they had grown up in.

Memories of walking down Grant Avenue holding Beth Ann's hand surfaced and almost made him cry. Why the hell did he come back to this war? Why hadn't he put her first? She'd begged him not to go. If he made it back now, what was to say she'd even want his sorry ass?

From the first time he'd seen her on the railroad tracks, she had melted his soul. Her little ramblings and puttering had become his window into her nervousness. Memories of making love to her for the first time flashed in his mind. His memory raced through different parts of his life. Maybe that's what they meant by your life flashing before your eyes. Did that mean he was dying?

No. He had to get back to Beth Ann. Getting out of this mess had to be his focus, but he didn't even know what day or year it was. It was hard for him to get any information. He had tried scratching the days in the ground, but the assholes had even taken that away.

Darkness came along with visions of his beautiful redhead standing by the ocean. Where was this place—Heaven? The beauty reminded him of the stories he'd heard. The ocean so green, the grass so lush. He felt a connection to this place. Beth Ann ran down a hill, her long hair blowing with the wind.

He said just above a whisper with his weakened voice. "Beth Ann, I love you."

Chapter Twenty-Two

Beth Ann and Blake stepped into the suite to find dozens of flower arrangements. Without warning, a chill went down her spine and she couldn't move as she heard Kaylob whispering to her again. One part of her wanted to scream to him, but instead she focused her attention back on the beautiful flowers and cards, trying to appear normal.

Blake touched her arm. "Beth Ann, you okay?"

She forced a smile. "Yes, I'm fine. Just glad to be off the bus and in a real room."

He took her hand and led her over to the flowers. "Look at all these. Some are from movie stars. Here's one from Cher."

"Did you say Cher? Oh my God." Beth Ann squealed and picked up the card.

Congratulations on a wonderful show. Well done.

Cher

They ran around the room reading the other cards. The fragrances combined with the energy generated by new experiences caused spontaneous giddiness. The emotion didn't last because her inner hallucinations made her teeter on lunacy. They opened the French doors that led into the bedroom.

Beth Ann squealed again. "Look, a real bed."

Blake didn't move and appeared to experience a hint of apprehension, but she couldn't help her excitement about the bed. She ran to jump on it, acting like a goofy child. After a few prolonged moments, he sat on the edge and gave her a sidelong glance.

"Sorry," she said, "I know I'm being silly, but it's been forever since I saw a real bed. I can't wait to take a real shower."

"Yeah, I was going to mention that," he teased.

She took a half-hearted swing at him before he playfully grabbed her and pulled her into his arms. The pizzazz from his touch surged, making her heart quiver.

His eyes slanted with desire. "I've thought about our kiss ever since that night."

His voice did surprising things to her, and his touch implored, enticing and suggestive. Temptation soared, and she had to do something before she jumped his bones. She folded her hands, not knowing what else to do.

"Beth Ann ..." Gently, he lifted her chin and moved his lips close to hers. When she didn't protest, their lips touched softly. His breath smelled sweet, with a hint of coffee. He pulled her close, and she didn't want to stop him, but she had to. It took all her strength to move herself off the bed.

"Shower." She pointed in that direction.

"Yes, shower." He nodded.

With shaky legs, she picked up her makeup case and walked into the bathroom, closing the door behind her. What had just happened? Blake Tanner was intoxicating, no question about that. One minute she'd been hearing Kaylob and the next she'd been in Blake's arms.

The shower called out to her, and she hoped it might help clear her head. She removed her clothes and stepped inside. Ahh, the warm water traveled down her body like a cozy hug from a long lost friend. The thought of the next four days off filled her with excitement. With everything she had been going through—the nightmares, the visions or whatever they were—she felt depleted and needed this time to recharge. Waiting for her outside the door was a hot, no, sizzling, no, seductive ... Oh, heck, Blake was all those things and more, wrapped up in one tantalizing package.

Yet even though Blake was a triple scoop of delicious, nothing could stop the thoughts of Kaylob. Suddenly, the memories assaulted her, and she could feel him washing her hair, holding her, kissing her. Like an old projector playing back their moments.

"Stop that, Beth Ann," she scolded herself.

She might never experience Kaylob's touch again, but whose fault was that? Not hers. She wasn't the one who'd gone back to that war. That didn't stop her from missing him. Most days she expected him to knock on the door and tell her it had all been some big mistake.

This had to stop. This was her first date since Kaylob had ... left. She wasn't going to screw it up with her craziness.

She turned off the water, stepped out of the shower and put on her robe. Blake had been sitting on the bed when she left, and she had a feeling he would still be there. She needed to go out there and get her clothes, but she changed her mind after glancing in the mirror at her wet, messy hair. At least it had grown enough to cover her shoulders again. She dried her hair and put on some makeup. After she finished getting glamorized with tips she'd gotten from Glamour, she stared at herself in approval and opened the bathroom door.

She found Blake lying on the bed with his eyes closed, arms behind his head. Holy cow. She stared at him, unable to move, heat radiating to the pit of her stomach. How could she keep from admiring his ... um, truly impressive body. Her brain needed to be washed out with soap. The surge of heat caused her tongue to move over her lips. His well-formed stomach and defined thighs made her drink all if him in.

"My God, his biceps and broad shoulders are amazing."

Oh, shit. Had she said that out loud? Holy hot flash, she wanted to run and hide, but she couldn't seem to tear her eyes away from his zipper. When she finally managed to glance up, she found him looking right at her.

"Yes, darlin, what can I do for you? My biceps interest you because ...?" Those twin dimples showed up again and made her flush.

"I, ah ... need to find something to wear."

He sat up propped on one arm and grinned. "Well, I'm not sure they would fit ya, but you can try them on if you like." He stood up and began to unbutton his shirt as he raised his eyebrows.

Dang it, she was busted with a capital B. Even though he was clearly having fun teasing her, his sense of humor was as tantalizing as the rest of him, approaching the edge of sarcasm but not falling off. It gave another sexy angle to his luscious looks. That part of him reminded her of Kaylob and attracted her even more.

"Very funny," she said, trying to sound dignified.

His grin widened as he walked toward her. "You want to go out or stay in? You could try on my clothes if you want. I'll share anything you desire."

"No, I have my own clothes, and no you can't borrow them." She tried to put some distance between them and moved to her suitcase.

"Yeah, but you seem to find mine much more ... entertaining." He slipped into her personal space and again the smell of his sweet breath so close made parts of her body tingle. "Beth Ann, I would be happy to stay in this room and do whatever you wanted. What would you like to do?"

Now this side of him was very different from Kaylob. She sensed that if she moved forward, he wouldn't stop her, and she liked the way it made her feel like an uninhibited woman. She definitely wasn't ready for anything like that.

It took her a couple of agonizing seconds to find her voice, but she managed to say, "Clothes, I need to find my own clothes." She flushed again to think she had nothing on under her robe. "I'd really like to go out."

He moved in front of her again and lightly touched her fingers. Overstuffed seconds passed before he politely retreated. Whew. If he had pulled her robe open, no telling what might have happened.

"Okay, then," he said, sounding disappointed. "Come on, let's get going." He walked over and sat on the edge of the bed again.

He had to know what he had just done to her. Since junior high, he'd ushered a cavalcade of females wanting to be close to him. Now Beth Ann understood more than ever the charm he'd had over those girls. He practically oozed sex appeal and charisma, and she couldn't help wondering what it would be like to …

No, she had to push that thought far away. Like maybe to the next country.

At last she found the right dress and brushed by him to enter the bathroom. Behind the closed door, she hoped she would be safe from her own desire. The white dress seemed a little sexier than what she had planned to wear, and a distant memory hit her of the time she had worn a sexy black dress for Kaylob. Yep, he would hate this little number because it revealed too much skin, but she thought it was groovy the way the dress showed off her figure and her B cups. Yes, this would do, along with her little white heels, gold earrings, and purse to match.

She had calmed down some, but just placing her hand on the doorknob made her nervous again. Oh, God, she couldn't stay in the bathroom all night. To hell with it. She was done being shy, and tonight she would prove it. With a determined lift of her chin, she stepped out into the bedroom.

Blake was sitting on the edge of the bed studying his shoes. She waited for him to notice her, and as soon as he glanced up, his eyes told her he liked her little white dress too. He stood and swallowed a gulp of air, and she couldn't believe the crimson she saw spreading over his cheeks.

Blake Tanner blushing? What the heck? Never once had she made Kaylob blush. He had always done that to her.

Crap, she had to push Kaylob out of her mind. This was her first date with anyone other than him. She needed to have fun, to laugh, and let her hair down. For too long all she'd done was suffer in silence. With her shoulders back and head held high, she embraced her ability to make this playboy redden.

He bent over and brushed what looked to be imaginary lint off his suit, obviously trying to collect himself and control his emotions.

"Elizabeth Ann Rose, I think I'd better check my shoes, because you just knocked my socks off. I'm pretty sure you've broken several laws by looking so good." His gaze meandered over her body, and a grin flaunted his dimples again.

God, give her strength not to attack him right now.

"Why, thank you, Mr. Tanner," she said, returning his smile.

He reached for her hand, and she slipped it into his. They needed to get out of the room while she still could. Just before they stepped out, he stopped and turned her to face him.

"One more for the road?"

She tilted her face up and kissed him, enjoying the taste of his sweet mouth and lips.

"Damn, Beth Ann, you are one sexy lady. We better get out of here now before I lose my ability to drive."

Off they went to the heart of the Windy City. While they explored the highlights around the hotel, she kept peeking at him from the corner of her eye, wondering if that kiss had made him delirious. He peered back and forth between the road and her face.

He told her he was taking her to a superb restaurant right down the street that had amazing food, beautiful music, and plenty of elegant ambiance. His words impregnated her mind with another memory—the night Kaylob had proposed. The atmosphere in the car changed instantly, and she was glad it was dark so he wouldn't see the tears building in her eyes.

She stared out the window, pretending to take in all the sights and sounds of the city. She couldn't let the memory steal the fun she might have tonight.

When they reached the restaurant, Blake drove up to the front door and switched off the car. "Are you okay?" he said. "You're really quiet."

She nodded and was glad when the valet jogged over to the driver's side and opened the door for Blake.

"Good evening, Mr. Tanner."

Blake got out and handed him the keys, surveying the area as though he were looking for someone.

The valet touched Blake's arm. "Got the word that all's clear. They took your limo and created a diversion."

"Thanks, Robbie." Blake moved to the other side of the car and opened the door for Beth Ann.

Confusion washed over her. What kind of diversion were they talking about? The questions must have shown on her face, because Blake grinned and held the door open.

"I'm here often, and they know me."

He took her hand and led her to the entrance of the restaurant. When they stepped inside, the elegance blew her mind and brought her to a standstill. It was like something seen only in a sophisticated Hollywood movie. Awestruck, she felt captivated by the chandeliers that sparkled like exotic gems above the lush, deep red carpet. The emperor stairs swept up to the dining room adorned with marble and cherry wood. After five seconds in the place, she knew any restaurant she'd ever been to with Kaylob didn't compare.

Blake placed his warm hand on the small of her back, guiding her away from the entrance. Live piano music floated through the room from somewhere off in the cavernous reaches. The ambience made her feel as if she had stepped back into the Thirties. Cherry wood tables and antique sofas lined the sitting area that featured what appeared to be a gas fireplace. Vases of fresh flowers bordered the walls and were tastefully scattered about.

Beth Ann mentioned to Blake that she needed to visit the ladies' room, so he motioned to the hostess who waved for someone to come and show her the way. The girl led her down a hallway to an ornate door and opened it for Beth Ann. The bathroom escort nodded, hesitated, then disappeared. A few minutes later, Beth Ann realized she should have tipped her when she overheard a woman in the bathroom telling a friend that she had given her a five-dollar bill. Wow, what a job—lavatory hostess.

The sitting area was larger than her apartment in Riverside. Several mini makeup tables lined the wall along with plush orange-and-red chairs. There were also some type of half-back sofas with ottomans to rest your feet. Beth Ann hoped that beyond the resting room was the actual restroom.

She walked into the lavatory and found another strange surprise in the form of a housekeeper seated on a stool whose apparent job was to keep an eye out for errant splashes, counter drippings, or any other mood-disturbing indiscretions.

Inside one of the stalls, she found some of the toilets were bidets that sprayed water where she least expected. That startled her, since she had not planned on any type of shower. Thank God the sink seemed normal. When she placed her hands under the running water, the room faded.

Oh, no. It was happening again.

A voice called out to her as the jungle came into view. Off in the distance, gun shots blasted and voices shouted in a strange language, "tra tan." A dog wailed. Dear God, she wanted to go save the poor animal.

Then she heard Kaylob's voice. "Beth Ann, please, I love you."

Mud covered the ground, but this time she was able to move. The humid stench swarmed around her, the air thick with heat. Birds squawked and other creatures continued growing louder.

"Kaylob." she cried over the sounds of the jungle. "Kaylob, please."

"Miss, can I help you with something?"

A woman's voice startled her, and Beth Ann was once again standing in front of the sink with the water running. Holy night. It was the splatter lady. How long had she been standing there? Faces of strangers stared at her while she tried to appear normal and wipe the sweat dripping from her face.

"Miss, can I go get Kaylob for you?"

Stunned, Beth Ann whipped around to look at the lady. "Excuse me? Why are you asking about Kaylob?"

The woman appeared puzzled. "You called out his name twice. Do you want me to find him for you?"

"Oh ... no. No, thank you." Beth Ann pulled out a towel, dried her hands and swept by the lady. In the sitting room, nobody acknowledged her, so she sat on a lounge chair to compose herself.

Why did she keep seeing the jungle and hearing gun shots? Was it possible God was trying to show her what had happened to Kaylob? She tried to collect herself so she wouldn't broadcast her insanity to Blake. Instead, she focused on the beautiful décor and pushed away the disturbing visions and what meaning they had. After ten minutes or so, she stood, released her breath and left the bathroom.

Chapter Twenty-Three

When Beth Ann came around the corner from the bathroom, she saw Blake speaking to a mature gentleman. Blake glanced up and motioned for her to join them.

"Peter, this is Beth Ann." He turned to her with a smile. "Beth Ann, Peter works with me. He's here to meet with a potential client who may want to buy one of our biggest complexes, and we need to go over a few ideas for just a minute. Is that okay?"

"Sure." She smiled at both men.

Peter took her hand. "Lovely to meet you." He wiggled his brown eyebrows to express approval and almost didn't let go of her hand.

"You too, Peter." After a few seconds she was able pull her hand away from the man.

Blake leaned close to her ear. "You were gone a long time. I was ready to send someone to check on you. Everything okay?"

"I'm fine. You go ahead. I'll go have a seat."

The luxurious couches lining the expansive lobby beckoned for her to take a seat and relax. The aromas from the unseen kitchen notified her tummy that she needed food. People dressed to the nines who were coming and going made her feel underdressed and overexposed.

Her thoughts went back to the scene in the jungle, and she remembered one of the words she had overheard in the vision, tra tan. She picked up her handbag and found a pencil along with an envelope to write down the word, although she wasn't sure how to spell it. What did tra tan mean, and what language was it from? As she tucked the envelope away, she knew she had to find out the meaning.

For now, it was time to enjoy her date. She had been through enough for one night. Somehow, someway, she'd make sure to have a good time. She had to find a way to overcome the guilt that seemed to slap her with stupid crap anytime she had a moment of fun. It was absurd, unfair, and needed to stop.

She had to focus on something else, and Blake Tanner was the perfect distraction.

Sexy, now that was a good descriptive word, but it didn't fully characterize Blake. All around her, women passed him and did double takes. Actually, women weren't the only people who ogled Blake. Several guys walked up and shook his hand. He was certainly popular.

Ooh la la. What would it be like to touch him under that suit?

Okaaay, where had that come from? Not only was she insane, now her mind had gone to live in the gutter. She giggled as she thought of how that would make a good country song title—"She Was Insane With a Gutter Brain." Gram would be so proud.

Well, if she had to lose her mind, she might as well do it with humor and a little fun. Blake Tanner fun.

A sound nearby caught her attention, and she turned to see a man who appeared to be in his thirties. He was staring at her as if she was an inviting appetizer. Self-consciously, she attempted to tug her dress over her knees, but there was nothing to pull down. To avoid looking his way, she pretended to study the material on the arm of the couch, but the predator slithered over to plant himself next to her.

"Hello there, beautiful," he slurred.

"Good day," she responded, immediately repulsed. She looked for Blake, but he was still talking to the older gentleman.

The intruder groped her with his bleary eyes. "I sure could go for some strawberry pie for dessert."

His breath and garbled speech told her he was drunk, but why would he be telling her what he wanted for dessert?

"Stwawberriess is my favorite disssh. You're quite a dish, little lady."

"Pardon me?" She didn't want to create a scene, so she scooted to the end of the couch. The guy scooted next to her and had the nerve to touch her knee.

A blur crossed her eyes, and Blake had the guy's arm. "Do we have a problem here?" he demanded, yanking him upright.

Beth Ann was certain the man had a sudden, uncontrollable bladder problem.

"No, no problem, sir. None at all." The man suddenly sounded as sober as a nun.

"You're right," Blake said. "We have no problem here. Don't make me kick your ass."

Beth Ann was glad for the rescue, but she didn't want an altercation. Things had been bad enough with her hearing voices and seeing visions. She pulled on Blake's arm.

"No, Blake, don't hurt him. Let's just go eat."

Within a minute, two large men appeared out of nowhere. The taller addressed Blake. "Mr. Tanner, is there a problem here?"

"I believe this man needs a rough escort outside," Blake answered, handing him over to the guys.

"Of course, Mr. Tanner. We'll make sure the rest of your evening is not interrupted."

The three vanished as quickly as they'd appeared, making her wonder about secret passages in the place.

Fortunately, people around them didn't seem to notice, primarily because the lounge was relatively empty except for an older couple who appeared deep in a conversation. Beth Ann turned toward Blake and watched him straighten his suit and tie. When he finished, he put an arm around her, and she felt his tension subside.

The hostess motioned for them to follow her up the marble staircase to the dining area where there was soft lighting and ambiance that spelled romance. The attractive hostess led them to a table near the windows.

"Someone will be right with you." She reached out and touched Blake's arm. "So good to see you again, Blake."

Beth Ann glanced between him and the hostess, making him squirm.

"I've, ah ... been here a lot," he said.

"Yeah, I can see that." She unfolded the napkin and enjoyed watching him fidget as he fixed his tie again. He had so much experience with women that it made her feel like a virgin. Hell, she was a virgin compared to him.

She looked out the windows and was astonished at how the upper floor gave a view of some of the most incredible buildings and dazzling lights of Chicago. A waiter appeared and handed them menus, and another young man brought them water and bread.

"This is stunning, Blake. I love it."

"I'm happy you like it, darlin. This is my favorite place to sit because of the view." He gave her his famous boyish grin as he opened the menu and pointed out the specials. "The Steak Diane is wonderful, but the Chicken Marsala is out of this world."

A few minutes later, a different waiter came over with a white towel draped across his arm and took their order. They ended up ordering the same thing—Chicken Marsala. It was scrumptious and melted in their mouths. Beth Ann was only able to eat half of hers, so Blake graciously finished the rest.

While they ate, sadness filled her heart again when it occurred to her that the last time she'd eaten that dish, Kaylob had made it for her. He had always been such a good cook. She missed him terribly, and the visions she kept having only made it worse.

With everything she could muster, she pushed the visions from her mind and concentrated on her date. After the entrée dishes were cleared away, a waitress came and handed them the dessert menu.

Blake took a sip of wine and smiled. "Listen, I'm sorry I lost my cool earlier, but how rude can a guy be?"

"You're right," Beth Ann said as she read the menu. "He said he wanted strawberry pie for dessert. They don't even have that on the menu."

Blake lowered his voice as if telling her a secret. "He said he wanted strawberry pie. Strawberry pie."

"It's not on the menu," she repeated.

His expression changed as he tried to stifle a laugh.

She put down the menu. "What's so funny, Blake?"

"Darlin, I'm pretty sure he meant your red hair. As in you, your pie, your strawberry pie. Yummy dessert." He looked at her face then moved his eyes quickly downward.

Heat crawled up her neck and across her cheeks. Damn. She wished she could control that. At least, Blake had told her. Frankie and Carol usually just left her in the dark. A light must have formed in her eyes to show she understood, because he nodded.

She leaned over and gave him a gentle kiss. "Thank you, Mr. Tanner. I'm sorry to be so clueless."

With a sexy grin, he touched her cheek. "Darlin, your innocence is part of your charm, and I've always loved the way you blush. You must get tired of everyone having some inside joke. I promise that when we're together, I'll tell you anything you want explained."

"Thank you. You have no idea how good that makes me feel."

While they waited for dessert, Beth Ann spotted a woman peeking around the corner at them. A few minutes later, the lady and a young girl walked up to the table. Beth Ann felt startled, but Blake acted nonchalant, as though it happened every day. What the heck?

"Oh, Mr. Tanner ..." The woman flushed and stuttered. "I've wanted to meet you for so long. Can my daughter Betsy and I take a picture with you?" She held up a camera in her hand. "Please."

Blake smiled and nodded. "Certainly."

Beth Ann noticed the same two guys who'd hustled the drunk away approaching fast. They grabbed the camera, and the poor lady let out a shriek. Her daughter took one giant step behind her mom. Beth Ann felt bad for the little girl who looked to be around twelve, and she wanted to hit the two big gorillas with a breadstick, but there weren't any.

Blake stood up quickly. "No, guys. I got this one. Johnny, stay with Beth Ann and keep her company until I get back. Lucky, come with me so I can get my picture taken with these two charming ladies."

Beth Ann was perplexed about the entire situation, but before she could ask any questions, Blake leaned over and gave her a kiss.

"Hold on tight, darlin. I'll explain everything later."

He took the older woman's elbow and winked at the little girl. A delightful smile spread across the mother's face. When the young girl grinned, she covered her mouth, probably to hide braces.

Blake touched the girl's chin. "Gorgeous."

In that moment, Beth Ann adored Blake Tanner.

He led them to an area across the room that appeared to have better lighting for photos. Beth Ann watched them go and then looked across the table at Johnny. He was very handsome—big with dark hair and dark eyes. Despite his imposing size, there was playfulness about him. He grabbed a dinner roll from the basket still on the table and took a very large bite.

Good God, he was chewing with his mouth open. Beth Ann stared at him in surprise, then he glanced up and shot her an impish grin.

"Oh, sorry, Ms. B. It's time for dinner and I'm starving." He chuckled.

Beth Ann couldn't believe the guy had just called her Ms. B. "Your name is Johnny?"

"Yes," he mumbled, his mouth still full of bread.

She picked up her glass of wine and took a sip. "So I take it you work for Blake."

He nodded and looked her up and down, curiosity filling his eyes. The man didn't even try to hide where his eyes were going. She tried to ignore the heat creeping into her cheeks and kept talking to take her mind off it.

"Blake seems very popular, so much that people want to get their picture taken with him."

Johnny laughed. "Well, of course, Ms. B. Everyone wants to get close to Mr. T. 'Specially the ladies, if you know what I mean." He raised his left eyebrow.

She wasn't really surprised by Johnny's statement since Blake had always had women fighting over him throughout school, but now it seemed his playboy reputation had brought him even more attention, probably from being a playboy mixed in with being rich and good looking. He had always been an overachiever—no surprises there. She had heard from Denny that he was a real estate king with companies all over the world, and she knew he'd been in a few magazines last year.

Beth Ann was just about to ask another question when Blake returned to the table. He stood watching Johnny stuff his face with the dinner roll for a moment

Johnny swallowed fast and stood up. "Hey, Mr. T. Anything else you need tonight?"

Blake said something to him in a language that sounded like French, then he said in English, "You and Lucky go get some dinner. Tell them to put it on my tab."

"Thanks, Mr. T. Nice meeting ya, Ms, B." Johnny winked at Beth Ann and left.

Beth Ann looked at Blake with eyes full of questions, but they were interrupted again by the arrival of their dessert—a delicious-looking slice of decadent chocolate cake with whipped cream and a cherry on top. Blake moved closer to her so they could share in the slice of heaven. Then he piled the perfect amount of cake along with whipped cream on his fork and held it up to her lips.

"Here, you go first." His eyes gazed into hers deeply as he leaned close to her ear. "Je veux vous embrasser beaucoup." He slowly put the fork between her lips.

The taste melted into utopia, nothing like she had ever tasted. The way he'd fed it to her was incredibly sexy. Kaylob had never fed her that way ... No, don't do that. Enough about Kaylob.

"So, Mr. Tanner, what language is that, and what did you say?"

He smiled again. "It was French, and I said 'I want to kiss you very much'." He gave her another bite, his eyes focused on her lips.

"I've never tasted anything so heavenly," she said.

He inched closer and gave her a deep, lingering kiss. "Vos baisers sont incroyables."

She was finding it hard to breathe, so she gave him a puzzled look.

He leaned close again and whispered, "Your kisses are incredible."

"Blake ..." She caught her breath. "Speaking French is very romantic."

He lifted her hand to his lips, and the heat spread all the way to her toes. How could she feel so excited over Blake when she still loved Kaylob? She had to blink back the tears as guilt found its way into her heart. Would she ever be able to be happy again?

She didn't want him to notice her distress and spoil their date, so she directed her attention back to the dessert. Never had she tasted such an enticing cake, and mixed with a kiss from Blake Tanner, it was truly irresistible. He gave her another slow, sexy bite, and she smiled at him.

"Is this how you seduce all your ladies, Mr. Tanner?"

He shook his head. "I've never fed anyone cake before in my life."

Her hand brushed against his leg, and she heard his sharp intake of breath. The way his eyes were enveloping her left her hungry for a different kind of dessert.

Almost immediately, another question came sneaking around the corner of her brain. She wanted to shut the door in its face or maybe seal it or cut it to pieces, but it refused to be ignored.

Was she ready to be with another man?

Less than an hour ago, she was standing in a jungle hearing Kaylob calling out to her. Should she even be here with Blake, especially when he was the guy Kaylob had always been most jealous of. Her heart sink as another question blasted her brain.

Oh, Kaylob, was she being disloyal to him?

Blake touched her hand, drawing her back. "Hey, darlin, did I lose you?"

She shook her head. "I was just thinking about how nice this is." She touched her nose to see if it was getting longer from all the fibs.

He kissed her again. "Wait until you see what else the night holds."

Her entire body reacted to his words. She decided she was going to do whatever it took to enjoy Blake fully.

When they finished their dessert, he took her to a sports bar—the only bar she'd ever entered. There, they danced the night away. Before they left, Beth Ann saw Blake stop in front of the mirror to adjust his tie and ensure he still looked perfect.

She had the feeling she was about to find out just how perfect he was.

Chapter Twenty-Four

When they arrived back at the hotel room, Blake took her key and opened the door. What amazed the heck out of her was how he stood there not asking to come in. Wow, he was actually nervous. The playboy was putty in her hands. That knowledge gave her the courage to do what she wanted to do. She placed her arms around his neck and gave him a soft, sensual, blow-your-mind kiss.

His face revealed his shock. Groovy. She decided to take it further and let her tongue glide over his lips.

It was her turn to be shocked when he moved away from her, although not before he let out a deep moan. "Can I call you in the morning?"

This was way more fun than she'd thought it would be. Blake Tanner, blushing and nervous. Unreal was the only word to describe it. Had he always been like this? Certainly not from the stories she'd heard all through her school years.

"Beth Ann, can I call you?" he repeated. "Are you going to answer me?"

Something then dawned on her. She couldn't answer him, because she didn't want him to leave and had no clue how to tell him. On one hand, she wanted to grab him by that sexy pink tie and pull him inside the room, but on the other hand she was still asking herself if she was ready. Could she really have sex with someone other than Kaylob? Blake was getting ready to leave, so if she didn't stop him right now, she was going to miss out on a night with him.

* * * *

Blake stood at the door of Beth Ann's hotel room, feeling unaccountably nervous and trying to sort out the distant expression on her face, especially after that mind blowing kiss. She faded away at times, which really frustrated him. He finally had a chance to be with her, and had no clue where he stood.

"Beth Ann, hello? Are you going to answer me? Can I see you tomorrow?"

Shit, why wouldn't she answer his question? She had always been so hung-up on Kaylob. Blake remembered another time when he'd stood trying to get an answer out of her. Damn, maybe he should just walk away. He didn't want to take advantage of her vulnerability. She'd been through so much losing Kaylob. He had no desire to push her into something she wasn't ready for. He decided to just give her another kiss and leave.

What the hell?

A thunderbolt of surprise almost knocked him off his feet when he realized Beth Ann had him by the tie and was pulling him inside. Good God.

Her lips moved unexpectedly on his, making his head swim. Christ Almighty ... her hands slipped down to his butt and pulled him close. His body responded, and there was no way in hell he could help it. What in God's name was happening? Her hands touched him in a way that made him rise for the occasion.

His voice was husky with desire. "Beth Ann, you better stop right now or ... we're gonna have a minor problem. I didn't bring a second pair of pants."

She walked back to the door, shut it, and locked it tight. He almost went to his knees when she grabbed his tie again and pulled him toward the bed. Lord have mercy, she was undoing his tie, and he was coming undone. He went from shock to desire in seconds as she pulled off his tie and tossed it on the couch.

"Beth Ann, are you sure you want to do this? Are you ready?"

This wasn't like him at all, although maybe with her it was. He had always been crazy about her and didn't want her doing something she wasn't ready for. Then there was the other thing that made it different with her.

His heart was on the line.

Okay, she was officially killing him. Her fingers had slipped down and were undoing his pants.

"Beth Ann, please say something. Are you sure?" He tried to keep his balance. "I don't want you doing anything you don't want."

"Yes, Blake, I'm sure and I'm ready. I'm here with you because I want to be, not because I'm still grieving. Yes, I still miss Kaylob, and I always will. That's not why I want you. I want you because of who you are. You're an amazing man, inside and out."

Her words caused him to melt. If she only knew how he felt, but then again it might scare her if she did. He wanted her, but he'd also noticed her spinning that engagement ring on her finger off and on all night. He remembered the time he had taken her out to dinner in Riverside while Kaylob was still alive. She had shown him the engagement ring then.

He picked up her hand and kissed it gently, making sure he kissed the ring finger. It was his way of letting her know how often she touched it. It was an unspoken question because she still had it on.

She removed her hand from his, and what she used it for next just about made him crazy, but it gave him the answer he hoped for.

"What about protection?" he said.

"I take the pill." She smiled.

There was no way to hide his desire. He watched as her eyes took in all of him. With a move that was both seductive and once again mind-blowing, she reached down to the hem of her dress and lifted it over her head. The dress hit the ground, then she slowly pulled off her lacy white panties. A surge of heat rushed through every nerve in his body. She was so beautiful. Hell, that wasn't the right word. She was the most exquisite woman he'd ever seen.

She reached out to touch his chest, letting her fingers trail lightly down his stomach. Looking into his eyes the whole time, her hand kept going until she was holding him in a way he had only dreamed about.

He gasped and moved her hand. "Darlin, if you keep that up, I'm not going to last long."

Her smile sent him flying to the edge of bonkers. She moved his hands to her breasts. How long had he dreamed about touching her? How many years had he been in love with her? All the women he'd slept with had never measured up. He had always been looking for her heart and soul in the eyes of other women, but he had never found anything close. Now here she was touching him, and he felt like a damn rambling virgin.

"Oh, hell, I'm a dead man. I can't believe—"

She put her fingers on his lips. "Shush."

They gazed into each other's eyes as he pulled her into his arms. He couldn't stand the wait anymore. When their naked bodies touched for the first time, he gasped again and picked her up. He carried her to the bed, shivering as he laid her down.

"You have no idea how long..." His voice faded as he lost the ability to form words.

"I know, Blake, I know." She sounded like soft silk that shimmered into his heart.

She seemed so alive, so brave, so grown up. She moved on top of him, the movement of her hips drove him out of his mind. Jesus, she was so sexy and sensual. Although he was perfectly willing to let her take charge, she climbed off him and turned onto her back. That alone almost sent him flying over the cliff. He'd been with some of the most beautiful women in the world, but the simple truth was that none of them had ever mattered, because he had always been and still was in love with the hometown girl from Novato, California.

Chapter Twenty-Five

When weeks passed without seeing Blake again, Beth Ann was surprised, but not devastated. Their night together must have been a fling to him, or maybe he was just the love-'em-and-leave-'em type. She didn't have a problem with a fling as long as she had a whole lot of more of it. She couldn't believe how much she had loved seeing the ladies checking Blake out when they'd been out together. Man, she had never even come close to feeling that way about Kaylob. Maybe she was more mature now.

Or maybe it was because she would never love anyone the way she loved Kaylob.

Blake kept tabs on where they'd be on tour, and his attentiveness honestly touched her. She was touched when flowers and cards from him showed up at the next stop. In the ensuing weeks, more gifts arrived, and she never knew what to expect. Sometimes bakeries in the area would deliver chocolate cake to the theater with a private note asking her to please remember their first piece of cake together. No way she'd ever forget the cake or the night.

The rest of the cast looked forward to the treats more than she did. None of them knew Blake, but they were always happy to get the goodies. He always signed the cards 'From B.T.', and she was often asked about her mystery man.

When Blake finally managed to make the shows, he came bearing more gifts. He would stash the things for Beth Ann at his hotel room, but he would have other stuff delivered to the cast, never making an appearance backstage. Beth Ann started to wonder if he was hiding from someone or something. She knew darn well he wasn't bashful.

He did really cool things like paying for dinners at expensive restaurants and having tickets set aside for movies or shows. While the cast was eating or watching shows, Blake and Beth Ann would sneak away to his hotel room and ravage each other over and over again.

She was happy for the distraction. All the work and constantly being on the road left her lonely. She never took the time to go out to eat. Instead, she cooked something on the tour bus. Most days she missed things like a home-cooked meal or watching TV. Hell, she didn't even know which programs were on anymore. Maybe what she needed was back in Riverside.

Her heart ached for all her friends, but what she longed for more than anything else was Kaylob. She had overcome her guilt enough to be with Blake, but nothing had changed about her feelings for the love of her life. She still hadn't found out the meaning of the foreign word from her vision and wanted to ask Blake if he knew, but she couldn't bring herself to do it. Besides the awkwardness it would cause, what if tra tan meant death? She didn't think she could take hearing that, so she didn't say anything.

Beth Ann's feelings for Blake deepened much more than she ever imagined they would. She was starting to depend on him, and those emotions scared the stuffing right out of her.

Then, as spontaneously as they had started, Blake's visits stopped without explanation. The flowers, cards, and gifts still arrived, but none of them held a clue as to why he no longer appeared. Beth Ann missed him, but she wouldn't allow his departure to interfere with her routine. Instead, she slapped herself mentally with the reminder that Blake had always been a playboy. She was a little pissed at him—okay, a lot pissed—because she'd thought she meant more to him than that.

Kaylob's voice continued to haunt her, and the visions took her back to the jungle. There was always a dog barking and the four trees, and now there was a new development—bamboo. In her dream, the doors always turned into bamboo, and now she was seeing bamboo in the visions too. What did it all mean?

Nothing could ever replace the love she felt for Kaylob, but it hadn't been quite as bad while Blake had been there to distract her. Memories of Kaylob never strayed far away, drifting just outside her consciousness. In moments when everything was still, she would ask the universe to bring him home. One side of her heart knew he might be gone, but the other side believed he was coming back. She'd catch herself often spinning the band on her finger, a symbol of their love. She didn't think she could ever bring herself to remove it.

The nightly shows in the Chicago area had taken a toll on her emotionally and physically. Usually they did three appearances per city, and then left for the next place. Their next stop was Milwaukee, and she was looking forward to three days off and a nice hotel room. When Danny asked her to go out to dinner, she jumped at the chance.

Even though she wasn't attracted to him, she thought he was sweet and cute. She knew his strawberry-blond hair and green eyes had gotten the attention of several of the other dancers, but she felt only friendship toward him. She worried a little about hurting him, because his reaction when she accepted the date reminded her of a child being told they were going to

Disneyland, but she still wanted to go. A distraction from missing Kaylob and Blake's confusing behavior would be good for her.

She decided to wear something casual and was ready when Danny came to her hotel door, holding a splendid bouquet of pretty flowers and wearing a wide smile. Beth Ann couldn't help feeling special to know she was making his life brighter, but it also reminded her of Rule Number One, Don't lead him on and deflect serious questions with suggestions to date someone who would be interested. She planned to persuade him to date Michelle, a fellow cast member who had a crush on him that was obvious to everyone but Danny.

The evening out was wonderful for both of them. They laughed, swapped road stories and enjoyed each other's company. Beth Ann was relieved when he was receptive to asking Michelle out and admitted he hadn't paid attention to the other ladies in the cast.

He stirred his coffee and cleared his throat. "You really are the sweetest and kindest girl, Beth Ann. I know you're not interested in me for more than a friend, but thank you for going out with me tonight and suggesting Michelle. I appreciate your honesty and would love to be your friend."

"I'm glad, Danny. You deserve someone who'll be crazy for you."

After dinner, he walked her back to the hotel. She was feeling comfortable with their newfound friendship, so she gave him a peck on the lips and put her arm through his as they walked. When they reached her hotel room door, she smiled up at him.

"I had such a good time tonight, Danny. Thank you for suggesting this."

"Thank you for going with me." He gave her a hug, then he reached out and opened her door.

The unmistakable sound of an irritated person clearing his throat made them both turn to look behind them. Blake stood in the hall staring at them, his face red and his eyes glaring. He clearly didn't share their appreciation for the festive evening. Holy hell, he was mad. His hands were wringing his gloves like a dishrag.

Danny stepped away from Beth Ann quickly. "I'd better go."

"I'm so sorry, Danny," she said. "I didn't expect Blake to be here. Last I heard, he was on the West Coast. Can I catch up with you later? Thank you for the lovely evening."

"Sure thing." He nodded, glancing at Blake as he briskly walked away.

"Don't hold your breath for another night there, Sparky." Blake shouted after him.

Beth Ann frowned at him. "Why would you say that to him?"

When all she got in reply was more glaring, she turned and entered the hotel room. He followed her in cold silence. Beth Ann thought the tension in the room matched his clenched jaw line.

"Have you been screwing him?"

Anger rolled down her spine as she moved to the couch and scowled at him. What the hell was his problem? He stopped coming around, didn't call, only sent gifts and then got mad because she had dinner with someone? Besides, he could have let her know he was coming.

"Not that it's any of your business, but I'm not sleeping with him. What difference does it make to you anyway?"

He paced over to the couch and threw down his gloves. "None of my business? What difference does it make? If you're going to date other guys, then maybe I should date other women too."

His reaction had her truly perplexed. "I assumed you were dating, considering I haven't seen you in weeks."

He flinched, almost as though he'd been kicked in the gut. "Screw this. I'm not taking this crap."

He pivoted on one foot and then walked to the door, but he stopped and turned to glare at her again. "For your information, you're the only girl I've had on my arm since our first night together. I assumed I was the only guy you were dating. If this is what you want, then fine, you have fun. I guess I was just a little amusement for you and some good old-fashioned experience."

He turned back to the door, but he didn't open it. He was clearly angry, but she could also tell he was hurt.

Kaylob had never walked out on her, nor had he ever threatened to break up except for once when he made her promise to go on with her life. She didn't know what to think about Blake walking out without looking back. Did he just not care, or did he care too much? She had enjoyed being with him and would miss him a lot, but he wasn't Kaylob. Before she could decide if she wanted to stop him or let him go, the door slammed and he was gone.

For a moment, she didn't move. Then she ran into the hall and saw him turning the corner.

"Blake."

He disappeared, and she wasn't sure he'd heard her. Slowly, she turned to go back inside.

"You called?"

She stopped and looked down the hall to see him and his dimples walking back to her.

Chapter Twenty-Six

When they were back inside the room with the door closed, Beth Ann put her arms around Blake's neck. "Please don't leave. I'm sorry if I hurt you. I'm not interested in Danny."

"Then why were you with him?" he demanded.

"He's been asking me out for a long time, and I thought it might be fun to go out as friends. Nothing more, just friends. In fact, I was trying to convince him to date one of the other girls in the cast." She felt him relax and decided not to mention Danny's crush on her.

He sighed. "I still don't like it. Do you know how close I came to punching him?"

His jealousy was flattering, and she couldn't help smiling. He sighed again and led her over to sit on the couch. She hadn't expected to feel so upset over the thought of losing him, but she couldn't deny the feeling of panic that had made her run after him, and her heart was still racing. She wasn't sure she wanted him to know how much he affected her.

He turned her toward him with his hands on her shoulders. "This isn't funny, Beth Ann. I don't want you dating anyone else."

"I only want to be with you, Blake, but I didn't expect you to change your lifestyle for me."

He took a deep breath and let it out slowly. He seemed to be gathering courage to say something.

"I want to change my lifestyle, darlin. You're the only woman for me."

Before she could react, he stood and pulled her into his arms. "I'm in love with you, Beth Ann. I have been for years. I can't handle you seeing other guys, and I don't want to see anybody but you."

Holy cow, he loved her? She had no idea what to say about that, so she tried to play it cool.

"Okay, no other guys. You're quite the handful anyway, and I hope you realize that you're only the second guy I've … you know." She laid her head on his chest and felt his muscles relax as he held her. She loved the way he smelled of Old Spice and vanilla. So different from Kaylob ...

Oh, Lord. She was doing it again.

He lifted her chin to face him. "I'm glad to hear that, Beth Ann. I love you, and there's something I need to ask you." He pulled a small box from his pocket.

"Oh, holy night no, Blake. I'm not ready for this." She took a step back from him, holding up her hands. "This is too soon."

His expression was a mixture of laughter and a hint of disappointment. "It's not what you think. Just open it." He handed her the box.

It was one of those moments when she wanted to hide. Her feelings instantly morphed from fear to oops. Carefully she opened the jewelry box and found a key.

He laughed at her obvious puzzlement. "I bought a townhouse in Riverside. That's why I've been gone for so long, I was looking for a place. I'll only be there part time, and I thought maybe you'd want to stay there when you get home. I wanted to surprise you."

"I can't give up my apartment," she said in a voice so low she didn't know if he heard her.

Her fingers unconsciously moved to her engagement ring and held it. Blake looked down at her hand and back up to her face.

"Don't then. It can be your second home. The townhouse is so I can be with you when I'm in town. We can make it our own little getaway. It's got two full amazing bathrooms and four bedrooms. It's over 3,000 square feet with the additions I'm having done as we speak. I bought the entire building, and my builders are turning two of them into one very large townhouse."

She smiled and let go of her ring. She knew Blake had seen her touching it, but hadn't said a word, and she appreciated his sensitivity.

"Okay, I'll spend time with you at your townhouse."

He over being angry. For the next few hours, he showed her why someone had coined the phrase make-up sex. They made up again and again, and she started to think fighting might not be so bad. While they were lying exhausted in each other's arms, Blake sat up and stared at her.

"Why didn't you respond when I said I loved you? Don't you love me?"

How was she supposed to tell him that she didn't know if she could ever fall in love again? She put her hand on his face and smiled at him tenderly.

"I care very much about you, Blake, and I only want to be with you," she whispered, hoping that would be good enough to soothe any possibility of ruffled feelings.

He looked at her intently for a moment, then he pulled her in his arms. After a while, the soft sounds of his breathing told her he had drifted off to sleep.

She lay awake and lifted her hand to study her engagement ring. It seemed a long time since Kaylob had been gone, but she wasn't ready to take it off. The truth was she wasn't sure she would ever be ready. She wanted to have it on when Kaylob came home. Lovingly, she lifted the ring to her lips and kissed it.

With her head on Blake's chest, it didn't take long for her to fall asleep. The emotionally charged evening had taken its toll.

* * * *

In the dead of the night, her nightmare returned.

Kaylob's voice echoed down a darkened hallway. Confused, Beth Ann ran and reached a pair of burnt red iron doors. She threw herself at them, but only bounced off. Unlike her earlier nightmares, she was stunned to see the doors fly open to reveal a broken and withering Kaylob. She tried desperately to go to him, but her legs felt as if they were churning in quicksand.

After struggling for what seemed like an eternity, she managed to reach him, and her heart exploded with agony to see him so emaciated and in pain. She heard his voice, but when she attempted to touch him, her hands went right through him. Then, right before her eyes, his image began to vanish.

"Kaylob, no. Please don't leave me again. Please God, don't take him."

"Beth Ann ... I love you. Don't forget ..."

Something or someone was pulling her away. "No, please. Kaylob, come back. Where are you?"

She opened her eyes and found Blake holding and rocking her.

"It was just a bad dream, darlin. I'll protect you."

"I have to save him," she murmured, still half asleep.

"It was just a dream," he repeated, huging her tighter.

For some reason she didn't fully understand, she pulled away and scooted to the other side of the bed facing the wall. Her only thoughts were of saving Kaylob, and because she couldn't, she cried herself to sleep.

* * * *

The next morning, she woke to find Blake staring at her with sad eyes. He ran his thumb down her cheek.

"You dreamed of Kaylob last night?"

The concern on his face touched her heart. "Yes, I've been having them for a while now."

He kissed her lips lightly. "I'm so, so sorry you had a bad dream. I tried to comfort you, but you pulled away and cried inconsolably. I feel awful that I couldn't help." He pulled her closer. "Please let me help when you have those dreams."

He was so kind and understanding. This was the Blake she had always known, but he seemed to hide it from almost everyone. She made a choice to trust him and told him about the recurring dream and how it had been different last night from earlier ones.

"Blake," she added, "I don't just have dreams at night when I'm sleeping. They also come when I least expect them in the daytime hours."

He propped his head on his hand and gazed into her eyes. "During the day?"

She nodded. "I hear him calling me, and sometimes I'm in a jungle. The last time I heard gun shots and a dog barking. There were tall trees and bamboo. I heard a word that I need to find out the meaning of—tra tan."

Fear mixed with confusion rolled across his face.

"Blake, I can tell you know what it means. Please tell me."

He was silent as a grave, and her heart sank. She had suspected all along the word meant death. Someone or something was trying to show her where Kaylob had died. Bile rose in her throat, and she struggled not to throw up. Oh, God. That was what the visions meant. Kaylob was dead and buried in that spot.

"It means death, doesn't it? I know it."

Blake shook his head. "No, darlin. It means torture, and it's Vietnamese." He put his arms around her. "I'm sorry you're still going through so much. Maybe together we can make it go away."

"Oh, Blake, do you think someone tortured him to death?"

She wept at the thought. Maybe Kaylob was reaching out to her, or maybe he was trying to show her where his body had been buried. All she knew for sure was that right now she needed to be held. Sharing her visions with Blake was a huge comfort to her. She was tired of suffering alone.

Blake's voice embraced her along with his arms. "I don't know, darlin. Just know I'm right here for you. We're going to chase these nightmares away. Do you hear me? We'll do this together."

She wiped her eyes and looked up at him. "Are you sure you want to be involved with a crazy person?"

He gave her a soft smile. "You're not crazy. You've just been through a lot."

It helped to hear him say she wasn't insane, but deep inside she knew she was either raving mad or being shown something important. She still believed he was coming home someday. Some things were better left unsaid, so she would keep those secrets to herself.

Chapter Twenty-Seven

The days danced into weeks, and soon her six months and three weeks on the road ended. On the last day she packed her stuff and looked forward to going home. Saying goodbye to all her friends in the show had been emotional, but saying goodbye to Mitch had been the hardest. Still, she was tired and ready for a long break.

She intended to keep her promise to spend time in the townhouse with Blake. He'd told her they would be flying from JFK to Los Angeles together. The chance to fly home with Blake on his company's private jet had been exciting, even though she didn't like flying. Then disappointment had knocked when she got a phone call from Blake the day before, saying he couldn't join her because of a last minute business snafu he had to fix.

Beth Ann and the rest of the cast were unloading the tour bus when Blake's limousine pulled up. The cast teased her, and she felt her cheeks heat as usual. The driver motioned for her to get in while he loaded all her stuff. To top it off, the driver didn't speak English. He tried to say a few words to her, but her blank stare must have told him she was clueless.

When they arrived at the private plane, the driver pointed for her to climb inside. She climbed up the small stairs to the door where an older lady smiled and waved her inside. The woman had dark hair and spoke a very small amount of English with a thick French accent.

She pointed to the sitting area. "You be comfortable and help you to any ting."

Beth Ann nodded and glanced around, totally astounded. This was beyond what she had ever imagined about private planes. Seats for seven people, along with a two-person couch. The gray leather seats had cloth inserts that matched the carpet on the floor. Hot coffee and pastries were waiting and ready.

The woman came back and handed her a pillow with a soft blanket. "For you if you need. You can snore." She smiled and left.

Beth Ann struggled not to laugh. At least this flight would be much faster than a commercial flight because they flew straight through with no stops, which was nice. She found herself gazing at her engagement ring during the flight. What would Kaylob think of her right now? Would he be proud of her for being on Broadway and getting this special treatment? Or would he be disgusted with all the ritz?

"Oh, Kaylob, I wish you would talk to me," she whispered. She rested her head back on the seat, and the next thing she knew, gentle fingers touched her arm.

"Miss, we've arrived and your driver is here."

Holy cow, she had slept almost the entire flight. She had to stretch to shake off her lethargic stupor. The minute she stepped outside, cameras blinded her and made her flinch. What in the world? She'd had no clue she would be met by photographers.

The limo driver took her arm and hurried her over to the car. He smiled as he opened the door. "Mr. Tanner told me to get you home safely. We need to dodge all these camera idiots, so let me get you inside the car."

He almost pushed her inside. Holy night, what the heck was going on? What had Blake not told her? Instant anger bubbled because she'd told him about the vision and voices, but he obviously hadn't thought it was important to warn her about this. He was going to hear about it for sure.

The limo driver opened his little window and looked back at her. "You seem surprised by all this." He arched an eyebrow. "You didn't expect it with Mr. Tanner being one of America's most eligible bachelors and all?"

Her face must have broadcasted confusion, because he pointed to three magazines on the seat.

"Relax and do some reading during the drive," he said.

She picked up the first one and almost gasped when she saw Blake on the cover with a headline calling him one of America's top ten most eligible bachelors. The article teaser read 'He's rich, powerful, and now in love.' Beth Ann flipped to it as fast as she could.

The media wanted to know who had won his heart, and there were even pictures of her in two out of the three magazines and pictures of the outside of her apartment. Holy stars. She didn't even know this had been happening. Now everything added up, like Blake wanting to stay inside when he visited. They hardly ever left the hotel unless it was well after dark, and then only if the limousine was at the door. Yeah, he had some explaining to do all right.

She put down the magazines and leaned forward to tap on the window. "Excuse me, what's your name?"

"Dean," the driver replied.

"Well, Dean, do you have any idea why Mr. Tanner wouldn't have told me he was rich, powerful, and famous?"

Dean shook his head. "No, but how is it you didn't already know? Where have you been living, under a rock?" He paused. "No offense."

She arched an eyebrow of her own. "I've been on the stage and rehearsing for the past six months."

He responded. "Oh. Well, don't you read the papers?"

"No, I did at first while on tour, but I stopped because all the critics made me nervous. I stayed away from the papers and had no time for TV. I remember a few people who saw Blake from a distance mentioned he looked like a movie star or someone famous, but I laughed it off."

He shrugged. "Well, I guess Mr. Tanner will have to tell you about it. He told me to help you get to your apartment safely. Those idiot camera people will be hungry to get as many pictures of you as they can. Mr. Tanner's never been tied down to one woman before."

She let out an annoyed sigh. "Just great."

How the hell was she supposed to deal with all this? What if they caught her having one of her visions? She could just see the headlines—'Most eligible bachelor has crazy girlfriend.' Just what she needed.

Sure enough, she spotted photographers skulking around the minute they caught sight of the limo. How in the world had they found out when she was getting home? This was not what she'd dreamed about for her return.

Dean stepped out and gave the guys a piercing glare that could kill, but they stood their ground. He opened the door for Beth Ann and escorted her quickly up to her apartment. She heard the cameras snapping all around her and saw the flashes. Dean made sure she was safely inside and told her he would bring her luggage up later when things calmed down.

The minute she stepped inside her tiny place, deep sorrow welled up, confirming her reasons for not wanting unexpected photos taken. She paused near the front door as memories swooped down on her. Her mind replayed past events. Kaylob in the shower, on the bed, standing in the kitchen, cooking a delicious meal. The watershed of emotions overwhelmed her. She walked over and plopped down on the couch. Putting her hands over her eyes, she willed the memories away. Would this ever stop hurting? So much time had passed, yet the pain was still so raw.

A knock on the door caused her to jump. Before she could move, the front door opened and Jack entered. Her heart swelled when he rushed over to pick her up and twirl her around.

"Look at you, Miss Sexy."

"Oh, Jack, it's so good to see you."

She did her best to hide her tears. He was just what she needed. She gave him a big kiss, and he backed up.

"Beth Ann, you're looking so good you could almost turn me on. Better be careful."

She laughed as much as her heart would allow. Jack leaned down to look in her eyes.

"What's the matter, honey?"

She knew it was useless to try to fool him. "Jack, it still hurts so much. When am I going to stop missing him?"

His arms went around her. "Honey, I wish I had an answer. I think it was good for you to be away from this apartment. You might want to think about moving somewhere that isn't full of painful memories, not to mention all those nincompoops with cameras. They've been waiting around for you all day."

"I think you're right." She sighed. "It's too painful here, and I don't like having my picture taken. I think moving is a good idea, and the sooner the better."

"Honey, you're involved with America's most eligible bachelor, and people are curious. I've seen your picture and this apartment building all over magazine covers. They even approached us asking questions about you, but you know Lenard. He told them off and walked away."

"Oh, God, Jack. I'm so sorry. I had no idea."

"Hey, it's no surprise. One of my best friends is a famous Broadway star, and you've snagged one of the sexiest men in the country. Not to mention you're a walking symbol of beauty and sex appeal yourself."

"Oh, Jack, stop." She slapped his arm. "I had no idea Blake was famous. He's just a guy I grew up with in a small town, and I'm just an average girl."

"Honey, there ain't nothing average about either of you." He wiggled his eyebrows. "How is it that you didn't know?"

She shrugged. "I stopped watching TV and reading papers, and you guys never said a word about it on the phone."

"True. Everyone figured you knew, and it's not like we spoke to you that often."

She scanned the apartment, and everything punished her heart.

"Aw, honey." Jack gave her a hug. "This place just isn't good for you anymore. Let's get out of here. We're cooking a wonderful homecoming meal for you tonight. What do ya say?"

She nodded, knowing she would leave first thing in the morning. Tonight she would say goodbye to her old life and her old friends, then she needed to move on.

"I'd love to, but do you mind if I come a little later? I'd like to shower and change."

"Sure, sweetie. Whenever you're ready." He kissed her forehead before he left, locking the door behind him.

While looking around the apartment, it was as if she were transported back in time, and it wasn't long before she heard Kaylob's voice calling her. Unable to move, she closed her eyes and imagined his face, his lips, and the way he'd held her. She wrapped her arms around herself, wishing they were his.

"Oh, Kaylob, where are you?"

As soon as the words were out of her mouth, the floor beneath her started to sink. Her tiny apartment faded, and she stood once again in the dense, murky jungle. It became hard to breathe. The heat and dampness from the ground made her skin clammy. Her eyes darted about, trying to get a more accurate picture of her surroundings.

Out of the blue, the fog lifted to give her a view of four large evergreen trees, along with bamboo and weeds. She could see a river flowing behind the trees, and once again a dog sounded an alarm. Off to the right, she caught sight of a bird. Was it a white pelican? She had seen one once on a magazine cover. The bird stared at her and did not move.

She heard someone calling her name. Kaylob again. She couldn't see him and couldn't tell where his voice was coming from. Over by the trees she saw someone, but it didn't look like Kaylob. Whoever it was appeared thin, ragged, and maybe ill. She tried to get out of the mud and run toward the figure, but the sound of a ringing phone stopped her, and she was suddenly back in her apartment.

Somehow she found enough strength to walk over and pick up the receiver.

"Hi, honey," Jack said. "Sorry to bother you, but would you like baked potatoes or mashed?"

"Either one, Jack. Really, whatever is easier."

"Okay." He paused. "Beth Ann, are you okay?"

"Yeah, sure. Why?"

"You sound funny, like you were sleeping or something."

"No, I'm fine. I'll be up in about thirty minutes."

After she hung up the phone, she just stood there a moment, wondering what she was being shown in the visions. Was there a clue or something she needed to see? Why did she keep having them?

She shook off the questions and went into the bathroom, trying to take her mind off the vision so she could enjoy her dinner with Jack and Lenard. Then, the shower brought a downpour of new memories. The totality of the tiny dwelling now represented all her lost dreams and rainbow wishes.

What had made the two of them so unique? Beth Ann could only describe it like a song. Together they had made a perfect melodious romance. There was more than one part of their love song, a connection that was a deep, spiritual root that joined them forever. They hadn't just held hands, they'd held each other's hearts, guarding each and every treasured secret. There had been an unmeasured trust.

One of the biggest factors that had bound them together was they had been a family and each other's safe harbor. Kaylob was her fog horn, calling her to his arms, and she had been his shining light. She guessed that was why the low, deep rhythm of the horn would always remind her of her one true love. She hoped the light from her love would guide him home someday.

A chill brought her back to the moment and gave her a start, but it turned out to be just the hot water running out. After she got out and was dressed, she headed up to Jack and Lenard's to spend time with two of her dearest friends.

The night was sweet and helped heal her heart. Jack had cooked a wonderful dinner and baked a chocolate cake, her very favorite. Nobody brought up Kaylob's name, but she could tell they were both walking around the subject. She was sure that more than once she caught Jack thinking about him.

When she finally crawled into bed, sleep eluded her. She kicked off the covers and stared up at the ceiling, unable to stop thinking about Kaylob. God, she missed his arms, his smell, even his breathing. Before she fell back into the darkness of despair, she decided to go to her happy place—the ocean. It had been so long since she'd been there, and it was just what she needed. Relax, take a deep breath, count down, then see the ocean in her mind. One, two ... Waves rushing to the sand.

As soon as she thought about the waves, the only waves that washed over her were the waves of pain. The ocean reminded her of the honeymoon that had never happened. Their wedding in Hawaii they'd never gotten to plan. The sun bright and glorious, mixing together with the ocean, trees swaying in the wind. Far off in the distance, the deep moan of a fog horn sang to her heart as she stood on the white sandy beach.

Stop. This is not helping.

She pulled her pillow over her head. Finally, hours later, sleep came and took her hand.

Chapter Twenty-Eight

The next morning, Beth Ann woke to the familiar sounds of the clock ticking and the rumble of muffled traffic. She glanced around the room, the place she had cherished as their place, hers and Kaylob's. She had loved sharing it with him, and now she couldn't bear to be there without him. She had to move out.

When she called Blake and told him she would move in with him for now, his happiness permeated his voice, and she could practically hear those twin dimples in his voice as well. She called Jack and Lenard after breakfast, and they helped her pack up the majority of her belongings.

While digging into her closet, she found the music box Kaylob had for her as teenagers hidden in the back. She hadn't seen it since he was declared ... gone. She hadn't been able to bear the reminder of her lost love, so she'd put it out of sight. Now, as she lifted the box delicately, she could feel the weight of a thousand memories.

As she opened it she tenderly touched the old notes from their childhood that she'd tucked safely away. As if compelled, she pulled one out and was surprised when an unfamiliar envelope fell to the floor. She just stared at it, inexplicably terrified, until Jack walked over picked up the sealed note and read the outside.

To be opened by Beth Ann in the event of my death.

She sensed Jack's eyes searching her face while Lenard had sadness in his. Had Kaylob somehow known he wouldn't be coming back? Did she want to read it? Finally, she glanced up at Jack and saw worry in his eyes.

"Beth Ann, do you want me to hang on to this until you're ready?"

After another long pause, she shook her head and held out her hand for the envelope. "No, but you can keep the jewelry box for me. I know it will be safe with you." Jack gave her the envelope, and she put it by her purse to read later when she was alone.

Neither Jack nor Lenard brought up the letter again, and she was grateful for their sensitivity. About thirty minutes later, a knock made everyone turn toward the door. Jack answered it, and they were all surprised to see Blake.

He walked over to Beth Ann and wrapped her in an embrace. "Darlin, let's get you out of here."

"Okay," she murmured.

When he released her, he looked at Jack and Lenard as if asking for some type of approval, and Beth Ann was glad when they gave an approving nod. The truth was apparent to all of them—once she walked out the door, it would be the last time she ever saw this place. A familiar pain crept into her heart, but when she looked at the three men gathered around her, concern in all their eyes, her heart swelled to know how much she was loved. She gave them the best smile she could manage.

"Blake, could you give me a few minutes before we go?" She stepped away and picked up the letter from Kaylob. "I need to read this."

She could tell he had questions about it, but he nodded. "Of course, darlin. Whatever you need."

Before they left, Jack gave her a gentle hug. "You sure, honey?"

She nodded. "I need some time alone."

The living room felt big and empty with just her in it as she prepared to say her final goodbye. She sat on the couch with the letter in her hand, and it seemed to feel heavier than before. She unfolded it with her heart pounding in her ears, and as she read the first words, she had to remember to breathe.

My dearest Beth Ann,

If you're reading this I must be gone, so I want you to hear my words. Please read this twice. I have no regrets about anything other than not growing old with you. I want you to know the many ways you colored my life. You were and will always be my rainbow. You colored my life with joy, happiness, and love. You are my forever love. The many different colors of your spirit that shine through for everyone to see will shine all the way up to the heavens and light up my life, even after I'm gone. You have given me so much happiness, Beth Ann. Don't forget that, and please keep your promise to live, shine, and grow. I trust you to keep your word to me.

I will love you forever and a day,
Kaylob

The letter was short but meaningful. She held it to her heart for an enduring moment, then she sighed and tucked it away inside her purse. Fragments of memories and conversations saturated the room. Reflections of Kaylob cooking and the amazing smells were like keepsakes in her mind. She moved over to the kitchen and ran her fingers across the old dishtowel. Her hand shivered when she touched it, as if his energy had been woven into the fabric. Closing her eyes again, she saw flashes of him wiping his hands, tossing his head back in laughter. Dear God, the shadows of those memories lingered all around her.

"Oh, Kaylob, how am I supposed to ever move forward when I miss you every second of every day?"

Never had she imagined that someday she would be standing in the middle of her apartment saying goodbye to the love of her life. The pain ripped through her like a sheet of glass being shattered. The memories were precious, but they tormented her heart.

She looked down at the ring on her finger. She was starting a new life and knew what she had to do. The ring had been her shining band of hope, but she had to let it go. Struggling to see through the tears, she slipped off the ring, placed her lips against the circle of gold and gave it a kiss goodbye. Then after a few seconds she tucked it away in her suitcase where it would be safe until she could return it to his family.

There was no way she could handle the pain anymore. It was time to move forward. Kaylob wanted her to live and let go. With that thought she walked to the door and paused with her hand on the light switch, summoning the courage to leave.

Looking around one more time she whispered, "I'll always remember you, Kaylob Shawn O'Brien. I'm so very proud of you, and I'll love you forever and a day."

A single tear slid down her cheek as she shut the door for the last time.

* * * *

As she walked down the stairs outside, the flash of cameras reminded her that she was angry with Mr. Blake Tanner. From the look on his face as he waited beside the limo, he knew he was in the doghouse.

Several of the damn camera stalkers jumped out of a van across the street and ran toward them. "Blake, Elizabeth," they yelled. "Let us get some pictures of the two of you."

Beth Ann had to laugh at the way Blake glared daggers at them. He covered Beth Ann with his jacket as he ushered them both inside the limo. Once they were safely inside and away from the cameras, he wrapped his arms around her, and most of her anger dissipated. Maybe she could never have what she had with Kaylob, but maybe this would be good enough.

"I'm sorry about all this, darlin. I hope you'll let me explain."

"Oh, don't worry," she said. "I'm expecting quite an explanation from you, Mr. Tanner."

As the limo pulled away, Beth Ann took one last look at the apartment building, knowing she would not be back. The camera jerks were still taking pictures when they pulled away, and she couldn't help shooting them a dirty look. For the first time in her life, she decided to shoot them something else. Kaylob had told her never to do it, but Kaylob wasn't there. She rolled down her window, held out her hand and gave them the one-finger salute.

"Darlin, what the hell are you doing?" Blake pulled her hand back into the car and rolled up the window.

"Something my friend Carol showed me a long time ago. I always wondered if I would ever try it."

"My, my." He shook his head, but she detected amusement in his eyes. "I don't think now is a good time to use it with the paparazzi."

"Why not? And what's a paparazzi?"

"Photographers. Darlin, I have a reputation to keep and investors to please."

"Yes, Mr. Tanner, I guess it slipped your mind to tell me you're America's most eligible bachelor, and what's this about being a millionaire? You did a very good job of covering it all up and making sure we stayed hidden most of the time."

He tried to glance away, but she reached up and turned his face toward her. He gave her an innocent look.

"I kept meaning to tell you, but…" He turned away again and pointed out the window. "Hey, look at that dog. Now that's cute. Wouldn't you love to have a dog like that? I think they're called Doxies."

"Blake Tanner, don't you dare try to change the subject on me. Yes, I love dogs, but right now we're talking about something important." After an awkward pause, she huffed out a sigh. "Well, are you going to say anything?"

She watched him shift in his seat and fidget with his pants, acting as if he had to smooth out the wrinkles that weren't there.

"Blake."

"Oh, hell, okay," he said. "I was afraid you wouldn't see me if you knew. I know I made an awful mistake. I promise never to keep anything from you again."

Beth Ann gave him her best villainess look. "You'd better not."

"Ah, darlin, can you forgive me? Besides, I was the most eligible bachelor. I'm no longer eligible, and I gave that statement to the press. Now I'm wondering if it helped or made things worse, because they want to know who the lucky girl is." He ran his fingers up her arm and gave her a sheepish grin. "I hope she still thinks she's lucky, and I hope I get lucky real soon."

Beth Ann slapped his hand. "I shouldn't be speaking to you."

He pulled her closer and put on a little boy pout. "I'm really sorry, darlin. Want to punish me? I have some handcuffs and a whip—"

Her shocked looked made him stop and laugh.

"Cream, darlin. I was going to say whipped cream."

She narrowed her eyes at him. "Blake Tanner, I have to watch my calorie intake. Just what do whipped cream and handcuffs have to do with each other? Is that some weird diet thing people are doing, like wiring their mouths shut?"

He howled in laughter. When he could talk again, he enlightened her to what he meant. She did her best to act mad, but she had to admit the punishment sounded interesting.

When they pulled up to the townhouse, Beth Ann could only stare for a moment. The limo driver took the back entrance to avoid more paparazzi. After he parked, he glanced around before he opened the door for them. They hurried inside, and Blake led her to the elevator where a uniformed guy looking like a band leader without the hat seemed overdone for a townhouse, and she had to suppress a giggle.

When the elevator reached the top floor, Beth Ann paused again to take it all in while Blake fumbled to open the front door, clearly nervous. Finally, he got it open and motioned for her to step inside.

She felt as though she had entered a palace. A voice echoed down the hall to greet them, then an attractive dark-haired woman with a Marilyn Monroe figure walked toward them carrying a clipboard.

"Hello, Mr. Tanner." The woman adjusted the glasses perched on her nose. "There's a crisis at work, and Mr. Freemont is on the phone." She motioned toward the hallway and glanced curiously at Beth Ann.

"Shit, darlin," Blake said, taking Beth Ann's arm. "I have to take this call. Gabrielle, this is Beth Ann Rose. Gabrielle is the house manager, darlin, plus she helps me with my business."

Gabrielle nodded. "Nice to meet you, Miss. Rose."

A pretty girl looking about maybe twenty walked into the room. She was tiny with dark skin and big, dark eyes.

Blake nodded at her. "Beth Ann, Dana is my personal housekeeper. Dana, could you show Beth Ann around please?"

"Sure, Mr. Tanner," she said with a smile.

"Look around, darlin. See how you like the place. Dana will get you anything you need." His voice faded as he hurried down the hallway with Gabrielle.

"Holy night and daytime too." Beth Ann remarked to Dana. "This place is fancy-schmancy."

Dana smiled. "Let me show you around."

"Thanks, but I can check the place out myself. Why don't you go back to what you were doing? I'll be fine."

"Are you sure, Miss Beth Ann?"

"You can just call me Beth Ann."

Dana's cheeks flushed. "Okay, Miss Beth Ann, I'll try to remember. Are you sure you're okay and don't need anything?"

"I'm sure. Thank you though."

Dana left toward what Beth Ann guessed to be the kitchen from the sounds and mouth-watering aromas coming from that direction. Beth Ann turned toward a large door with a doorknob in the center and gasped when she opened it. Holy grasshopper, she had thought the hotel penthouse floor had been fanciful, but this was unreal.

The windows surrounding the living area gave a panoramic view of the city below, almost as though she were flying. Every electronic gizmo she'd ever heard of perched against one wall, flanked by behemoth speakers. On the other side of the room was what looked like a very large family area that held the most enormous television ever made. There was a fireplace in the center of the room surrounded by couches, loveseats, and recliners.

When she went upstairs, the paintings on the walls immediately caught her attention. Then, she wandered into the master bedroom. Blake must've had it professionally decorated. The curtains and bedspreads matched, and all the furnishings were stylish and expensive looking. The bed was humongous, and the story of Goldilocks came to mind as she gingerly sat on the edge of the bed.

This was nothing like she had ever imagined. Riverside sure didn't have townhouses this elegant. Blake had told her he'd ended up expanding three townhouses into one, letting the other tenants stay and surprising them by having their homes completely remodeled. Those who'd left had been given money to rent another place, and he'd paid for their move.

The bed felt so inviting she couldn't resist stretching out on the exquisite piece of furniture. She almost didn't hear the door open when Blake entered. She opened her eyes to see him smiling down at her while dangling a set of keys.

"What do you have? Keys to Gabrielle's house?"

He rocked back on his heels and laughed. "No, they're for you, silly." He pulled her up with a smile. "Follow me, darlin."

He led her downstairs and back into the parking garage. There, he walked her over to a1973 Mercury.

"Holy crap, Blake. What did you do?" She stared at him in complete shock.

He opened the door and handed her the keys. "This is my gift to you. I need you to fill out the registration, then it will be all yours."

Whoa, how could she consider accepting such an extravagant gift? Sure, she had made the choice to move in with him, but it wasn't like they were married or anything. Maybe she should move somewhere else. Besides, she still had her car from graduation that had hardly been used.

"Blake, this is too much. I can't let you put this in my name."

He reached out and touched her cheek. "Yes you can, and I really hope you will."

She stepped closer and looked into the car. "Blake, you shouldn't—"

He placed his fingers on her lips. "Please let me do this."

Touched by the expression on his face, she sighed and climbed into the driver's seat. "This is unreal."

"It's real, darlin. Just like my love for you."

That gave her a jolt. His gesture was wonderful, beautiful, and so very thoughtful, but could she accept it? She'd known all along that Blake had money, but she'd had no clue how much. Who had airplanes, private housekeepers, house managers, and gave cars as gifts? She wasn't sure how to deal with all the luxury. She didn't want Blake to think that her moving in meant more than it did. All those memories at her old apartment had hurt far too much, and that was the real reason she'd agreed to the move. Maybe things would evolve into more with Blake, but only time would tell.

She looked up at him. "Give me a few days to think about it, okay?"
"Take all the time you need, darlin. I'm not going anywhere."

Chapter Twenty-Nine

With Blake's help, Beth Ann settled into the townhouse, and she was truly happy to be there with him. He had her laughing more than she had in a very long time and doing funny things like slipping on her nightgown and strutting through the bedroom. She had never seen him so playful, and she loved that side of him. Normally he was all about business.

Her first night there, the staff prepared a wonderful dinner while she and Blake watched a movie. After dinner, the house people all discreetly vanished, and Beth Ann found out later that Gabrielle had her own place in the building. Blake said he wanted her close by, and Beth Ann couldn't help wondering if they had ever slept together.

When it was time for bed, Blake led her to the master bedroom where they made love for hours. Afterward, she lay with her head on his shoulder, listening to the sound of his heartbeat. She really did like being there with him, but it was so different from life with Kaylob. She would get used to this new way of living in time, wouldn't she?

* * * *

Saturday morning, she awoke to see Blake putting on cuff links as he got ready for work.

"You're working on a Saturday?" she observed.

His twin dimples flashed. "Yes, darlin. In real estate there are no set days off, but I hope to be home early. What would you like to do?"

"Hmm, let me think." She yawned and stretched. "Oh, wait. How about a repeat of last night, at least the last part of it?"

He bent to give her a soft kiss. "Now that's what I like to hear. I'll do my best to grant your request." He walked to the door, turned, and gave her a sexy wink before leaving.

She couldn't help thinking of all those Saturdays with Kaylob before he left for the army. Most days he got up early and started breakfast, but never before he had kissed her and told her how beautiful she was. They would spend the mornings cuddling or puttering, then later they would go to the park, have a picnic, or buy a hot dog. They'd had a simple life, and she missed everything about it.

Before she knew it, she'd lain there for over an hour, dreaming of the past. When would she ever stop comparing her new life to the life she'd had with Kaylob? That life no longer existed. She had to find a way to move forward. He'd told her to do that in the letter. Yet regardless of what she told herself, thoughts of Kaylob ate away at her soul. It took her another hour before she shook off the feelings of loss, and still her eyes burned with tears that she wiped away angrily.

"Stop this, Beth Ann." She threw back the covers and stepped out of bed.

What the hell? Her feet went into thick, wet mud. She looked down and couldn't believe it was happening again. She was no longer in the bedroom and instead stood barefoot in the jungle. She could see the same four trees and heard the same dog barking as well as the rushing sound of the river. The same thin, withered guy was by the trees, but this time she could see he was carving something in the base of one tree with a sharp rock.

"Hello," she called out to the man, but didn't know if he heard her because he just kept carving. She shouted louder. "Hello. Who are you?"

She was startled when he stopped carving and turned toward her. He searched all around as though he had heard her, but couldn't see her.

"Hello, I'm over here." she yelled and waved.

His hand went up to shield his eyes as he gazed right at her. "Beth Ann?"

A shiver went all the way down her spine, and she almost passed out. Oh, God, it didn't look like him, but the voice was his.

"Kaylob?"

Fear ripped through her. Dear Lord, that couldn't be him, but it had been his voice. She tried to walk toward him but couldn't take a step, her feet remained stuck in the mud. Frozen, she was forced to watch in horror as two short men in some type of uniform came out of nowhere and grabbed Kaylob then started dragging him away while they laughed.

For the first time in her life, Beth Ann wanted to murder someone. She could hear Kaylob yelling, calling for her. He was fighting and kicking, screaming her name over and over again. Then one of the vicious men hit him over the head with a club, and Kaylob fell silent. The evil monsters said the same words over and over again, both of them laughing hard.

"Dine thing nagoc."

Why were they doing this? She yelled and screamed for them to stop, but they kept dragging him out of sight. She forced herself to repeat back what they had said. What did it mean? She would find out later. Right now she had to find some way to see what was on that tree. She tried to pull her feet from the mud, but it was like glue. Finally, with a surge of pure adrenaline, she got free and made it to the trees.

She bent down and touched the ground where Kaylob had sat. What she saw broke her heart and made her cry out in anguish.

KAYLOB LOVES BETH ANN

Her hand went to her throat as sobs ripped through her. She had to find him. She screamed his name. "Kaylob."

How could this be? Was she witnessing the way he had died? Why in hell would God make her experience his death?

"Oh, Kaylob ... Oh, God no. Please no."

"Miss Beth Ann, are you okay?"

No, go away, she wanted to stay and search for Kaylob. She knocked away the hands touching her and turned to see Dana's eyes filled with shock. She had just hit the housekeeper.

"Dana, I'm so sorry. I ... I had a nightmare."

Her expression softened to concern. "Your eyes were open. I've been trying to shake you and bring you back for a few minutes. It was like you didn't hear me."

Beth Ann walked over and sat on the chair by the window, still shaking from the incident. "Dana, could you please do me a favor?"

"Sure, anything."

"Could you get me a notepad and pen? I need to write down my dream. It's important for me to write it down when this happens."

Dana nodded and left, still looking confused. A few minutes later she returned with the items. "Would you like me to call Mr. Tanner?"

"No, please don't. He has important clients today. I'll tell him about it when he comes home tonight."

"Well, okay." Dana nodded. "Would you like me to stay with you?"

"No, that's not necessary. I'm okay now. I just need to write down the dream. And, thank you so much."

Dana didn't seem convinced, but she turned and left.

Holy shit. She was insane.

Beth Ann waited for the door to shut, then she wrote down the words from the vision and repeated them to herself, dine thing nagoc. She thought Blake would know the meaning because he knew a lot of languages, but that meant she'd have to tell him about the vision. Great, just what she needed. He'd think she was crazy for sure.

There was nothing to do but try not to think about it until he got home. Maybe a walk outside or shopping would take her mind off Kaylob. Her insides still trembled at the memory of the vision, and she couldn't bear to think that he had been beaten. She needed to get in the shower or take a bath and try to get grounded.

After a very long bath, she got dressed and headed down the stairs to eat breakfast even though it was almost noon. The rustle of hushed voices stopped her dead in her tracks, but not soon enough. Standing at the entrance to the kitchen, she saw Dana and Blake whispering to each other. When Dana pointed upstairs, Beth Ann knew what she was telling Blake. She tried to step back, but the noise caught their attention and they turned to look at her.

"Oh, Miss Beth Ann." Dana's forehead creased with worry. "I called Mr. Tanner because I was worried about you. Please don't be mad."

Beth Ann's instinct had been right on. Dana hadn't bought her story, and she couldn't blame her. Fear twisted Beth Ann's stomach as she looked at Blake. What would he think of her? All she wanted to do was run away and hide, but she forced herself to step all the way into the kitchen.

Blake walked over to meet her, and he pulled her into a hug. "I'm here, darlin. Everything's going to be fine. It's time for a vacation, so I'm taking the next three weeks off."

Beth Ann opened her mouth to protest, but he placed his finger softly across her lips.

"Hear me out. I have two associates that I totally trust. They'll handle things while we're gone. I'm going to take you on a vacation you'll never forget. You need it, I need it, and I won't take no for an answer."

How had she had gotten so lucky to have this sweet man to take care of her, and why had she doubted him? A vacation sounded wonderful after being on the road for so long, always rehearsing and almost no time for play. It had drained her, and she needed to recharge, but she wasn't sure she could go away with him. She was supposed to start working as a vocal coach the following week. When Carol had called and told her the Lakeside School of Performing Arts wanted to hire her, she had been excited and jumped at the chance.

Blake kissed her. "Well, what do you say, darlin?"

"I'm supposed to start my new job next week. How long would we be gone?"

"At least two weeks, but you can call and tell them you need more time. Please, just see what they say." His look was pleading. "You know you don't have to work. We have plenty of money."

"I want to work, and I don't want to lose this job."

He walked over and picked up the phone. "Call and see what they say."

167

Much to her surprise, they agreed. The singing coach whose place she was taking was pregnant, but wanted to work right up to her due date, which was three weeks away so everything worked out perfectly.

Blake and Beth Ann spent the next two days getting ready for their trip. He wouldn't tell her where they were going because he said he wanted to surprise her. What if he wanted to take her to the ocean or anyplace near water? That would remind her too much of Kaylob. She had to tell Blake, so she mustered her courage while they were in the bedroom packing.

"Blake, I have to tell you something. I can't go to the ocean or near water."

He nodded. "Got it. No ocean, no water. You told me that before, so I made sure that wasn't in our plans." He winked at her and continued packing.

God, he was so understanding. She watched him with fondness that quickly turned to amusement as she realized that everything in Blake's life had to be in order and done according to color and organization. Even his stupid socks had to be perfect.

She went back to her own packing and sensed him watching her too. She tried to ignore him, but when he started making sounds of disapproval, it began to get on her nerves. Each time she put something in her suitcase, he would groan and sigh. Soon she was annoyed, and when he walked over and emptied her suitcase on the bed, she put her hands on her hips and glared at him.

"Blake, what the heck do you think you're doing?"

"Darlin, the way you're doing this isn't proper, and you can't get everything you need packed doing it that way."

She snagged a pair of her underwear from him. "I can pack my own clothes, thank you very much."

He picked up a pair of her socks and folded them. "Look at the space you'll save if you do it this way. If you coordinate by color, it really helps."

"Blake Mitchell Tanner." She snatched them back and gave him the best evil eye she had.

His hands went up in surrender. "Okay, I see you don't want to learn the correct way. Go ahead and just stuff everything in."

She wanted to stuff something all right, and she knew just the right spot.

He continued to wince each time she threw a pair of socks into her bag, so she made sure to put everything in extra messy. After a few minutes, she started to sing a song about improper suitcases while she packed.

"Oh, despair, I folded my underwear. Shameful as it was, my suitcase was a buzz. The media sent out an alert when I had wrinkles in my skirt ..."

His eyes squinted, and her gave her an ornery look that told her she needed to run.

"You're in big trouble now." He laughed as he started toward her.

She let out a little scream and ran like hell, but he chased her down the stairs. The more he ran after her, the louder she sang. When he finally caught her, he hoisted her over his shoulder and carried her back up the stairs, casually saying hello to members of his staff along the way. Beth Ann felt her cheeks flame hot and watched as Dana covered her mouth, trying not to laugh. Several others looked as though they knew Blake well enough to know what her song meant.

Back upstairs, he shut the bedroom door and locked it before he put her down.

"Now I'm gonna get you out of that skirt that caused the media alert." He pulled her closer. "Ah, darlin, see what you do to me."

They both looked down at what she did to him and chuckled together. They threw all the suitcases on the floor, and he suddenly didn't care if everything in them was in perfect order. She was sure nobody downstairs expected to see them for a while, and nobody did.

* * * *

It was no newsflash that Beth Ann ended up packing her own way. She and Blake were both discovering that she didn't like being told what to do. She was becoming a strong, independent woman, and she had to admit that she liked the new Beth Ann.

Blake finally told her he was taking her to the Swiss Alps, and she was overwhelmed at such an extravagant trip. Luckily, she had kept her passport from when Kaylob had gone into the service. The flight was long, but her first glimpse of the Alps blew her mind with their beauty.

When they landed, the magnificence of the rugged mountains overlooking the green meadows and shaded woodlands was breathtaking. June was a beautiful time to visit—not too cold and not as crowded during snow season because of winter sports. The resort was amazing with rustic elegance, and their room was embellished with a modern style mixed with old world charm, like stepping back in time. Adorning the room was a canopy bed, with the most beautiful bronze lights that flickered throughout the room and gave it a warm feel of burning candles. The living room was decorated with golden furniture, like something from a historical magazine.

The Monday morning after they checked in arrived with hints of sunlight flickering through the window. Beth Ann awoke to the curtains fluttering from a gentle breeze as she was serenaded by the sounds of birds twittering. She quietly rose and moved over to the window, feeling enchanted as she gazed out at the picturesque beauty. The sun shone across the cap of snow that still covered the mountains and displayed a stunning view of all the colors of a rainbow.

She inhaled and slowly let it out. "Rainbows ..." she whispered

An unexpected swell of pain rushed through her. Would Kaylob ever see this kind of beauty? Would he ever hear birds singing again or enjoy the touch of a gentle breeze? Her stomach twisted as tears blurred her eyes. How could so much time pass and the pain still be so raw? How could she ever think she could move on after that last vision?

"Hey, darlin. I missed you."

She turned to look at Blake, and she could tell he saw her tears. "The beauty is so overwhelming." She waved her hand toward the window.

He pulled her into his arms. "I'm glad you like it, but I didn't expect a reaction like this."

Okay, so she lied to him. Maybe it was wrong to mislead him, but how could she let him know the truth after all he had done for her? She didn't want to hurt him.

Apparently, he bought the explanation of her tears, because when she looked up at him, she saw desire heating in his eyes. She knew what he had in mind, and what a beautiful mind Blake Tanner had. She slipped her nightgown over her head and let it fall to the floor. The next thing she knew, she was in his arms being carried back to the bed. Before the passion of his love took her to another place, a place where she didn't hurt so much, she had one last thought.

She hoped God would give her the strength to push Kaylob out of her thoughts at least for this vacation.

Chapter Thirty

The days melted away like the snow melted by a warm breeze, leaving behind memories. Beth Ann and Blake discovered even more hidden desires and ways of pleasing each other. She loved every minute of their time together, but her guilt still lingered. Not one day was she able to push Kaylob completely from her thoughts. She wondered if Blake knew. Did he feel that three people lived in their relationship? At least the dreams and visions had stayed away on their vacation.

After three weeks of rest, beauty, and fun, it was time to go home. As soon as they returned, Blake resumed his busy schedule. Weeks passed and Beth Ann did the best she could to settle in her new life. The rich and famous lifestyle was harder than she'd ever imagined. Weekends of relaxation became a thing of the past. It seemed they were always entertaining, having dinner parties, or meeting new clients, never just being lazy or spending weekends alone.

One morning in late August, Beth Ann woke and decided she needed some time with Carol and Frankie. She'd been surrounded by all Blake's friends and none of hers for too long. If they weren't hobnobbing with other wealthy people in Hollywood, they'd fly off in his company's private jet, trying to dodge the media and cameras.

The word for the way Blake spent money was ridiculous. People were starving while they squandered money on trivial things. The other word for it was decadence, and it was hard for Beth Ann to get used to that. She didn't have much in common with some of the rich people because she had always been a simple small-town girl. She missed her friends, her old life, and things like shopping at garage sales.

Reporters called daily for private interviews, and it about drove her crazy. Blake thought they should go ahead and do the interview so the reporters would stop hounding them, but Beth Ann wasn't sure about any of it.

One morning he watched her sitting on the edge of the bed drinking water, and her unhappiness with his lifestyle must have shown on her face.

"Darlin, is everything okay?"

She was angry and wanted to make damn sure he knew it. "No. I miss my friends. I haven't seen Frankie and Carol since I got back."

"We will soon," he said. "I just have so much going on right now, and I need you with me."

He leaned down and kissed her forehead as though she were a child. She glared at his back as he walked out the door. A storm was brewing, and not the outside kind. She was tired of him brushing her off. This wasn't just his life. She had a life too. Her friends counted and were just as important as his. Did he think money made him the center of the universe? Well, she'd just see about that.

Blake stayed so busy for the next week so she bided her time as the days hurried by and summer came to an end. Even for a hot place like Riverside, the beginning of September was cooler than normal. Trees began to lose their leaves, and the cool breezes made her pull out some sweaters. Yet although the temperatures outside were cooling, Beth Ann's anger was still heating up. When another weekend passed entertaining Blake's friends with no mention of hers, she finally reached her boiling point. Enough was enough.

She woke up Monday morning determined to change things. "Blake, I've had it. Either I'm going to have my friends over for dinner here, or I'll go meet them on my own."

She stomped off to the bathroom, slamming the door behind her. This was their first fight as a couple, but she was holding her ground and putting on her boxing gloves. A few minutes later, she heard a light knock on the door. Ding, she was ready for round one.

Blake leaned his head in. and surprised her when, "Sweetheart, I'd love to have your friends over," he said. "I'll change my plans for this coming weekend."

His expression appeared guilty and eager to make things right. Holy cow, if a little tantrum was all it took for Blake to give in to her, she'd be sure to have one more often.

After she got dressed and made her way downstairs, she overheard Blake in the kitchen giving the staff orders on what to cook for dinner. Yep, he was kissing up to her by having them prepare her favorite foods, Mexican chicken enchiladas and chocolate cake.

She pranced out the French doors and stood on the balcony that overlooked the city, but her good mood didn't last. The loneliness suddenly swallowed her. She missed her family and friends, but more than anything she missed Kaylob. Before her emotions suffocated her, she felt Blake's arms around her.

"I'm sorry, sweetheart. I've been selfish, and it won't happen again. From now on, we'll make time to do the things you like to do and have your friends over." His sweet lips brushed across her neck.

Oh, Lord, she needed him. She turned and gave him a lingering kiss.

He let out a low growl. "You'd better stop or I'm going to carry you upstairs right now, and I'll never get anything done."

She didn't stop, and he was almost late for work. Watching him get dressed, her earlier happiness returned, and she felt excited again that her friends were coming next weekend. Just thinking about spending time with Carol and Frankie made her feel alive.

After Blake left, she slipped out of the house for some fresh air—just what she needed. Then, when she entered the garage, she made a sudden decision and climbed in her new car, heading toward some secondhand stores. Blake spoiled her, but she didn't know if she liked him doing that or not. If she vaguely glanced at something in a store window, he would have it gift wrapped for her the next day. It made her feel uncomfortable after the umpteenth time, so she tried to stop looking.

She guessed her uneasiness came from her life with Kaylob, when diligent frugality had meant more food on the table. She had loved their simple lifestyle and missed being able to walk to the corner store without those stinking flash bulbs going off in her face. Blake probably wouldn't like it when he found out where she was going, but why should she care what others thought? She loved going to used places and wouldn't stop.

She really enjoyed herself, and the afternoon faded away before she knew it. She also had a great evening with Blake, and dinner was a real hit. Almost as wonderful as Blake making up to her a little more when they went to bed.

When she went down to breakfast the next morning, Blake looked upset. He frowned and showed her the morning newspaper. 'Millionaire's girlfriend forced to shop at thrift stores.'

"That's ridiculous," she said. "I wasn't forced. I love going to those places. I can get great deals, so why should I pass them up?"

Blake sighed, folded the paper, then he leaned over and kissed her. "Okay, we need to do an interview and clear this up."

"Why do we care what they think?" She waved her hand, dismissing the article.

"I have to care, darlin. I have investors who need to think I'm a good guy."

"You are a good guy."

He handed her the paper and poured his coffee. "Not always. I broke some hearts unintentionally and played around a lot."

He gave her the naughty look she knew so well. She arched her eyebrow and slapped him with the newspaper, and they both laughed.

Blake set up the interview with a television journalist and her cameramen for that afternoon at the townhouse. Beth Ann was pleased that the reporter wanted to know why she loved shopping at secondhand stores. She emphasized how they kept her in touch with her roots and explained her personal feelings about them.

"I think it's something people of wealth should do because it helps out those organizations so they can help people in need." Beth Ann felt cool and calm while looking into the camera, and she was proud of herself for not letting them intimidate her. In fact, after being on stage, it felt completely normal.

The interview was a hit with viewers, and Blake's reputation soared, but the magazines were a different story. They always had Blake cheating with some other woman or saying Beth Ann was having an affair with a guy who lived in her old building, which ended up being Jack. That made them both laugh.

Everything seemed to be going somewhat better. She hadn't had any visions in weeks and thought maybe she was back to being sane again. As she lay in bed on Thursday morning, she felt thrilled that her friends were coming the following night. She wished Jack and Lenard were coming too, but they were going on vacation.

Beth Ann had taken both Thursday and Friday off to prepare for Carol and Frankie's visit. Thank goodness her co-worker Jennifer had agreed to handle things for the next two days. With that thought, she lay back and let complete peace flow over her. It felt so good being in that place again. The stress in her world was finally leaving.

A knock at her bedroom door brought her into the here and now. She pulled on her robe and opened the door for Dana.

"Miss Beth Ann, there's a phone call for you."

"Oh, who is it?"

"Someone by the name of John Patterson. He said he knew your fiancé."

Beth Ann couldn't move. She stared at Dana and felt the room start to spin.

"Are you okay?" Dana grabbed her arm. "Should I tell him to call back?"

"Could you tell him I'll call him later and get his number, please?"

"Of course." Dana nodded and left.

Beth Ann stood there a moment longer and inhaled when she realized she wasn't breathing. Why in the world was this man calling? Did he have information about Kaylob? Was she ready to find out whatever he wanted to tell her? Maybe she was being a coward, but she couldn't talk to him now. She'd call him later like she said.

Just when she thought she was finally getting a break, this had to happen. Fear hit, and she was terrified that it would bring back the visions and nightmares. The last thing she wanted was to get upset when Frankie and Carol were coming.

Chapter Thirty-One

The darkest days in the jungle camp had come upon Kaylob. He thought the year was 1973 from what he could understand from the other prisoners. After two years of being in hell, he knew now he was in one of the worst types of prisons, isolated and deep in the jungle. As the new prisoners came in, they brought information about the war. From what he gathered from their tapping code, southern Vietnam had some the worst POW camps. One guy had told him they were fighting with Northern Vietnam. These assholes weren't following the rules and made up their own. Lucky him, to be at what they called 'the resort.'

He was spending more time out by the trees than in his bamboo hut. At times, they would bury his body in the putrid ground with just his head sticking up. Insects climbed all over him, biting and stinging his lips, nose, and even his eyelids. They would leave him buried for a couple days with maggot-ridden food in front of him. They'd dig him up a few days later and toss his ass on the ground, his body covered in insect bites, leaches and open sores.

He knew he was burning up with a fever, and he sensed that his time was coming to an end. For the last few days, he'd felt as though someone was watching him, but he figured it must be his fevered mind playing tricks. Without warning, vomit ran from his mouth down his body. He tried to wipe it off, but it did no good. The stench of his body and knowing he was rotting on the inside made him feel sicker.

Death hovered all around him. Was that who was watching him? Darkness wanted to swallow him and carry him away, and he was almost ready to let it. Then he saw her standing in front of him, the angel he loved.

"Kaylob, please ... is that you?"

Oh, God, it was his Beth Ann. "I'm here, baby ... Beth Ann ..."

Tears streamed down her face. "Kaylob, where are you? Please come home."

Before he could say another word, she faded, and his words turned to sobs. He'd give anything to be with her again, to hold her one more time and tell her he loved her.

"God, please ..."

He tried to get on his knees and look toward heaven but wasn't sure where it was. Right now his idea of paradise was back home with Beth Ann. Out of the corner of his eye, he saw the Cong known as 'pig's ass' heading toward him again.

"Oh, you calling her again? She with new man, she love him now." He kicked Kaylob in the leg and spit at him. "You die soon. She be with other men and never think of you again."

His wicked laugh made Kaylob want to kill him. In the next second, Kaylob felt heat scalding his head from liquid that smelled like hot lard. In another instance a lit cigarette pushed into his scalp, followed by another.

"Aaaaaaa, you son of a bitch."

He tried his best to fight him off, swinging at the idiot but missing. When he looked up, two other guards had come to join the fun.

"Go ahead and kill me, you bastards."

They started beating him with bamboo sticks. Someone pushed his face down in the mud, forcing vomit and dirt up his nose. He gasped for air, and all he could do was close his eyes and let it happen.

"You bastard pigs," he said as he spit the filth from his mouth. "Screw you to hell."

Their sick laughter burst all around until they walked away. He rolled onto his back and looked up at the sky, a silent prayer going up to God. If only God would take him now. He was so tired of hurting. What had he done to deserve this type of torture?

Once again the sound of the dog barking drew his attention, followed by movement in the bush. It was like before. He sensed someone out there but couldn't see anything.

"Who's there?"

Tears streaked his dirty face. If it was death coming to greet him he didn't care, not anymore. Anyplace would be better than this hell hole. This time he knew he heard noises. He couldn't stand up, so he crawled toward the sound. His eyes scanned all around trying to find whoever it was.

Then he saw someone dart behind a tree. He knew his mind was playing tricks on him, because it looked like a man in an American uniform. He crawled back to the tree and leaned his battered body against it, certain that he was dying. Why else would he be seeing American soldiers hiding behind trees?

He let his eyes close and drifted off, hoping he wouldn't wake up again. If this was his last minute of life, he wanted to sing his song with the little strength he had left.

"Oh, my love ..." He tried to sing for her, his angel. "Beth Ann, I need ..."

His voice broke as he cried to think this was his final moment and he would never see home or the love of his life again. He was so sorry he'd broken his promise to her. At least he had carved the words in the tree that he loved his Beth Ann. Hopefully someday she would find out she had been his last thought.

Chapter Thirty-Two

Friday morning, a chill hit Beth Ann hard. She felt Kaylob and felt him strong.

Then reason set in, and she knew it was probably because John Patterson had called her, and she had to shake it off. She wanted her friends to see her happy and laughing, not the basket case she'd been before. She wanted them to see the new, stronger, more confident Beth Ann.

When she made it downstairs after Blake had left for work, she was pleased to find the housekeeping staff had cleaned everything, getting things set up for her guests. After breakfast, she decided to go clean her room herself and pick out what to wear. She kept trying to push the phone call from Patterson to the back of her mind by finding distracting things to do.

Morning rolled into afternoon, and everything looked beautiful. When Blake got home from work, he headed upstairs to get ready. For whatever reason, she felt nervous and started puttering. Like a light bulb going off in her head, it dawned on her that Kaylob had been right all along when he told her she always puttered when she was nervous.

Finally, the doorbell announced Frankie and Carol's arrival. Beth Ann took a deep, cleansing breath and opened the front door. Frankie grinned at her and held up a bottle of wine, and Carol opened her arms for a hug. Beth Ann let out a squeal and hugged them both, swallowing her tears.

"It's so great to see you both. I've missed you so much."

Frankie held her at arm's length. "Wow. How is it possible for you to be even more beautiful?"

She hugged him again and motioned for them to come inside.

For once, Frankie was at a loss for words as he looked around, clearly awestruck by her new pad.

"You have to give us a tour of this place," Carol said, her eyes wide.

Both of them followed Beth Ann while she gave them the grand tour. Frankie walked with his hand around her waist and then he turned her to face him.

"Girl, you've been plastered all over the gossip magazines, but they don't do you justice. We've missed you so much. It's been too long."

Beth Ann couldn't help the mist that formed in her eyes. He was right. It had been way too long.

Carol winked at her. "How does it feel to see your picture all over the place?"

Beth Ann shook her head in disgust. "I honestly don't like it. There's always some cameramen or women waiting to snap a picture of me on my worst day, or I do something they make into a downright lie."

When they finished the tour, Beth Ann took Frankie upstairs to show him the rest, but Carol decided to hang out in the kitchen with the hors d'oeuvres. The staff had cooked enough food to feed an entire football team.

When they were alone upstairs, Beth Ann and Frankie acted like the childhood friends they were. He pulled her into his arms, swung her around and kissed her innocently on the lips. His friendship meant the world to her, and it had been a long time since she'd giggled that hard and felt so giddy. With Frankie she felt a natural high just being with him. His silly humor brought out the little girl in her, and she made up her mind never to be away from him for that long again.

Yet when he put his hands on her shoulders and looked into her eyes, she knew it was question time.

"What, Frankie? Why are you looking at me like that?"

"Is everything okay, sweetheart? Are you happy? Is he treating you good?"

She smiled and nodded. "Yes, he treats me wonderful, but I miss Kaylob every day."

"I know you do, sweetie."

She laid her head against his chest while he stroked her hair. Just being in his arms and knowing how much he loved and missed Kaylob too brought her so much comfort.

* * * *

Blake had been on a business call in his office when the doorbell rang. When he came out and walked into the kitchen to see Carol glaring at him, he almost turned around and left. She was clearly not happy to see him, and he didn't know why. He had only met her once at Beth Ann's opening night.

"Hello, Carol." He tried not to sound nervous.

She just nodded and continued to stare at him.

He couldn't believe his palms were starting to sweat. "Where are Frankie and Beth Ann?"

Still no trace of a smile. "She's giving him a tour upstairs."

Why the hell was she alone with him upstairs? He didn't like that a bit, but Carol was still surveying him, and he sensed that something was coming. What it was, he had no idea. He didn't know Carol, but the look on her face made him sure he didn't want to be on her bad side. The woman could easily intimidate a Sumo wrestler.

Before he had a chance to say anything else, she walked over and poked his chest. "Hurt her and you die, Blake Tanner. I don't know you, but if you hurt her I swear—"

"It's not her you have to worry about getting hurt," he said. "It's *my* heart at stake."

"Yeah, well, I don't give a damn about your heart. It's hers that has been ripped apart, and I don't want some playboy hurting her. If you do, I'll come kick your rich ass."

She stuck a carrot in her mouth and chomped it in half. Blake took it as a warning that she was about ready to devour him, and not in a good way.

He held up his hands in surrender and stepped back. "Message received, but you don't have to worry. I've loved her since we were kids. I would never hurt her."

Carol turned back to the food and muttered, "You've been warned. Don't make me kill you."

"I told you I love her."

She scowled at him. "From what I've read, you've loved a lot of women. You just remember my warning about this one."

He nodded and decided he would rather be anywhere but there. "I'll go see what's taking them so long upstairs."

Jesus holy Christ, this woman was not someone he wanted to test. Besides, he didn't like the idea of Beth Ann alone with Russo. And why the hell had she left him alone down here with Miss Night of the Living Attitude?

* * * *

Beth Ann and Frankie were hugging again in the hall outside her bedroom when Blake came upstairs. She didn't know he was behind them until he coughed. She could tell he didn't like their embrace and didn't care. His damn jealousy was a pain. She was glad he kept his cool enough so that Frankie didn't notice there was a problem.

Dinner was pleasant enough. They entertained Carol with some of their school hi-jinks. While Frankie and Beth Ann reminisced and told stories, Blake stayed quiet but polite. When it was time for Frankie and Carol to leave, they both hugged Beth Ann and kissed her goodbye. She and Frankie agreed to meet for coffee in a few days.

181

After she closed the door, Beth Ann spun around and let Blake know with a look that she wasn't happy with him. She waited for the housekeepers to pick up the food trays and take them into the kitchen before she raked him over the fire.

"Holy smokes, Blake. What is your problem?"

He didn't answer and stalked toward the stairs. No way was she letting him ignore her like that. She rushed past him so he would face her and glowered at him, but before she could say anything, one of the housekeepers came in and started cleaning up.

Blake lowered his voice but didn't hide his anger. "I saw the way Frankie was touching you, and I don't like it. I heard about you two kissing when you were kids. He's always had a thing for you. I can't believe you don't see it when you walk in or out of a room. He can't take his eyes off you."

She put her hands on her hips. "What are you talking about? Frankie's one of my best friends, and I don't have eyes in the back of my head."

"Maybe I should get a best friend who kisses my lips and holds me the way he holds you to see how you'd take it."

"Blake Tanner, knock it off. It's friendship and nothing else."

His eyes were dark with anger, and she couldn't believe he was acting this way. What the hell was he doing? This was the first time she'd been around her friends in months, and he decided to flip out like a jealous idiot.

"Oh, wait," he said, his voice rising. "I got that wrong, because you wouldn't give a shit if I had a friend like that. I'm just a fill-in, right?"

Another housekeeper walked in and looked like she wanted to run. Blake looked at both of the women and cleared his throat.

"It's okay, no need to do that right now. Give us about thirty minutes and you can finish up in here later."

"Yes, Mr. Tanner. I'm sorry." The poor lady backed out of the room as fast as she could.

"Blake, what are you talking about?" Beth Ann said when they were alone. "Of course I care about you."

"Bullshit. You care so much you let other men kiss and hold you?" He took a step up the staircase then turned to look at her. "How am I supposed to feel? I hate it when someone—anyone—puts their hands on you."

A memory of her tantrums surfaced. She had always been jealous of Kaylob and had stomped around the room tossing pillows and yelling. Now she was getting a taste of what it felt like to be on the receiving end.

"I'm in love with you, Beth Ann," Blake went on. "I tell you that all the time, but all you ever say back is that you care about me. How am I supposed to feel? It hurts that you never give a crap who flirts with me, but boy did I hear about the temper tantrums you used to throw when someone glanced Kaylob's way. Yeah, I know where I stand."

The air felt weighted with concentrated emotions. She walked up the steps to get closer to him and was stunned to see tears pooling in his eyes. She did love Blake in her own way. Maybe she wasn't in love with him, and she'd never love anyone the way she loved Kaylob, but she could be honest and tell him how she felt about him and how important he was to her. That's what Kaylob had always done for her when she'd thrown jealous tantrums, and it had always calmed her down.

"You have a special place in my heart, Blake. I don't want anyone else."

A tear spilled over onto his cheek, and it about broke her heart. Yes, it was time to let him know that she loved him. She put her hand on his cheek and smiled up at him.

"You are so important to me, Blake. I do love you. Very much."

His eyes softened, and all trace of his anger melted. "Do you mean that, Beth Ann? Did I hear you right? You really love me?"

"Yes, I do. I'm sorry it took me so long to tell you. I love you, Blake." She moved closer and put her arms around his neck. "You're the sexiest man in the world, and have I ever mentioned how wonderful you smell?"

She was glad she'd said she loved him, but this felt better, talking about how sexy he was and how he affected her. She wanted to get away from the love topic. Was it really possible to love one man while being in love with another? Hell, it must be, because it was true for her.

He brushed his lips across hers, then he lifted her in his arms and carried her to their bedroom. Slowly, they undressed each other, and while they made love that night, she gazed up into his eyes and knew she had told him the truth. She loved Blake Tanner deeply.

Yet it was also true she would never love anyone like she did Kaylob. There was a part of her heart that only belonged to Kaylob, and sadly for Blake, it was the biggest part.

Chapter Thirty-Three

The next morning, Blake wished he didn't have to leave to take care of business. He looked over at Beth Ann and pinched himself to see if he was awake. She loved him and had finally told him. He wanted to spend the day in bed with her—hell, he wanted to spend the rest of his life with her. Hot damn, she was steaming. She was a little tiger in bed, and he loved every minute of it.

"Stop staring at her and get your horny ass in the shower," he muttered to himself.

Damn, leaving their bed was hard. She kept many things hard these days. He moved her long hair off her neck and gave her a gentle kiss. She stirred and whispered something that he couldn't quite make out. Or did he not want to? Jesus, did she just say Kaylob's name?

He listened again and realized she was speaking Vietnamese. What the hell? Finally, she stopped talking, and her breathing told him she was asleep.

He got up and went into the bathroom. Standing under the water in the shower, he tried to sort out his thoughts. As happy as she had made him by saying she loved him, he knew something was going on with her and had been for a long time. She was talking in another language in her sleep, not to mention the way she zoned out all the time. The other day she had been sweaty and hot to the touch, and he'd had to call her three times to get her attention. Could she be pregnant? He wouldn't mind that at all.

Not many people had lived through what she had. He knew all about her nervous breakdown and how she'd stopped talking and eating for months. Some people had thought she would never be normal again. He also knew about her hacking off her hair and jabbing holes in her scalp.

He turned around and let the hot water hit him in the face. Hell, look what she did after everything she went through, going on to get a lead role in a Broadway production. What a strong girl she was. He was damn proud of her and wanted to make all the pain from the past fade away. Still, his last thought before he stepped out of the shower was to wonder if Beth Ann would ever be over Kaylob completely.

Since his master closet was attached to the bathroom, he didn't have to wake up Beth Ann when he got dressed. When he went back to the bedroom, she was propped up on her elbow with her sexy little smile and those rosy cheeks. Good God, she had to be the sexiest woman he had ever known. He could easily spend the rest of the day in bed with her.

"I hate to go, darlin, but I have a big day today. I have to run."

She giggled and threw the covers back, crooking her finger at him.

Jesus, Mary, and Joseph, the redhead was hot as fire. He held up his hands and stepped away from the bed, turning away to grab his keys. He tried hard to not to look at her before he stepped out of the door, but he stuck his head back in.

"Bye-bye, buttercup."

He heard her laughing after he closed the door and had to stand there a few minutes to compose himself. The last thing he wanted was to walk through his house showing the staff what she did to him.

The hour drive to his office gave him time to cool down. Damn, he seemed to live in a permanent state of need these days. Nobody had ever made him feel the way she did just from being naked. Of course, it was way beyond sex for him, and he hoped he wouldn't end up with a broken heart, because she sure as hell had the power to do just that.

He knew how much she still loved Kaylob, but Kaylob was gone. He was willing to gamble that in time she might grow to love him as much. Nobody could have ever tempted her away from Kaylob. Hell, even at an early age, no other guy had stood a chance. Now he had to compete with the memory of Mr. Perfect.

He arrived at his office an hour after he left home. Not too bad of a commute. He had bought one of the best places in Palm Springs. He'd owned his townhouse there for a couple of years but hadn't stayed there much. Maybe he should sell it, but then again, if he had clients from out of town, he could offer them a place to stay.

Riverside held very little appeal due to the lack of high end properties. Blake was mostly into commercial real estate and had places all over the globe, but Riverside had never been a place he serviced. He wished Beth Ann was willing to live in a better area. As he glanced around, he observed the deep green lawn with approval. The landscapers were hard at work in full force. They started early because of the heat. The palm trees looked good, and so did the rock waterfall that had just been finished.

He parked his car and made his way upstairs to the office. When he got there, Mellissa, his front office manager, was shuffling through some paperwork. She was an attractive little blonde right out of high school, with deep brown eyes and maybe an inch over five feet. Her dad was a bigwig broker who wanted her to learn responsibility. She was a nice girl who reminded him of Beth Ann, probably because it didn't take much to make her blush. All he had to do was smile or wink and she turned red.

She looked up at him and grinned, her cheeks flushed as soon as she saw him. She was cute, but his rule number one had always been to never get involved with employees with the exception of Leslie.

Oh shit. She was coming back this week after being gone for over six months. He'd started dating Beth Ann a few weeks after she left. Why the hell hadn't he called before now to let her know his situation? Christ, this was so Blake Tanner.

"Mellissa, is Leslie back yet?"

"Yes, Mr. Tanner. She got in last night. She's been down twice looking for you. The note is on your desk."

"Mellissa, I told you that you don't have to call me Mr. Tanner. I'm not that much older than you. Call me Blake."

She nodded and blushed a deeper red. "Okay, Blake."

"Thank you. I was beginning to feel old." He stepped inside his office and shut the door. He was just about to pick up the phone when the door flew open. He turned and forced a smile.

"Hey, Blake." Leslie beamed at him.

Oh, Christ, she was much too happy to see him. Before he could say anything, she rushed over and threw her arms around his neck.

"Oh, Blake, I want to take you home right now. I've missed you so much. I stayed at the townhouse last night and waited for you to come home, but you never did." A cute little pout formed across her lips.

He stepped back and held her at arm's length. "It's good to see you, Leslie, but we need to talk."

He walked over and closed the door, then he sat on the couch and patted the seat next to him. He waited for her to sit beside him, then he told her everything about Beth Ann. He finished by telling her how wonderful she had always been, and the he wished her the very best.

She listened to him in silence, staring at the rug while he talked. When he finished and she looked up at him, he felt slapped in the heart to see tears misting her lashes.

"I'm sorry, Leslie. The last thing I ever wanted was to hurt you."

The room turned chilly. "That's fine, Blake. I guess I really shouldn't be surprised. I read the stories about you but thought they were just a publicity stunt. I figured you would call me if it had been true, but I guess I was wrong. I don't think I can work here anymore."

He reached out to touch her hand, but she jumped up.

"As a matter of fact, I quit as of now." Her face was getting red, and he thought he saw steam coming from her ears.

Damn, he hated to lose her. She was the best sales agent he'd ever had. She had overseen his company in Europe and done a superb job. Before she'd left, he'd studied with her to get her license in Europe as well, so he knew how sharp she was.

"Leslie, please don't quit. We need you. I'm such an ass. Please forgive me."

She turned away, and he could tell she was crying. He felt like a first-class heel.

After a minute, she sighed and turned to look him in the eyes. "It's my own fault. I let myself fall in love with you even though you made it clear from the beginning about no ties."

Man, talk about clueless. He'd had no idea she had fallen in love with him. Why hadn't he seen the goddamn signs? Honesty had always been the name of the game for him with his ladies. He'd told Leslie no commitments, no attachments, and no falling in love. Then he'd let her have a key to his Palm Springs townhouse and had taken her to Hawaii and on a few other vacations. He should have known better. What a joke that they'd called him the most eligible bachelor. More like the most eligible hound dog.

He walked over to her and took her hand. "Would you consider working full time at the firm in Europe? We'll buy you a private condo of your choice, put it in your name and throw in a new car. I'll throw in housecleaning for three years and a nice-sized bonus. All you need to do is sign a five year contract to stay with the company."

Her lips still quivered, but he detected the hint of a smile. "That would be great. I would have taken just the job, Blake, but throwing in all the extra stuff is very generous."

He tried to kiss her cheek, but she pulled away.

"No, don't do that. Maybe later. And thank you for this opportunity. You won't be sorry." She turned and left his office.

He glanced at Mellissa, but she kept her eyes on the papers on her desk. He'd gotten off easy with Leslie, but now he had to face the wrath of his redhead. He needed to call her before somebody leaked the story to the press. Sometimes it was bullshit, but other times it was right on.

He spent the next thirty minutes on the phone with Beth Ann, telling her everything about Leslie. When he finished, he held his breath while he waited for her to say something.

"Blake, do you think she'll be okay? I mean, it has to be hard seeing you every day and being reminded of what you two had. I feel bad for her."

Damn it to hell, he should have known. She wasn't jealous even a tiny bit. In fact, she was worried about Leslie.

"She's going to work at our office in Europe." His hand gripped the phone in irritation. "She'll be fine. She loves the place."

"Oh, that's good, Blake. I hope she'll be happy, the poor thing."

He had to hang up the goddamn phone before he said something he'd regret. She made it too obvious she didn't care. He'd always heard the running joke about how she threw pillows when women tried to pick up Kaylob. Hell, not only had she never thrown a pillow, but she'd never shown one ounce of jealousy. She would more than likely be fine with it if he had another girlfriend.

In truth, he had never given her a reason to be jealous, and maybe it was time to test her. Yeah, he knew it was childish, especially after she'd just told him that she loved him. His parents had said the words too, but he'd never once felt love from them. They'd bought him things, but when it came to sharing emotions, they were stiff and rigid.

Maybe that was why he'd always been afraid to fall in love.

Chapter Thirty-Four

Beth Ann sank onto the edge of the bed and rubbed her hand through her hair, staring at the end table with the phone on it. She knew what she had to do, but that didn't make it any easier. What should she say to John Patterson? Even if all he wanted was to thank her because Kaylob had saved his life, how the heck could she act nice and pretend to be happy if he said that to her? Nobody had saved her fiancé.

She walked over to the nightstand to get the number and started to open the drawer when the phone rang. Relieved, she ran to answer it.

"Hey, you wild thing," Blake said. "How would you like to go to Vegas this weekend?"

She sighed. "I can't, Blake. I have so much to get done before Monday."

The main thing she had to do was call John, but she also couldn't take time off work again. She didn't have her own business like Blake. He could do whatever he wanted.

"Sonny and Cher are going to be there," he said cajolingly. "I can get us front row seats."

"I can't, Blake. I'm sorry."

She heard the disappointment in his voice, but she couldn't help it. She had to make that phone call, and she had no way of knowing how she would respond after talking to John Patterson. Since Blake had extra clothes and luggage at his townhouse in Palm Springs, he told her he was going to leave for Vegas from there. She really hated to miss the trip. In all her travels, she'd never gotten the chance to see Vegas.

Okay, enough with the delays. It was time to face the music.

She opened the nightstand drawer and pulled out the phone number. Holy night, her stomach ached with fear already. She picked up the phone and slowly dialed. A man's voice answered.

"Is John Patterson in?"

"Yes, I'm John."

"Hi, John. My name is Beth Ann. You knew my fiancé, Kaylob Shawn O'Brien."

There was a long pause along with a nervous cough. "Thanks for calling me back, Beth Ann. I wanted to check in with you since I heard you had a very hard time of it for a while. I tried to get in touch with you last year, but I could never get you on the phone. I tried for months."

"Oh, I was on tour and gone for over six months."

"That's what I heard. How are you?"

"I'm better now."

Another pause. "Kaylob was a good man. He saved my life along with a lot of others. Is there anything you need or anything you'd like to ask me?"

"That's very nice of you to ask, John. Thank you, but I'm okay." She tried to sound upbeat. "I mean, things are going better in my life right now."

He cleared his throat. "So, you're sure you're okay then?"

What could she say? Hell no, she wasn't okay. The man she'd loved all her life was missing, and he kept coming to her in dreams and visions. Waking up sometimes in a jungle and not knowing how she got there. He would call the loony bin.

"Beth Ann, you still there? I'm sorry if my calling has upset you. I just wanted to be sure you were all right. Well, actually ... I hope this is okay to say, but I had a dream and Kaylob asked me to check on you. It felt so real. I know that sounds crazy."

"No," she said, struggling to breathe normally. "No, it doesn't sound crazy at all."

Could she tell him about her visions? Maybe Kaylob had reached out to him so she could have someone to tell what she had been going through.

"John, I need to share with you about some things that have been happening to me. I hope you won't think I'm crazy."

She told him everything, every detail and even about the word tra tan. She told him about the river, the mud, and the four trees, and even how one had a carving near the bottom that read 'Kaylob loves Beth Ann'. How on the very top of the mountain off to the east was a large wooden cross.

"The last time I had a vision, I saw a white pelican and could tell that the place looked like they'd hacked away at bamboo and made some sort of prison."

He went silent, and she had a feeling he thought she had lost it.

"I'm speechless right now and don't know what to say," he said. "The wooden cross on the mountainside is something I saw once while I was in Vietnam. I can't be sure it's the same one, but the white pelicans are common around the river."

She sighed deeply. "I know it sounds crazy, and maybe I am. I just thought—"

"No, you don't understand. I'm at a loss because some of the things you're describing are indigenous to Vietnam, and the fact that you heard the word tra tan, which means torture, is amazing. Can you tell me anything else about the area?"

"I heard more words in the last vision," she said, almost afraid to believe he didn't think she was insane.

"Beth Ann, can you tell me the words? I know the language pretty well."

"I wrote them down. Hold on and let me get them." She ran to get her purse and took the paper back to the phone. "The words were dine thing nagoc. I think that's how it's pronounced." A long, overstretched pause made her nervous, but she had to know.

"John, do you know what they mean?"

"Yes." He paused again, and she heard him sigh.

"Please tell me what they mean."

Another sigh followed. "It means crazy idiot. Beth Ann, are you sure you don't know the language?"

"The only language I know besides English is sign language, and very little of that. The only reason I knew the first word is my boyfriend speaks several languages and told me what it meant. I know you must think I'm nuts. Maybe I am."

"No, I don't think you're nuts. I'll tell you what. I'm going back over there. The description you gave me sounds very much like the place where we got ambushed. The water, the birds, a dog barking, and a wooden cross on the mountain. I'm going to check it out to see what I can do."

"When do you leave?" She was glad he believed her, but she felt sad that he was going back again.

"In two weeks. I'll call you before I leave."

She had to ask him one more thing, something she hadn't asked anyone else.

"John, do you think Kaylob could still be alive?"

"Sweetheart, I have no clue, but I do know he loved you. All he wanted to do was get back home to you. There wasn't a day that went by that he didn't mention his redhead back home."

Emotion moved through her. She tried unsuccessfully to keep it out of her voice, but John must have heard because he spent the next few minutes talking softly to her, murmuring words of comfort. He seemed like such a good guy, and she liked him already. After they said their goodbyes, she held the phone and stared at it a minute or so before placing it back in the holder.

She took a deep breath and tried to let go of all the resentment she still felt at the unfairness, all the pain, and anger hidden inside her. Hell, she was furious at everyone, but the army most of all. As far as she was concerned, they had given up on Kaylob way too soon. She hadn't realized how mad she was about it until she had to call John. Maybe the truth lived right in front of her, but she hadn't wanted to see it.

Those unhealthy emotions had prevented her from calling him right away. Now someone finally believed her, so how could she dare resent John for being alive? What kind of person feels bitterness at another human being for surviving? Kaylob would be so disappointed in her.

Jesus, she needed to push away the visions, dreams, and guilt. Kaylob had vanished, but she was still going through so much hell, and she was so tired of it. She couldn't even remember what it had been like to have a life that didn't hurt. To wake up in the morning and not feel sad.

She lay on the bed and thought about how it had been traveling with her family as a child, waking up in the car, never having a home while her dad chased his dreams. It hadn't been much of a life, but there had been bright spots. Cole would smile at her or make her laugh, and the entire world would light up. She needed to see her brother and feel his strong arms around her. She made up her mind to call him soon and ask him to come for a visit.

In the meantime, maybe going to Vegas with Blake was just what she needed. She'd go see Sonny and Cher and have fun and forget about all the anguish for a while at least. She could take Blake's private plane if it was available and surprise him when she got there.

She was on her way by early afternoon. Her excitement grew while she was on the plane, and she was practically buzzing by the time they landed in Vegas. When the limousine pulled up in front of the Sahara, she understood why it was so famous. The big neon sign lit up the sky and announced Sonny and Cher's appearance, and it made butterflies swarm in her stomach when she read it.

The driver took her to the front of the hotel and escorted her to the main door. When she stepped inside, she had to stop and take in the magnificence of the place. The sparkling chandeliers and the overall elegance was mind blowing. The front desk lined two walls, so she moved to the end of the line and waited her turn.

When she told the hotel clerk who she was and who she would be joining, he acted as if they had been expecting her. Probably because Blake had always been such a playboy and so many women had joined him throughout the years. The clerk rang Blake's room for her, but there was no answer.

"Excuse me for eavesdropping," said a female clerk at the other end of the desk, "but I saw Mr. Tanner going into the bar a little while ago." She pointed in that direction.

Beth Ann turned to look, and a sly idea blossomed. She'd surprise him in the bar and make him take her out for a night of fun, then bring her back for a night of passion. She smiled as she strolled through the busy lobby filled with the sound of bells and laughter that lit up with tons of flashing lights.

The bar was dimly lit with lots of mirrors that made it hard to see, so she stopped at the entrance to wait for her eyes to adjust. There were people talking loudly and men smoking cigars. It shocked her to see ladies dressed in outfits that showed off their breasts, and not just a little bit either. A tall blonde with a voluptuous figure in a tight red dress drew her attention, and recognition hit a second before the sirens pierced her thoughts.

The woman was standing next to Blake. Beth Ann froze, watching them while they continued to laugh and have a grand old time. When the woman's fingers combed through his hair, Beth Ann felt her temperature gauge start to climb. Blake didn't touch her back, but he sure as heck didn't remove her hand either.

With her face on fire, Beth Ann watched the obvious floozy keep touching Blake. She leaned over to get a straw and pressed her ample chest against Blake's arm. When she put her arm around him and whispered in his ear, it took all of Beth Ann's restraint not to pick up one of the liquor bottles from the bar and throw it at the back of Blake's head.

Luckily for Beth Ann's blood pressure and Blake's skull, he turned around and looked right at her, and he had the nerve to flash those damn dimples at her. He said something to the harlot and then walked over and kissed Beth Ann on the cheek.

"I'm so glad you came, darlin. What a nice surprise."

"Looks like I got here just in time," she said, glaring daggers at him. "Don't let me break up your important meeting."

He ignored her remark, which only made her madder. When he tried to put his arm around her waist, she wiggled loose and moved away from him. He didn't even flinch and just took her hand without a word, still smiling like nothing was wrong. Damn him.

"I was just about to go get something to eat. Let's go, darlin."

Too angry to even speak, Beth Ann followed him silently as they walked away from the lounge and went around the corner into the café. After the hostess seated them, Beth Ann continued to glare at Blake while she waited for him to explain, but he said nothing other than idle chatter about what he wanted to eat, which made her even more furious.

She was silent throughout the meal, but Blake rattled on about work and didn't seem to notice. At one point, he reached over to touch her hand and stroke her fingers, but she jerked them away. She thought of a very bad word to call him. One that started with ass and ended with hole.

This was not what Beth Ann had thought Vegas would be like, and she wanted to get up from the table and run back to Riverside. What a mistake it had been to come. Now she knew what he had been doing while he traveled. Guess he wasn't off the market after all, and maybe those magazines weren't so far off about him seeing other women. Kaylob would never have done such a thing. He had always been true blue all the way, and Blake was nothing like him.

Finally, she couldn't take it anymore and said, "Can I have the key to the room? I'm tired and I want to go to bed early."

"Sure, darlin. Let's go."

"Sure you don't want to go back into the bar and finish your tall drink of blonde?"

His smile looked a little off, and she guessed he finally knew he was caught. Then he let out a little laugh as they walked to the elevator, all the while behaving as if there was nothing wrong. He even whistled.

Beth Ann's arms crossed over her chest as she glared at his obliviousness while they were in the elevator, but he didn't say a word. How could he not notice how upset she was? Did that hussy's boobs have a built-in stupid beam that had made him clueless?

When he opened the door to the room, she took an exaggerated step back. "Are you sure there's not some evidence you want hide from me first? Maybe I should wait at the door while you run in and check to make sure you don't have any more big boobs hiding under the bed."

He just smiled and motioned for her to come in. "After you, my love."

She tried very hard not to notice the beauty of the suite. It was enormous, with every plush trimming you could think of, with wall-to-ceiling windows that revealed the spectacular view of the city. A marble-topped bar lined with white wood stood against the far wall.

Then she noticed Blake was chuckling.

"What's so funny?" She felt her face heating up again.

Instead of answering, he rocked back on his heels and held his stomach in laughter. "Darlin, is there something you want to say?"

"No. What would I have to say other than I hope you enjoyed letting some woman Velcro her body all over you while she pawed at your hair. I have nothing to else to say to you, Blake Tanner."

She was done. She wanted to go home and get as far away from him as possible. He could have his tall blonde with the obscene chest. She picked up her suitcase that had been delivered.

Blake laughed again. "What are you doing, darlin?"

"I'm going home. You can stay here and laugh your ass off all you want."

He took the bag from her hand and smiled. "Okay, I have a confession to make. I knew you were coming hours ago. I get notified every time someone uses the private jet. I even saw you walk in the door looking for me. I was just about to tell her I was taken when I decided to see what you would do. You've never showed any jealousy before, so I wanted to see if you even cared what I did."

She folded her arms again. "Well, it worked, so you must be ecstatic. Goody for you. You made me jealous, so let's throw a party."

He didn't laugh, but he still looked way too amused for her taste.

"Listen, Mr. Blake Tanner. I'm angrier than I've been in… I can't even remember when. I have half a mind to dropkick you off the balcony. Enjoy the results of your manipulation. I hope it keeps you warm tonight." She snatched the suitcase back from him and headed toward the door.

"Wait, wait. Don't leave. I'm sorry. I won't ever do it again."

She stopped, but then he let a chuckle slip out. She turned and narrowed her eyes at him.

"You don't look sorry. All you're doing is laughing and acting like an asshole. You want to feel sorry, watch me walk out the door."

She grabbed the doorknob, but before she could twist it, he put his hand over hers and stopped her.

"Beth Ann, I'm sorry. I couldn't help myself. It just felt so good to see you get jealous and… I can't believe you called me an asshole. Such language, me oh my. I think I'm getting the vapors." He placed his hand over his heart as though he were in shock. "I've never heard you say words like that before."

"I never called you an asshole. I said you were acting like one."

"What was I thinking, making a redhead angry?" He took her hand off the knob and held it in both of his. "I'll admit I loved it, but I promise it won't happen again. I don't blame you for being mad, but it was so cute to see you finally get jealous."

She felt her anger receding. "It better not happen again, or some temptress might lose her hand next time. By the way, mister, why did you think you needed to test me?"

He let go of her hand and straightened his tie. "I guess I just needed to know you cared."

"Okay, now you know, but you're in the doghouse."

"I know, but it was worth it. You are so damn cute."

Was he crazy? Didn't he know her well enough to realize he had just stepped on a verbal land mine.

"Cute?"

Blake looked puzzled while she continued seething at his word choice.

"I'm cute compared to that bimbo? Did you see her chest?"

He put up his hands and shook his head. "No, of course not. I never even noticed."

Well, he clearly wasn't dumb after all. He proved that by his answer.

Chapter Thirty-Five

After three days of Vegas action, excitement, and loud noises, Beth Ann was ready to go home. The highlight of her trip was seeing Sonny and Cher. Going backstage to meet them was even more of a thrill then she could have ever imagined.

On her way home she realized that her past fear of flying didn't bother her in Blake's private jet, and she even enjoyed the thrill. They landed in Ontario, then were driven back home, and she relished the quiet time with Blake.

A week after they got home from Vegas, Beth Ann walked into the kitchen to find the most recent issue of Starlight magazine with the rest of the mail on the kitchen table. A picture of her with Carol was plastered across the front page. They were walking out of school, laughing with their arms entwined. The headline read 'Bachelor's lovely redhead butters her bread on both sides?'

Beth Ann stared at the magazine and then slammed it down on the table. Why in the world would they care which side of her bread she buttered? How stupid could they be? God, they must really be hard up for stories to write about something so meaningless. She left it on the table for Blake to see then continued to go through the rest of the mail.

As soon as he walked into the kitchen, she handed him the magazine. "Can you believe they care about how I butter my toast?"

He looked from the magazine to her face, and it was obvious he was trying not to laugh.

"You think it's funny?" She sighed and turned to walk away, but he wrapped his arms around her and kissed her neck.

"Ah, darlin, you're just so damn cute." He chuckled and turned her around to face him.

She squirmed, but he wouldn't let her go, and his hands began moving in a way that made her body tingle. She forgot all about the toast and the article. Since Blake had the morning off, it was Beth Ann who was late for work this time.

Later that afternoon when she got home, she found Blake had put away the rest of the things from her old apartment that had been sitting in the same spot in their spare room for months. The only boxes he left unpacked were the ones labeled Kaylob, which brought on a wave of loneliness. Blake was wonderful, but he hadn't stopped the pain that lived deep inside her. He filled a void in her heart, but it didn't keep her from missing her true love. Dread filled her as she pulled up the lid on one of the boxes, afraid to even peek at the contents.

She could do this. She needed to do this.

Cautiously, she stuck her hand inside without looking and gasped when her fingers touched weeds and mud. Once again, everything faded. The temperature shot up to tropical, and sweat formed on her back. The revolting air swirled with a thick, nauseating smoke that made her head spin. She heard the dog barking off in the distance and saw the pelican watching her. She wanted to go to the trees, but the smoke got thicker. Jesus, that god-awful smell made her want to throw up. Her stomach churned and finally erupted.

Vomit went everywhere. The jungle vanished, and she was again standing in the spare room. Tears burned her eyes, and not just from being upset. They stung from the smoke that had filled the air. Before she could move away from the mess, she heard a gasp behind her.

Dana stood in the doorway with her hand over her mouth. What the hell would she tell her this time? The only thing she could do was lie. She was getting really good at that.

"Oh, Dana, I think I must have the flu. What a mess I've made. I need to clean this up."

"No, you go to bed. I'll call and have maintenance take care of it." Dana helped her to the stairs. "Can I get you anything, Miss Beth Ann? How about if I bring you up some Seven-Up and some chicken soup?"

Beth Ann smiled. "Sure, that would be great."

Now she had to act sick, but that wouldn't be hard since she was still nauseated from that horrible smell. She wasn't sure what it had been, but she guessed it was the stench of death.

She had to talk to someone about it, so she called John Patterson. A woman answered the phone.

"Hi, my name is Beth Ann. Is John there by any chance?"

"Oh, sure. Hold on, Beth Ann."

She heard the woman call his name and then the phone being picked up.

"Hello, Beth Ann," he said. "What a nice surprise. I didn't expect to hear from you so soon."

"John, I needed to tell you about another vision. I hope you don't mind me calling. I don't have anybody else to talk to about it."

"Of course I don't mind. What happened?"

"I was in the jungle again, and this time I ended up getting sick. There was this awful smell and smoke. This is so hard for me to say, but it smelled like ... death. Don't ask me how I know that, but I do. I know it sounds crazy."

He cleared his throat. "No, it doesn't. I've seen a lot of strange things happen in my life, so you can't rule anything out. I just don't want you putting your life on hold waiting for something that might not even be real. You deserve to move on, Beth Ann. It's been a long time, and they did find Kaylob's dog tags and his boot."

"Then why do I keep seeing these things?"

He sighed. "I don't know. Maybe he's trying to tell you something. I promise I'll check into it like I told you before."

They spent a long time on the phone talking about Kaylob, and when she hung up, she knew something for certain from what she'd heard in John's voice. He had no hope that Kaylob was still alive. She realized he was right, and she needed to move on. She just didn't know how she was supposed to do it.

There had to be something that could take her mind off Kaylob. Her new goal was to find out what it was. She would get busy, take up mountain climbing, swimming, hiking, anything. She picked up the phone to call Blake and heard the bedroom door open.

"Dana said you were sick." Blake stood in the doorway looking pale and worried.

"I just have the flu. It's nothing serious."

His eyes showed something more than worry, and it almost seemed like anger. He didn't touch her, and he stayed across the room. What was wrong with him? She stood up to look at him.

"Are you going to say something or just stand there staring at me?"

He still didn't answer.

"Blake."

He glared at her. "When were you going to tell me about these visions? Or did you have any intention of telling me you were talking to someone about searching for Kaylob?"

Oh, shit. He must have overheard her conversation with John. Now she could see hurt in his eyes along with worry.

"I didn't want you to worry," she said in almost a whisper.

He ran his fingers through his hair and clenched his jaw. "Too damn bad. I'm goddamn worried about all of it. What visions were you talking about— new ones? Who was this person you were talking to and how long have you been at this?"

"Blake, please—"

"Don't argue with me, Beth Ann. I want you to see someone. You need to get this out of your system. You're living with me, but you're still obsessed with your dead fiancé. Kaylob is always there, the third person between us. I'm fed up."

Her heart told her he was right. How could she expect him to put up with a ghost? Kaylob wasn't there. He was either gone or missing, and as hard as it was for her to think that, she had to face it. Maybe she did need to see someone. It just wasn't fair at all.

"You're right," she said. "I need to let go and move on. I love you and want to get over this. I want the visions to stop, and if it happens one more time, I promise to get help. I'm so sorry, Blake. I know I shouldn't have kept this from you, but I didn't want you to think I was crazy." She plopped back down on the bed and grabbed the pillow, clutching it for dear life.

For a minute he just stood there taking in what she had said. At last, he walked over and sat down on the bed beside her and took her hand. "I'm glad you agree. I've been struggling with three of us in this relationship for a long time. Now, will you tell me about these new visions?"

She told him everything, right down to why she had thrown up. When she finished, he wrapped his arms around her and held her tightly, stroking her hair. How in the world could she not be in love with this man? He was so supportive and kind. How did she get so lucky? A lot of women never found one good man, and she had been blessed with two.

Chapter Thirty-Six

The next weeks blew by with no visions or dreams. The end of October approached, and they had a small celebration with a few friends and family members for her birthday. Blake spoiled her as usual and bought her a diamond and tourmaline necklace with matching earrings and a bracelet. He also lavished her with a pink mohair sweater that had authentic pearl buttons. She made sure to show him that night just how much she loved what he had done for her.

Something seemed to shift after that between Beth Ann and Blake, and she felt they had a deeper connection with mutual respect. They moved into a settled life, and in her heart she knew they would be together for a long time. Nothing would ever be as beautiful as her life with Kaylob, but what she and Blake had was remarkable in another way.

November marched in and so did chilly weather in Riverside. One Sunday afternoon, Blake and Beth Ann were watching a show on TV about a dad and his son. Blake turned down the volume with the clicker while Beth Ann enjoyed the foot rub he was giving her.

"I hope we have one of each when we have kids," he said with a wink.

Uh-oh. She'd been dreading this conversation. It had been hard to tell Kaylob that she never wanted children, but she'd made it clear. Kaylob loved kids, but she told him he could get some himself if he wanted them.

Blake must have felt her tense. "What's the matter?"

"Blake, I know we never talked about this. I don't want children."

"But you work with children," he said. "I thought you loved those kids."

"I do. I love them because they're not mine. They go home every night to their parents, and I get to come home to peace, quiet, and our life."

"You don't ever want children?"

She shook her head. "No, never."

He was quiet for a long time, and she could tell her announcement affected him. He stared blankly at the program, obviously not watching anything. When the show ended, he clicked it off and turned to her.

"I've always wanted children, but I want your happiness more. I can go without." He paused a moment. "Plus you might change your mind someday, right?"

"Kaylob always said that too, but I don't think so."

He let out a long, defeated sigh. "I know Kaylob was a part of your life for a long time, and I know you'll always love him, but does he always have to be part of our conversations? Like I said before, I feel like he's in the room with us most of the time."

She couldn't deny anything he'd said, and she knew it needed to stop for Blake's sake and for her own. She wondered if there would ever be a day when just saying Kaylob's name wouldn't be so painful or he wasn't always in her thoughts. At least the visions had become less frequent, but in some odd way that disturbed her and she wondered why.

She remembered something important about one of the visions she definitely wasn't going to tell Blake. When she'd gazed through the window of the abandoned building, she had seen a little girl, and there was no doubt the child had been hers and Kaylob's. It had only been a vision of what their life might have been like, yet there had been a child.

"You're right, Blake. I'm sorry. I know you guys never liked each other, so I appreciate how good you've been about me bringing him up and dealing with all the things I've gone through. It's getting better, but I'll try harder not to mention him." She put her hand on his face. "I love you, Blake. You mean so very much to me."

He touched her lips lightly with his finger. "I love you, too. You know, I don't think you've heard about all the history between Kaylob and me. I lost my cool with him more than once, and I told him to fu ... to screw off a couple of times too."

"Are you serious?" She pulled back to look at his face.

"Serious as Watergate."

"What happened?"

"Are you sure you want to hear it?"

She nodded.

"Our run-ins happened a lot," he said, "but there was this one time when I genuinely wanted to deck him. You don't know how many times I watched you cry and wait for him. For five years he strung you along. Anyway, at your Sweet Sixteen party, I found out he still hadn't asked you to be his girl. That's why I thought you might be tired of waiting for him and want me."

"Do you know why he didn't ask me to be his girl?"

He sighed. "I know it had something to do with a promise, but that's all."

"Yes it did, but it wasn't just a promise he made to himself. He was forced, or should I say coerced, by Cole not to touch me until I was twenty or we were married."

His eyebrows shot up. "Really? I didn't know that. I could see how Kaylob wouldn't want to break a promise to Cole. Your brother would've pounded him into the ground."

"Maybe, but Kaylob didn't keep the promise because of threats. He kept it because he had integrity. He gave Cole his word." Her voice trembled and she tried to hide it with a cough.

"Well, anyway," he said, "the night of your birthday party, I was standing out back when I heard you and Kaylob come outside, so I hid behind the old oak tree. I saw you reaching out to him. At first he pulled you into his arms and kissed your forehead, then he moved you away from him. The expression on your face broke my heart."

She had been sure that would be the night Kaylob asked her to go steady, but she'd had no clue anyone else knew. That party had been full of fun but also full of disappointment, because Kaylob had never asked her to be his girl.

"You went back inside, but Kaylob stayed in the yard. I was so angry when I stepped out from behind the tree that I let him have it. I called him an asshole and a few other names. He calmly told me he wasn't trying to be an asshole, but I wasn't having it. I told him he didn't deserve you and pushed him. I think the guy was channeling Billy Jack or something, because he remained so calm. He said he couldn't tell me his reasons for making you wait, but that he was deeply in love with you. He said something about a promise. Then he went back inside."

This was all new information to her, and she felt tears stinging her eyes. No wonder Kaylob had always been so jealous of Blake. This made everything clearer to her.

"He said you were his universe, that without you he wouldn't have wanted to be born. What kind of guy walks away like that after I'd pushed him around and swore at him? That's when I knew he was a standup guy. Of course, that just made me hate him even more since I could never compare to him."

The emotional confession brought them both to tears. She could see how difficult it was for Blake to both hate and respect Kaylob, and his openness about it gave her a newfound respect for him.

"You may not be like Kaylob, but you're a wonderful man, Blake. I love who you are."

"Thank you, darlin. To be honest, it was his words that changed my life. I knew I couldn't be the kind of man he was, but I knew I could change and become a better person. He inspired me."

Beth Ann couldn't stop the tears spilling down her cheeks at the thought that Kaylob would never know he had inspired the one person he'd hated. Her relationship with Blake deepened after his confession, and she loved him more.

Despite how fantastic Blake was, the hole in her heart from losing Kaylob remained.

Chapter Thirty-Seven

The dreams came again that night. Beth Ann woke up crying, and once again Blake held and rocked her while he wiped away the tears. She wondered how many men would put up with this. She wanted to stop, but how did you stop dreams that haunted you?

"Darlin, you okay?"

She cuddled closer as he stroked her hair. "I'm better now in your arms."

"I love you so much, Beth Ann. I wish I could take away all your pain."

"Me too."

His touch was warm and tender as he brushed the hair out of her eyes. He held her that way until she fell asleep again.

The next morning, he spoke about her seeing someone, and she promised she would after the holidays. A little later, Beth Ann's mom called and begged her to come down for Stanley's birthday party since she hadn't been home to Novato in over two years. With those words from her mom, Beth Ann knew it was time to go back. Hearing the excitement in her mom's voice when she agreed made it worth it.

Blake's company plane wasn't available, so they would go commercial. While they were packing, Beth Ann made sure the ring from Kaylob was safely in her suitcase and ready to take back to his family. Before she could finish packing, Blake handed her a new suitcase designed in a floral print.

"What's this?" she asked.

"I bought it just for you, darlin. Look inside and see how much space there is."

She unzipped it, and there was a small box inside. He was always buying her gifts and hiding them like that. She sighed and looked up at him, and she noticed how nervous he looked. What had he done?

She opened the box, and her heart skipped a beat when she saw what it held—a beautiful ring with the biggest diamond she had ever seen. There was also a note, and when she looked at him, he nodded for her to read it.

My love,

You don't have to say yes, but please keep the ring and think about it for a few days. I love you with all my heart and would love for you to marry me. You have my heart, and I want to spend my life with you.

Love always,
Blake

She held the note and the ring with Blake watching her, wondering what she was going to say. Spending her life with him would be wonderful, but what about Kaylob? There had been no word on him from John, and she wondered if they would ever find his body. After so much time, she knew she should accept he was more than likely gone, but how could she just give up on him? Marrying Blake wouldn't take away her love for Kaylob, but it would still feel like a betrayal to her. Kaylob had told her to love again, but she didn't think he'd meant with Blake.

When she looked up at Blake and saw the tears pooling in his beautiful blue eyes, there was no way she could hurt him by telling him no. She wrapped her arms around his neck.

"Yes, Blake."

"Tell me I'm not dreaming," he said ecstatically. "You did say yes, right? You'll marry me?"

"Yes, I said yes," she said with a laugh.

He picked her up and swung her around, then he swept the suitcases off the bed. They made love to a point that they almost missed their plane.

Of course, the paparazzi followed them to the airport, snapping pictures the whole time. A few of them even yelled out about the ring on her finger. Figuring it would be news soon, they decided to announce their engagement themselves as soon as they got to Novato. They found out later that the jeweler had tipped off the paparazzi, no doubt for a good-sized fee.

Beth Ann's mom had always liked Blake and seemed very happy about the news. She gave them both a big hug when they told her. "When's the date?"

Beth Ann laughed. "No date yet, Mom. We just got engaged a couple hours ago."

Blake smiled. "Well, I was hoping for Valentine's Day, but I'll settle for whatever date Beth Ann wants."

"Valentine's Day sounds nice." Beth Ann tried to sound happier than she felt.

Before she could think about wedding plans, there was something she had to do, and she had to do it now before they read about her engagement in the papers.

It was time to go see Kaylob's parents.

Jean told Beth Ann she could use her car. Blake was out back with Stanley fixing the fence, so she walked out to tell him she was going.

He wrapped his arms around her. "Are you sure about this?"

"Yes, it's time." She kissed him and said goodbye.

Driving over, she noticed the neighborhood looked the same. The oak tree in front of Kaylob's house hadn't changed. Even the fence Kaylob had painted still had the same paint. A knot formed in her stomach as soon as she pulled into the driveway. Memories lived everywhere, and she wasn't so sure she was ready for this after all. Her legs felt like lead as she got out of the car and walked up to the door.

She knocked and heard shuffles inside. The door opened, and Kaylob's dad Harold stood there with a soft smile on his face.

"Oh, Beth Ann," he said. "It's been too long."

"Who is it, dear?" Kaylob's mom called from the kitchen. When Jackie came out and saw Beth Ann, her hand went over her mouth as she tried unsuccessfully to push back the sobs. Beth Ann swallowed her own tears. After a lengthy hug, Jackie stopped.

"I just wanted to come over and see how you guys were doing, and, well..." She reached into her purse and pulled out the box that held Kaylob's ring. "I wanted to return this to where it belongs."

Jackie took it from her and wiped her eyes with her apron. She glanced meaningfully at the ring on Beth Ann's finger. "You're engaged?"

Beth Ann nodded and looked at the floor. She felt Harold's hand on her shoulder and then Jackie cupped her face in her hands and made her look at them.

"We know how much you loved Kaylob, and we understand you have to go on with your life. We're happy for you, Beth Ann. I know this is what Kaylob would've wanted."

Harold cleared his throat. "Who's the lucky guy?"

"Blake Tanner."

"Blake?" Jackie did her best to smile. "Does he treat you good, sweetheart?"

Beth Ann nodded. "Yes, very."

Jackie hugged her again. "Then I'm happy for you. We love you, Beth Ann. We want your happiness."

Beth Ann couldn't hold back her tears. "I'll never love anyone the way I loved Kaylob. Blake knows I love him, but I think he understands it will never be like my love for Kaylob. I can't give what I no longer have."

Jackie took her into the living room, and they both sat on the couch. Being there felt like stepping back in time to Beth Ann. Everything looked exactly the same as when Kaylob was growing up, except for one corner of the room that seemed to beckon her. She stared at it a few moments, then she got up, and walked slowly over to it.

Jackie and Harold had made a shrine to Kaylob. Beth Ann's hand gently brushed over the tightly folded United States flag encased in glass, then she carefully picked up the framed picture of him in his uniform. Surrounding the picture were other snapshots and trinkets, reminders of a son lost way too soon and who happened to be the love of her life.

She picked up one of the photos as if fearing she would awaken dormant spirits. The photo showed Kaylob and Beth Ann in front of the pool hall, and she remembered what a fun day it had been. They had hung out with all their friends, gone to the movies, and eaten pizza.

"This was the first time he held my hand, and the first time I fell asleep in his arms," she whispered.

The memory made her feel queasy, and her body started to tremble. Nausea ambushed her and she took a deep breath, trying to ease her stomach.

Jackie walked over and carefully guided her back to the couch. "Are you all right, dear? Can I get you some water?"

"I'll be okay. It's just … I haven't seen a picture of him in such a long time."

Beth Ann swallowed hard, trying to fight the nausea. No way did she want to throw up in front of them.

Harold got her some water, and she put a mint in her mouth to soothe her stomach. It seemed like forever before she could regain her composure.

Jackie gave Beth Ann's hand a gentle squeeze. "He was so lucky to have had your love."

"To have my love," Beth Ann corrected. "It's never going to be gone. I'll love him forever and a day and then some."

Beth Ann knew they were worried because of her breakdown. Everyone was still walked on eggshells around her, afraid she would slip back into the pits of hell.

She changed the subject and asked them about old friends they had in common. After a few minutes of catching up, she knew it was time to say goodbye. Being at Kaylob's house reminded her too much of what she had lost, and she had to get out of there before she fell apart in front of his parents.

As she drove away, Beth Ann glanced in her rearview mirror and caught sight of Jackie waving goodbye. When she turned the corner, she had to pull off the road when she saw the train station. She folded her arms over the steering wheel and laid her head down with her eyes closed. She had no choice but to bid her entire childhood with Kaylob farewell.

The crying began as memories took her back. All around her, shadows of their lost love danced in her mind. She and Kaylob holding hands, sharing an ice cream, herself laughing while climbing on his back, all their sweet kisses.

Tears drenched her cheeks and she whimpered. "Oh, Kaylob."

"Beth Ann, I will love you forever and a day."

Her eyes flew open and she glanced around. Oh, God, she was hearing his voice again. That was it. She had to see someone the minute she got back home.

For almost an hour, she sat there deep in thought. Had she made the right decision to marry Blake? Would it be fair to him if she was never able to love him like she did Kaylob? Could it ever be just the two of them in the marriage?

Oh, for God's sake, of course she had to marry him. No way could she hurt him by changing her mind. In time she would grow to love him almost as much as she loved Kaylob. Wouldn't she?

She'd forever be attached to Novato, the town she and Kaylob shared. Novato was the place their hearts had embraced and would always tug restlessly at her fraying heart strings.

At last, she made it back to her mom's. It must have been obvious that she had been crying, because Jean wrapped her arms around her daughter.

"You okay, honey?"

Beth Ann nodded, looking around for Blake. "It was harder than I thought it would be."

"I can only imagine, sweetheart. The men are still out back working on that fence." She motioned toward the kitchen. "Why don't we go get some sun tea and talk?"

Her mom poured two glasses and set them on the table. Beth Ann loved her mom's tea, it was always so tasty. She took a drink, then she spilled her guts about the doubts she was having.

Jean took her hand. "Honey, all love is different. Kaylob was your first love, and that's always more intense. Just like your daddy was mine. They're always special."

"Daddy was your first love? I didn't know that. It must have been hard for you to leave him. I could never have left Kaylob."

Jean looked into her daughter's eyes. "Yes, it was very hard, and I'm not a hundred percent sure I'll ever stop loving him completely, but I had to put my children first. I had to move on."

Beth Ann held her mother's gaze. "So you're telling me it's time for me to move on."

Jean squeezed her hand. "Yes, honey."

"I understand, Mom," Beth Ann said. "I know you're right."

Jean took a long sip of her tea. "It's time to let go, but I'm not saying you should or shouldn't marry Blake. Only you can make that choice."

Beth Ann nodded. "I'm going to marry Blake on Valentine's Day. I do love him, Mom."

Jean got up and walked over to the cabinet. "How about we take those boys some tea so they'll stop drinking all that beer?"

They both laughed in spite of the sadness and headed out back. Beth Ann's mind was made up. She loved Blake and was determined that they would have a good life together.

The rest of that winter weekend in Novato brought some subtle ripples of uneasiness when everyone found out she was marrying Blake. Beth Ann knew it was hard for them to think of her with anyone but Kaylob. She was glad they had Stanley's birthday celebration to distract everyone. They were all happy to see Beth Ann smiling again, and that's all that seemed to matter. When the weekend ended, she felt she was finally leaving the past behind and moving into her new life.

When their return flight landed, Beth Ann and Blake spent the drive back from the Ontario airport talking about wedding plans. They had decided to go somewhere electric, where they could have fun dancing the night away and watching Broadway shows. Of course it had to be Chicago where they'd spent their first night together.

As the weeks rolled by and they got caught up more in the wedding plans, Beth Ann realized she would probably never hear from John Patterson regarding Kaylob. She would find a way to focus on what she had now. She heard Blake taking a shower that morning when it hit—a chill from her heart all the way to her spine. Once again she felt Kaylob and felt him strong.

Oh God, it wasn't over. In that moment she knew it was never going to end. She would just have to learn to live with it and try to hide everything from everyone.

Chapter Thirty-Eight

Kaylob couldn't believe he was still alive and was sure each day would be his last. He had hung on longer than he expected. At first he had only wanted to get back home to his Beth Ann, but he had a pretty good idea that she had probably moved on by now, which gave him one less reason to try. Taking one last pain-filled breath would be a release. The afterlife had to be better than here.

As he lay on the ground trying to eat his rotting food, he listened to the sound once again of a dog barking. It sounded like the same dog he'd heard for a long time. For some reason, the barking sounded fiercer today, making Kaylob wonder if the poor animal was suffering too.

He was outside in the cold, dank squalor, on the ground by the same tree he now considered his tombstone. That was why he'd carved *Kaylob loves Beth Ann*, so someone would know he had been there.

Asleep and awake were so similar he never knew which state he was in. He hallucinated at night and dreamed throughout the day. His thoughts were fragmented, his body fractured. The only thing clear to him was the knowledge he was no longer a whole man. Sometime later, maybe noon or maybe in the dead of night, he felt hands tugging at him and heard alarmed whispers like distant echoes ricocheting off his dulled brain cells. Maybe the guards were dragging him away to a killing field like they did some of the other sick GIs.

Kaylob couldn't bring himself to care. The blurs that followed left him dizzy and nauseated, and he just wanted it to stop. He heard automatic weapons firing, people screaming, and what sounded like Grunts. His body was jostled and it felt like there were needles piercing his bony arms and thighs.

He faded in and out and had flashes of blinding lights, warm blankets, and muffled voices. His complete helplessness combined with the struggle of straddling life and death caused him to zone out.

Wait, was someone placing him on a litter? Did that mean he was dead? Either that or he was delusional. It felt like he was being rescued, but he couldn't allow himself to even hope.

Was that the sound of Hueys?

He blacked out again, and in his next moments of clarity, he heard a voice speaking English and he knew it was an American because the Southern drawl was unmistakable. Could he really be getting rescued and going home? Dare he dream that he would see his Beth Ann and family again?

Someone leaned over him, and a voice in the darkness shouted over the Huey blades. "It's okay, soldier. You're gonna be fine. We're gettin' you to a 2E a couple clicks from here. Man, it's good to see y'all alive."

Dear God, it was true. He was being rescued.

Tears ran down his cheeks as someone spoke to him again. "You're safe, soldier." He felt a hand touch his shoulder. "You're going home."

Before he faded out again, he mumbled "Beth Ann, baby, I'm coming home."

* * * *

John Patterson felt apprehensive as his troops arrived in a tank along with four others behind them. They had to do a sweep on a rescue that had taken place at 2300 hours the night before and make sure there were no soldiers left behind. They had been told the Cong had fled, but not before the US troops had killed more than a dozen of them. The idiots weren't following the release of POWs in Operation Homecoming. You never knew what you might be walking into. These Cong weren't like the ones in Northern Vietnam. They just kept the prisoners and hid out.

Patterson could see the troops leaning over the dead bodies and collecting the dog tags. They had to get the soldiers identified and home to their families. He saw a guy holding a clipboard and recognized him from boot camp, so he climbed out of the tank and walked swiftly over to him.

"Hey, Hunter, good to see you." They shook hands. "Got names and a count there?"

"Good to see you, Patterson. We got seven that made it out alive, and so far we've recovered fifteen bodies, one without tags. We've scanned the entire area."

Patterson nodded and looked around. Something about the place seemed familiar—the trees, the river, and the sound of a dog barking. Then it hit him and his stomach twisted into a knot. This was exactly like the place Beth Ann had described. He looked off to the east and saw a wooden cross up on a hill. After the last conversation he'd had with her, he'd thought she was losing her mind, but hell, this was the goddamn place.

Hunter touched his shoulder. "Patterson, you okay, man? You look like you've seen a ghost."

Patterson walked over to a group of four trees. Jesus H. Christ, it was unbelievable. He bent down and ran his hand across it. *Kaylob loves Beth Ann.*

"What is it?" Hunter said from behind him. He leaned down and looked at the carving. "Shit, did you know this guy?"

Patterson yanked the clipboard from Hunter's hand and looked for Kaylob's name, but it wasn't listed. "Goddamn it, he was here. Look at the tree. Where's the guy with no dog tags?"

"Right over there." Hunter pointed. "He's a short black guy about 5' 6". Looks like he's about twenty-eight or so."

Patterson shook his head. "Kaylob was over six feet tall. That's not him." He hung his head and looked at the carving on the tree again. "Man, I hate to call Beth Ann, but I need to let her know. He was here, but he's gone."

"Sorry, Patterson," Hunter said. "Did you know him well?"

Patterson nodded. "Yeah, he saved my life and about ten others. His name was Kaylob Shawn O'Brien." He pointed at the tree. "Beth Ann is the girl he left behind, his childhood sweetheart. I have to call her to let her know he didn't make it. She was hoping he might still be alive."

"Man, that's tough. I wish we could have found him in time. Sounds like Kaylob was some kind of hero."

Patterson nodded again. "Hero and good friend."

Damn, Kaylob had been there just like Beth Ann had said. He'd been alive, for a while at least. Should he tell her about the tree, or would that make it worse? He would have to think about that. Right now they had to retrieve the bodies and gather the burned remains so they could be identified. That way they could get home to their families. He wished he could at least do that for Kaylob.

They spent the day combing the area once more, but they found no more bodies. Kaylob Shawn O'Brien had died, but they'd never know how. Patterson hated what he had to do when he got back to camp, but it had to be done. He went to see his commander and explained why he had to get to a phone. Commander Jackson told him that it might take some time, maybe even weeks, but he would do his best to help.

Patterson thanked him and was almost glad for the delay. He was in no big hurry to break Beth Ann's heart all over again.

* * * *

Kaylob lay in a hospital in Vietnam, fighting for his life. Pain ravaged his body from his head to his toes. He had to fight even harder to live so he could make it home to Beth Ann. The line between awake and asleep was still blurry, and voices all around him drifted in and out of his consciousness.

As the hours went by, parts of his brain slowly switched back on. Voices started to make sense. The downside to this was the return of the debilitating pain, intermittently replaced with narcotic numbness. The plus side was that the numbness no longer clouded his thoughts. He wasn't dreaming and wasn't delusional. He was rescued.

He fell asleep and woke to a nurse shaving his face while humming a song. His eyes opened and blinked at her.

"Hey, blue eyes. You're awake," the nurse said.

He strained to speak. "Beth Ann … tell her …"

She smiled and finished shaving him. "Nope, I'm not Beth Ann, but whoever she is, she's one lucky gal."

After his shave, she began sponging him down. The warm water brought wisps of memories of Beth Ann washing him. God, he missed her touch.

He dozed again and woke later to find the same nurse looking at him curiously. Shit, he sure as hell hoped nothing had come back alive while she'd sponged him down. His mind was giving him clearer thoughts and allowed him to make out more of her face. She had dark green eyes and a stunning smile. Seeing a pretty face after enduring such horrible ugliness made him appreciate beauty so much more.

"Are you awake, Private First Class Connolly?"

"Who?"

"Connolly, Matthew T," she replied.

"No, ma'am. I'm Sgt. Kaylob O'Brien. Connolly didn't make it." He blinked back the tears.

"Oh." The nurse looked both surprised and alarmed. "You get some rest. I'll go talk to personnel and get this straightened out."

"Wait, Nurse?"

"Yes?"

"How long have I been here?"

"Fifteen days. You go on and get some rest now ya hear, sweetie?" She headed hastily for the double doors.

Fifteen days. He took a deep breath and struggled to stay awake, but the drugs were stronger than he was. His last conscious thought was no one at home knew he was alive.

* * * *

The next time Kaylob woke, he found a sergeant with a clipboard anxiously staring back at him.

"Sgt. O'Brien?" he said, glancing down at his clipboard then back to Kaylob.

"Kaylob Shawn, one each," he replied, trying to lighten the mood.

"I'm Sgt. Robert Smith, Army Personnel. I've tracked down your files. You were classified as KIA/BNR, but we've reclassified you as POW recovered. Now if we—"

"Sergeant, listen," Kaylob interrupted. "I'm still a little fuzzy upstairs. Can you explain the acronyms slowly please?"

"Damn, sorry about that. I'm not used to these types of circumstances. Okay, you were a Prisoner of War, then the Army declared you first as Missing in Action, then Killed in Action/Body Not Recovered. It was documented that your..."—he looked down at the clipboard—"bloody dog tags were found embedded in a boot." When you arrived here, it was assumed you were PFC Connolly who was classified as MIA and then reclassified as a POW. Intel from several recons found the camp where you were being held and ID'd you as Connolly before the Gooks bugged out. His dog tags were found on you."

Kaylob nodded. "I took them off his body so I could return them to his family. What does all that mean now, Sergeant?"

"What it means, Sgt. O'Brien, is that we have to bring you back to life administratively."

The way he said back to life would have been funny if it were happening to someone else. They had to crosscheck his fingerprints with his personnel files, then after more questions and at least three hundred forms that had to be filled out, in triplicate, Sgt. Smith told Kaylob he'd notify Mortuary Affairs to get the ball rolling on his reinstatement. In the meantime, he was officially dead as far as the Army was concerned.

After another week, the Army finally got their act together. The nurse who'd been taking care of him notified him his parents were going to be contacted via the Red Cross and informed he was alive. He should be going stateside any day.

When she gave him the good news, his hand reached for hers to thank her. After all he'd been through, the kindness she had shown him made her seem like an angel of mercy.

He was glad the Red Cross was going to contact his family for him even though they had been having issues getting in touch with his parents. He wouldn't have known what to say or how to say it. His mind was still too messed up, and the jarring nightmares made him nervous about facing the outside world. His rescue from hell was followed with being dropped into everyone else's reality, and he pictured the mountain of obstacles he'd have to overcome in order to fit in again. All the rules he'd needed to survive as a prisoner, to survive period, weren't the same back in the real world, but he decided he wouldn't let what he'd been through chart his present or guide his future.

"Nurse, could I see a shrink? I need to talk."

She looked at the chart hanging from the foot of the bed. "Dr. Stein is scheduled to see you tomorrow at 1300. He'll be able to talk to you."

In the meantime, Kaylob's restless mind wouldn't give him any peace. What if Beth Ann had moved on? Throughout his torture, throughout his pain, he had walled off all the what-ifs and just focused on staying alive. Now that he knew he was going home, he had to tackle the questions head on. The answer was simple: If she moved on, he would fight like hell to get her back.

He began concentrating on healing when he could stay awake, and noticing the bare white hospital walls and the smell of disinfectant. At least they had put him in a private room because of his nightmares and screaming all hours of the day and night.

When he finally saw Dr. Stein, the shrink seemed too quick to want to numb him with drugs. Kaylob needed someone to sit down and listen to him, not drugs. He'd heard of too many guys getting screwed up taking shit like that. No way in hell would he let that happen.

The nurse gained more colleagues the more alert he got. It seemed like every one of them stopped and asked if he needed anything, checked to see if he needed bandages changed or just fluffed his pillow. He wouldn't pretend he didn't like the attention. All the nurses looked scrumptious in their uniforms after spending two years in a place where the best view of the world had been straight up at the sky. Despite the attention and the scenery though, he couldn't wait to get home.

One of the nurses over all the others continued visiting more often, and sometimes she would read and sing to him. Her voice was pretty, but she wasn't Beth Ann. Kaylob would doze off and wake to hear himself calling to Beth Ann again.

"What's your name?" he finally asked her one afternoon.

She smiled and showed him her nametag. "Marilyn Meyers."

He took her hand "Marilyn Meyers, thank you for being so kind to me."

She leaned over and smoothed his brow. "It's been my pleasure, soldier. We've heard you're quite the hero. I'm proud to have helped." She adjusted his blanket. "So who is this lucky Beth Ann you're always talking about? She must be someone very special."

"She's been the love of my life ever since I was a kid. We're going to get married if she'll still have me. Me looking so handsome and all." He tried to laugh, but it made his bones scrape together. Morphine deadened the pain but only slightly.

"Oh, I'm sure she will. I bet she's been waiting for you to come home. Any girl would be foolish to give up on you."

He drew a heavy sigh. "She's what pulled me through that hellhole."

The nurse smiled and said. "She'll be one happy girl to see you."

He felt his mind drifting back to sleep and hoped his dreams this time would be of home and of Beth Ann.

Chapter Thirty-Nine

After the phone call from John Patterson, Beth Ann sat on the edge of the bed sobbing. She hadn't thought her heart could break anymore than it already was, but she was wrong. It shouldn't have been a surprise that he'd found the carving on the tree, but it still hurt to think how long Kaylob might have suffered.

Now she understood the visions had been Kaylob trying to show her where he had died. Always the hero, he'd wanted someone to save the other POWs. Patterson had told her they would more than likely never find his body. God, how that hurt. She covered her face with her hands and wept until she ran out of tears.

Blake had gone downstairs to watch TV, and the last thing she wanted was for him to find her crying over Kaylob again. God knew she had put Blake through enough already. Kaylob had been declared dead over two years ago, so the news from Patterson really shouldn't have been such a shock. Still, she would have to tell Kaylob's parents about the call when she got to Novato that weekend. If they were home from a rare vacation that Lisa had mentioned they'd taken. Beth Ann knew they needed that vacation and wasn't about to try and contact them until they were home.

She went to wash her face and then finished packing for her trip. It was supposed to be a girl's weekend to pick out the bridesmaid dresses. Blake had seen to it that she had the wedding dress of her dreams, and it was being designed by one of the best. Of course, none of this had ever been her dream, but she was glad to have him take care of it all.

Blake had wisely bowed out of the shopping weekend and planned to stay home. He wanted her to take the private plane, but Beth Ann wanted to drive. The drive alone would be good for her. She had always loved driving, plus her poor car had been sitting for so long and needed to be driven. It was her graduation car from her parents and over three years old. It hardly had any miles on it, and looked brand new. She hoped this trip would be a good way to lay all the memories to rest.

When she finished packing, she carried her suitcases downstairs and set them by the front door. She walked into the TV room and found Blake sound asleep on the couch. God, he was so handsome. The look on his sleeping face was one of complete contentment.

Yes, maybe someday she would love him as much as she loved Kaylob. After all, she already loved him more than she'd thought possible. They'd had such a wonderful Thanksgiving and Christmas. He had flown out Gram and her brothers on his private plane, but her parents had driven because they took a trip after leaving. Beth Ann had tried so hard not to remember Christmas had marked the two-year point. She didn't want to spend the rest of her life being sad at Christmas.

Now, January was here, and the wedding was just around the corner. She had to get busy. The bridesmaid dresses should really have been bought. She'd used the holidays as an excuse, but the truth was she had been procrastinating while she waited to hear from John.

Blake's eyes opened and caught her looking at him. A slow, sexy grin moved across his face and summoned his dimples. He opened his arms to her.

"Darlin, you're making me the happiest man in the world. I love you."

She bent over to hug him. "You make me very happy, and I love you too, Blake. But there's something I want you to do while I'm gone." She gave him a stern look. "Behave."

He chuckled. "Do I have to?"

He loved her to tease him like that, and the look in his eyes made it worth it. They walked down to her car holding hands. All her things had been packed inside by Blake's amazing staff.

"Call me as soon as you get there, and keep the doors locked while you're driving." He hugged her again. "I'm gonna miss you, darlin."

"I'll miss you too."

She climbed inside and looked up at him through the window. For some reason, a feeling of loss jarred her heart, and she almost got out to hug him again. What was wrong with her? Blake wasn't in any danger. She was probably just overly emotional because of having to face Kaylob's death.

She should have told Blake the whole story, but it was too late now. She had people waiting on her in Novato, and she didn't want to take the chance of crying again. With one last glance at her handsome fiancé, she drove away.

She occupied her time on the drive by going over the wedding plans, but no matter how hard she tried to think of seating arrangements and menu choices, her mind kept going back to her precious time with Kaylob. She had promised herself to stop dwelling on what might have been, but she couldn't stop. Memories of when they'd made love for the first time surfaced—the way he cried at the end and how he'd made her scream. Blake was a wonderful lover who gave her pleasure over and over again, but he had never made her scream or cry in ecstasy.

She tried to replace those torrid memories with lighthearted ones of when she and Kaylob had been kids and all the fun they'd had, but she couldn't help thinking about how he had died sending her messages from beyond. She knew nobody else would believe her, but at least John did.

Her life had been so blessed to experience the pure kind of love she and Kaylob had shared. She sighed and felt a chill run down her spine, the kind she had always felt when Kaylob was nearby. Looking around the car, she wondered if there was such a thing as ghosts. Maybe he was in the car watching over her. Tears spilled down her cheeks.

"I miss you, Kaylob Shawn O'Brien."

She cried most of the way and was glad her tears dried by the time she pulled up to her parents' house. Maybe she'd gotten it all out of her system so she could talk about her wedding. When she got out of the car, she was perplexed to see three other cars parked in front of the house and recognized them as belonging to Kaylob's parents and Lisa.

As she started up the walkway, she saw them through the large living room window, huddled together with serious looks on all their faces. What was going on? Why were they there?

Then it hit her. They'd found his body.

She froze and was just about to turn and run when the door opened and Lisa came out, visibly shaken. She took Beth Ann's arm and tried to lead her inside, but Beth Ann pulled away and ran back to the car. She couldn't listen to them tell her they'd found Kaylob's body. She had to run away and hide.

"Beth Ann, stop." Lisa yelled.

"No, I don't want to hear it. I know they found his remains. I can't, Lisa. I just can't."

Lisa blocked the car door before she could get inside. Beth Ann saw everyone standing on the porch watching them, then her mom ran out to the car.

"Sweetheart, you need to come talk to Jackie. Please, honey." Jean took her daughter's hand and guided her to the house.

Beth Ann followed her mom as if in a trance. When she was sitting on the couch, Kaylob's mom came over and sat beside her, but Beth Ann couldn't look at her.

"Kaylob's alive, honey. He's alive." Jackie squeezed her hand. "He's been in a POW camp, but he's been found safe. The Army rep said he should be in San Francisco in a few days. We got notified now because we just got home from our trip."

Beth Ann slowly turned to look at her as the whole world seemed to stop. For a moment, she couldn't speak or breathe. Then, as if her darkest recesses had been christened with a brilliant spotlight, her heart awakened and tried to soar out of her chest.

The shock caused her to collapse.

* * * *

When she woke, she was on her childhood bed surrounded by familiar, concerned faces.

"Are you okay, honey? Please say something," Jean begged.

Beth Ann sat up and took the warm washcloth from her forehead, and the news finally sank in to her overwhelmed brain.

"Kaylob's alive," she said, joyful tears cascading down her face. "He's really alive?"

"Yes, honey," Jean said. "It's true."

"I want to see him now. I want to talk to him. Please take me to him." Beth Ann moved her legs over the side of the bed and tried to stand.

Kaylob's dad stepped forward and took her by the shoulders. "Sweetheart, he's not back in the country yet. We have to be patient."

He might as well have been trying to reason with a charging rhino. Beth Ann's single-minded thought was to see the love of her life. Little things like oceans and distance were meaningless. She wanted to see him now. She had to touch him again and feel his arms around her.

Lisa spoke to everyone in the room. "Can I have a moment alone with her?" After they all left, she closed the door and got Beth Ann to sit on the side of the bed with her.

"What about Blake, honey? What about the wedding? You have to call him. He needs to be told about this as soon as possible."

"Oh my God," Beth Ann cried. "Poor Blake. He'll be so hurt over this."

Her heart ached at the thought of what it would do to him, but the pain was quickly replaced with joy again because Kaylob was alive, and she couldn't think of anything but going to him.

"You have to call him, Beth Ann. He has to hear it from you."

Lisa was right, of course. She couldn't go to Kaylob without talking to Blake.

"What am I going to say, Lisa? It's going to break his heart no matter how I handle it."

"Just let him know Kaylob's alive," Lisa suggested. "You don't have to tell him anything else yet. He'll understand that you're in shock and won't expect you to make any decisions right now."

"Maybe you're right." Beth Ann nodded. "I need to call him, but I want to talk to him in private."

"Okay, we'll all go out back and let you make your call." Lisa hugged her before she left.

Beth Ann headed to the phone in the kitchen with dread, wishing the phone was still in her bedroom. While she dialed the number, she knew each revolution of the dial brought her closer to breaking the heart of someone she loved. Oh, God, she wished she didn't have to hurt him. The happiness she heard in his voice when he answered the phone sent another jab of pain to her heart.

"Blake, it's me."

"Hey, darlin. How are you? I bet you're tired."

She thought she was going to throw up. "Blake, you need to sit down."

"What do you mean?" She heard the shift in his voice. "Is something wrong? Are you hurt?"

She opened her mouth, but nothing came out as the tears rolled down her cheeks.

"Beth Ann, are you crying? What's wrong? You're scaring the shit out of me."

She summoned every bit of strength she had. "Blake, they found Kaylob." She paused before she said the words that would crush his heart. "He's alive, and he's coming home."

"He's alive? How ..." She could already hear the pain in his voice. "How did they get it wrong?"

She gave him the details and when she finished, he was silent for several seconds. Then she heard him take a ragged breath.

"I understand you have to see him. Just remember that I love you very much, and I know you love me. We've spent over a year together. Promise me you won't forget how happy we've been and you won't throw us away. Please promise me, Beth Ann."

His voice broke before he finished, and she wished with all her heart that she could take away his pain.

"I can't promise anything right now, Blake, but you're right. I do love you, and I know you love me, but—"

"Go see him and take all the time you need." He cut her off as though he was afraid of what she'd been about to say. "I'll postpone the wedding. Just please call me when you can."

"It might be a while, Blake. He's sick and still in a hospital. He's been in a POW camp for over two years."

"I know. I hope he'll be okay."

"Thank you for being so understanding."

He was crying when he said goodbye.

She hung up, and immediately her thoughts were consumed with seeing Kaylob, even though her heart hurt over Blake. She opened the sliding doors that led to the back yard and stepped outside. Nobody said a word. The only sound was the far-off laughter of children that reminded her of growing up with Kaylob.

* * * *

While Beth Ann and Lisa sat in the back yard watching the sunset, Beth Ann thought about how many times they had done the same thing. The beginning of January gave notice that winter had arrived at last. It was always been a slow transition in Novato. The temperatures grew slightly colder every day, the fall colors had faded, and the leaves were off the trees. Yet nothing had ever faded about the love of her life. She'd loved him as a boy, as a teen, and as a man. Her Kaylob was finally coming home to her.

Lisa looked at her. "Penny for your thoughts."

Beth Ann released a long breath. "I knew Kaylob wasn't dead because I never felt him die. I kept telling everyone that. Frankie thought my mind was just trying to protect me. I kept hearing Kaylob's voice calling to me, and it was so clear. Then there were the dreams, and there's more. Something I haven't told anyone except Blake and John Patterson. He's the guy that Kaylob saved."

She told Lisa about the visions. Lisa's mouth was open the entire time Beth Ann talked.

"Wow, what a connection you guys have." Lisa showed Beth Ann her goose bumps. "That's incredible and even more amazing that Patterson found the carving in the tree." She looked up at the dark sky. "It's like two stars forever burning bright, that's you and Kaylob. From the moment you two were born, it was destiny for you to meet."

The back door opened and Jackie called to let them know that dinner was ready. Jackie and Harold stayed late into the evening, talking about Kaylob and what they needed to get for his homecoming. They'd donated all his clothes and everything, so they made plans to go shopping for him the next day. Beth Ann hoped the clothes they bought would fit since he'd probably lost a lot of weight and she no longer had any of his clothes either.

* * * *

Over the next few days, minutes passed like years for Beth Ann as she paced her parents' house waiting for the call that Kaylob was home. The Army and the VA only had conflicting, inaccurate, or misleading information, if not all of the above. Kaylob's parents got the runaround no matter who they called. More than once some bureaucratic pinhead told them he was dead.

The waiting took a toll on Beth Ann, but she tried not to complain although she was about to lose her mind. Blake spoke to her a few times to make sure she was holding up, but it was so hard talking to him. She could hear the pain in every word he said. To top it off, the gossip magazines had gotten wind of her long lost love's return. The headlines read things like 'Who will she choose—the most eligible bachelor or her childhood sweetheart war hero?'

Sunday morning, Kaylob's parents finally called to tell her Kaylob had been admitted to the San Francisco VA hospital.

"You want us to pick you up?" Jackie said.

"Yes." Beth Ann tried not to shout. "Yes, please. I can't wait to see him."

"Okay, we'll be right over."

When she hung up the phone, she caught sight of her mom and Stanley watching her from the doorway. Her mom's lip trembled when she smiled and opened her arms for her daughter. Beth Ann walked into their embrace, and the three of them cried with happiness.

Beth Ann forced down a piece of toast and a cup of coffee while she waited for Jackie and Harold. She paced and looked at her watch every few seconds. When she finally heard the horn outside, she ran so fast to get out the door that she almost forgot to tell her parents goodbye.

The drive to San Francisco passed in slow motion, and every minute took longer than the minute before. For over two years, all she had done was dream of seeing Kaylob again. Although he'd been across the world, he'd never been far from her, and she was finally going to see him again.

Chapter Forty

When they arrived at the hospital, Beth Ann was shocked at the size of the place. It was a Goliath of government architecture, almost menacing to anyone brave enough to step inside. They entered the enormous building and, after some missteps, found out where Kaylob had taken. At the nurses' station on his floor, they directed them to his room.

Incredibly, after waiting an eternity to see him, Beth Ann was so overcome with the prospect that she had to let Jackie and Harold go first. While she waited for them in the visitors' area, she paced with trembling legs, trying to collect herself so she wouldn't faint or fall apart when she saw him.

After about five minutes, Harold came out of the room and walked down the hall to her.

"He's asking for you, but you need to be prepared," he said. "He doesn't look the same. He's lost a lot of weight, and his skin is very pale. He told me he still has two broken ribs and screwed-up shoulders. His lungs are still healing, and he has two broken fingers."

"Okay, thanks," she said, starting to get impatient now.

The way he looked didn't matter a bit to her. She wanted to touch him. She wanted to look in his eyes and hear his voice.

Her legs couldn't move fast enough now. When she got his room, she stopped and had to grip the sides of the doorway so she wouldn't fall. Kaylob was sitting propped up, looking at his mother on the other side of the bed. When Jackie saw Beth Ann, she waved for her to come in, and Kaylob turned to look at her as if in slow motion.

Their eyes met across the room, and everything around them disappeared. A lifetime's worth of shared memories flashed through her head, and her legs moved as if they had a mind of their own, carrying her to the man who owned her heart. She had to touch him, to put her hands on his beautiful face and prove to herself that he was alive. That he'd really come back to her.

"Kaylob ..." Her hands moved over his tear-drenched face, his eyes, his lips.

"Beth Ann, baby ..." His fingers slipped through her hair and pulled her face to his.

Neither of them could say anything for the next few minutes while they wept and held each other. There were no words for what they experienced. There was only the two of them and this moment. No other time or place mattered.

Finally, he took her face in his hands and swept his thumb under her eyes to wipe away her tears. "Baby, I love you so much."

"Oh, Kaylob. You're really alive. I've dreamed of this for so long." She put her head against his chest so she could hear his heartbeat. This wasn't a vision or a dream. It was her Kaylob, and he was alive.

"I love you more than you'll ever know."

"You don't know how good that makes me feel, baby. I love you too."

She sat down on the edge of the bed carefully, afraid she would hurt him, but he pulled her into his arms.

"Let me hold you, I need to feel you."

With his arms finally around her for the first time in over two years, she knew she was home and would never let him go again. Her sweet Kaylob, the man she had loved her entire life. She had never been able to imagine living without him, and she knew now that she could never have done it. She had been empty without him, a container full of nothing. Now the warmth and fullness of their love filled her again and flowed into every crevice of her being.

"Kaylob, I knew you weren't dead. I never believed it when they told me. I felt you and saw you and heard you calling my name."

He leaned back to look into her eyes, as though he were reading her soul. "Me too, baby. I saw you in visions and my dreams. I'd hear you crying out for me, calling my name. I even saw you barefoot one time, stuck in the mud."

"Oh, God ..." she gasped. "Kaylob, I had a vision of being barefoot in the mud. I saw you and tried to get to you, but the bad men dragged you away."

He lifted her chin and lowered his lips to hers. "Oh, sweetheart, you're the light that guided me home."

She'd always known they had a connection no one else understood, and now they had proof. They both knew it was real, but they both didn't want to talk about it in front of his parents. There would be time later to share everything with each other. Right now she just wanted to be close to him.

She could feel his sweet, wonderful breath when their lips met again, and their tongues sought each other hungrily as the kiss deepened. She never wanted to let him go, but his parents' sniffles reminded them both that they weren't alone. Their love was clear to the world, but they'd have to wait to share all of it.

She made herself leave his arms and took a step back to get a good look at him. His dad had been right. His skin was pale and tightly stretched over his body, and his arms were covered in scars and discolorations. His hair was much thinner than when he left, and she almost cried out when she saw what looked like burn marks on his scalp.

"I know I look bad, baby," he said, taking her hand.

She touched his hair gently and kissed his head. "You're the most beautiful thing I've ever seen."

"No, you are, Beth Ann. You're even more beautiful than I remembered."

They looked into each other's eyes again, and it was as though the last two years had never happened. No time, distance, or other person could ever change that. As she kissed him again, she knew without a doubt there had never been a choice for her to make between Blake and Kaylob. Her only choice, her life, was right there in the hospital bed. Love had brought him back home to her, and there was no other love for her in the world but him.

* * * *

The doctors and nurses warned Beth Ann that Kaylob would have some type of stress disorder, but she told them together they could handle anything and would battle through it. How much worse could it be than what they'd already been through?

That night, as she sat by his bedside, she was awakened by his screams.

"Get away from me, you bastards."

Kaylob's arms lashed out, and the rolling table went flying through the air and almost hit her in the head. The nurses came rushing into the room, and Beth Ann watched in horror as it took three nurses and one doctor to hold him down and inject him with some type of medication that made him go quiet and pass out.

One doctor looked at her and shook his head. "He might never be the same. We just don't know."

While she watched him sleep, she knew that they could get through anything. Sure, the journey might be rough because of his stress disorder, and when he finds out about Blake, she knew he wouldn't be happy. However, she made up her mind to hide it from him as long as possible, at least until he was stronger and better able to deal with it.

Blake was the guy Kaylob hated most, so how was she supposed to tell him she had almost married him? Her stomach did a back flip just thinking about it. What had the doctor meant that he might never be the same? How long could a stress disorder last? He was home now, so surely he'd move past it.

Then, what about Blake? She had to end things with him and break off their engagement, and she had to do it soon because she couldn't string him along and hurt him even more. She hoped he would take it well, but she secretly knew it was going to be an ugly scene she would give anything to avoid.

She couldn't think about any of that right now. She had to believe that everything would be okay, because tomorrow was a new day with a whole new beginning. She would face everything head on and hopefully remain standing.

She took Kaylob's hand and kissed it. Now that she had him back, she could face anything.

* * * *

Blake fought to remain sane as he paced his living room, wondering if he had lost the only girl he'd ever loved. Why hadn't she called him from the hospital? Yes, she had gone to see Kaylob, but that didn't mean it was over between them. It couldn't be over. He wouldn't let it be over.

She loved him, he knew she did. She'll come home soon. He knew she would.

Beth Ann had been his true love since he was a teen, and he couldn't lose her now that he'd finally gotten her to love him back. When she came home, he would make her see that they belonged together. After all he was the only one who could give her everything she deserved.

He was Blake Tanner, damn it. He loved her and there was no way he'd ever let her go.

THE END

Coming Soon

December Road, Book 2 of Seasons of War

About the Author

Brenda Ashworth Barry's first book was a memoir titled, Healing the Voices Within, which was never published but sponsored on a local TV station and flew off the shelves at her Healing Center in Redding California.

Her most recent work is a four-part saga of star-crossed lovers separated by the war in Vietnam, entitled Seasons of Love and War. Brenda worked for over five years to bring the four part Saga alive.

Brenda lives in Roseburg, Oregon, by the Umpqua River, and has raised four children three birth children and one adopted born in her heart. Her husband, who was in the military for 21 years, gave her help and encouragement while writing her novel. When she's not writing she can normally be found walking the trails with her husband and their little dachshund, or in their RV enjoying nature.

Twitter- @sunsetsky52
www.brendaashworthbarry.com
https://www.facebook.com/pages/Seasons-of-Love-and-War-Author-Page/411210412247684
http://brendabarry.blogspot.com/
http://brendabarryashworth.wordpress.com/